P9-DHQ-065

Brewing Up a Storm

Brewing Up a Storm

A JOHN THATCHER MYSTERY

EMMA LATHEN

ST. MARTIN'S PRESS
NEW YORK

A THOMAS DUNNE BOOK.
An imprint of St. Martin's Press.

Design by Ellen R. Sasahara

Library of Congress Cataloging-in-Publication Data

Lathen, Emma, pseud.
    Brewing up a storm : a John Thatcher mystery / Emma Lathen. — 1st ed.
        p.   cm.
    "A Thomas Dunne book."
    ISBN 0–312–14554–3
    1. Thatcher, John Putnam (Fictitious character)—Fiction.   2. Bankers—
New York (State)—New York—Fiction.   3. Wall Street—Fiction.   I. Title.
PS3562.A755B74   1996
813'.54—dc20   96–22116
                                                                              CIP

First Edition: December 1996

10 9 8 7 6 5 4 3 2 1

Brewing Up a Storm

1. At the Bar

W ALL STREET IS THE unrepentant bastion of one form of seg-
regation. A privileged minority deals constantly with asset allocation, cash flows and leverage. The toiling masses farther
down the pyramid contemplate high finance once a month, when
their bills arrive.

Historically, communication across this divide has posed problems. The Sloan Guaranty Trust, for example, was a great money
center bank where John Putnam Thatcher, senior vice president, always knew what ailed capital markets from Hong Kong to Frank-
furt. Like most of his peers, he was shakier about Main Street USA
and the malls off the interstate.

This had led to precautions whenever fanfare about a new retail
product reached his desk. In the dark days before the microwave
oven, when Crock-Pots were being touted, Thatcher had taken
counsel with Miss Corsa, his secretary.

"Yes, I know the food is supposed to cook while you're at work,"
she had said, wrinkling her nose over rave reviews from one of Wall
Street's premier researchers. "I'd rather stop on my way home for a
pizza."

Furthermore it developed that Miss Corsa's mother did not like
gadgets and that her cousin Louise, a schoolteacher in Yonkers,
cooked over the weekend and froze.

"Thank you very much," Thatcher had said.

Since then Miss Corsa and her family had become his private data

1

bank about real life. When the first Toyota appeared among them, Thatcher knew that Detroit was in trouble long before the analysts.

"Rose is worth her weight in gold," Charlie Trinkam, Thatcher's second-in-command, often observed.

"True enough," Thatcher would say. "If we could only chart how she and her family spend, or plan to spend, their hard-earned money, the Sloan would know more about GDP than it does. But there are limits to what I feel I can ask."

Charlie fully appreciated the link between consumer behavior and the profits at the Sloan.

"Ask me anything you want," he said cheerfully, ready to bare all secrets.

But contributions from this quarter, although colorful, came with one drawback.

"You spend too much time in Tiffany's," Thatcher pointed out. "And not enough at Wal-Mart."

"That's why I'm here on Wall Street," said Charlie happily. "If you want to hear the heartbeat of America, you have to go someplace else."

Even to improve intelligence gathering, Thatcher was not ready to relocate. Nevertheless, the next ripple in the consumer society reached him within days of their conversation. Curiously enough, it arrived by way of a prominent trial attorney, not Miss Corsa and her invaluable relatives.

Thatcher encountered Paul Jackson in the lobby of their lunch club. Since Jackson was one of the livelier members, this was all to the good. Jackson did, however, tend to assume that everybody shared his current enthusiasms.

"You know I hated to recess for lunch today," he said, despite the excellent meal he had just finished. Still talking rapidly, he selected mints from the bowl on the library table, popped one into his mouth and pocketed several others for later use. "This is going to be one helluva case. Even the preliminary hearing is a laugh a minute."

The zest with which Jackson defended white-collar criminals had made him famous—or infamous—in certain circles. Thatcher himself applauded anybody who obviously enjoyed his work, and so, although his appetite for legal pyrotechnics was modest, he po-

2

litely inquired about the nature of the current litigation.

". . . a nineteen-year-old got himself beered up and wrapped his muscle car around a utility pole out in Astoria. They could get him for damaging Nynex property, but Wayne Ludlum, Junior, isn't with us anymore. Luckily it was two in the morning, so Junior didn't take anybody with him when he went."

Tragedies like this are common enough, but they did not normally figure in Jackson's lucrative practice.

"Who's suing whom?" Thatcher asked.

"It's Ludlum—that's the parents—versus the Kichsel Brewery," said Jackson with a wicked grin. "I'm representing Kichsel."

"Oh, really?" said Thatcher. The Kichsel Brewery, while not a national giant like Anheuser-Busch, ran a respectable second or third. More to the point, George C. Lancer, Thatcher's nominal superior at the Sloan, sat on the Kichsel board, returning from all directors' meetings to report solid performance and earnings by a conservative old-line firm. From Lancer, this was high praise.

However, it was not this tenuous connection with the Sloan that stirred Thatcher's curiosity. Retaining Paul Jackson indicated that Kichsel was bringing heavy guns to the fray.

"Am I correct in assuming your opposite number is not a recent graduate with a night-school degree?" he asked.

"Arthur Cleve," said Jackson, naming a rival legal superstar. "He's got a psychiatrist and a team of clinical psychologists lined up. I think he may be hoping to make Court TV. And it wouldn't bother me a bit."

As Thatcher knew, when the courtroom is transformed into theater, either large sums or weighty issues are involved.

"Is the senior Ludlum a man of substance?" he asked, thinking of Arthur Cleve's fees.

"He's a dispatcher for Citycab," said Jackson. "But he has friends with deep pockets and they think they've got the test case of the century."

Obviously there was more to *Ludlum versus Kichsel* than met the eye, and Thatcher asked what it was.

"I don't want to spoil the fun," said the lawyer. "You've really got to see this for yourself, John. If only for an hour."

As a result, instead of diligently returning to duty, Thatcher found himself accompanying Paul Jackson uptown. Given George Lancer's role at Kichsel, this detour could be defended as a prudent allocation of time to almost anybody except Miss Corsa.

The fun began on the steps of the courthouse, where Jackson halted and, figuratively speaking, doffed a sombrero.

"Mrs. Underwood!" he cried, gallantly leaping forward to swing wide the door of a taxi from which a woman was alighting.

"Thank you," she murmured, pausing on the sidewalk as her companion paid the cabby.

"And may I present John Thatcher from the Sloan Guaranty Trust," Jackson continued. "John, this is Mrs. Madeleine Underwood."

Neither young nor old, Mrs. Underwood was expensively dressed in a spring coat of green linen that complemented her short brown curls. Her large blue eyes were the best feature in a face that was photogenic, if not otherwise remarkable. Her lips were a shade too thin but that, Thatcher suspected, might be attributable to Jackson's approach.

As he shook hands, however, Thatcher realized that Mrs. Underwood was more than an attractive matron come to witness legal shenanigans. She was the center of a retinue that had discharged from attendant taxis. Hovering discreetly in the background was a band of business suits awaiting her pleasure. Even in the absence of this entourage Thatcher would have guessed that Mrs. Underwood was a force to be reckoned with. She carried herself with the quasi-regal self-possession that, forty years ago, would have signaled an heiress or world-famous soprano. Nowadays it could mean anything.

"Mrs. Underwood is the founder, the director and the guiding spirit of NOBBY," declaimed Jackson with suspicious gravity.

But Madeleine Underwood knew how to deflect even incipient mockery. "That stands for 'No Beer-Buying Youngsters,' Mr. Thatcher," she amplified cheerfully. "You probably haven't heard of our organization yet, but I'm happy to say that our activities are beginning to attract the support of responsible institutions, and I'm sure the Sloan—"

"Oh, no you don't, he's mine," Jackson interrupted. "Keep your fund-raising hands to yourself, Mrs. Underwood."

"There's no mine and no yours on this issue. Before I'm done we'll even have enlisted you, Mr. Jackson," she predicted with a subdued twinkle. "It will of course take a great deal of time and education for NOBBY to—"

Before she could continue, the slight young man who had accompanied her in the cab detached himself from a nearby group and came hurrying to her side.

"Sorry to interrupt, Madeleine," he began, "but the people from Channel Twenty-five would like a few words from you. I've explained that you can only give them two or three minutes."

"This is Sean Cushing, our administrator for NOBBY," she said, already withdrawing. "I'm afraid you'll have to excuse me now."

Belatedly Thatcher saw that, in addition to those entering the building, there was a tiny clot of reporters and one lone video crew stationed at the base of the steps.

"Wait until you get an earful of this," whispered Jackson, leading Thatcher to the circle forming around Mrs. Underwood.

"NOBBY is a grassroots organization of volunteers and concerned parents devoted to protecting our children from the terrible ravages of adolescent alcoholism," she began with practiced fluency.

Thatcher eyed his companion sternly. "If you've dragged me down here to listen to a latter-day Carrie Nation . . ." he began.

"Nope," Jackson assured him. "It's more complicated than that. Just hear Madeleine out."

". . . no quarrel with beer or non-alcoholic beer sold to adults," she was saying quietly. "The danger that NOBBY is confronting comes from Quax."

Without bothering to ask the obvious, Thatcher simply turned to Jackson.

"Quax is the non-alcoholic beer that Kichsel introduced two years ago," the lawyer supplied sotto voice. "Basically it's just another soft drink."

That was not the way Madeleine Underwood saw it.

". . . to target young children deliberately as a market for Quax, to promote it as a safe and wholesome alternative to sodas is un-

5

conscionable. As the Ludlum family has learned to its sorrow, Quax is merely the first step in an inevitable progression to early consumption of alcohol. By packaging Quax as a clone to Kix, its heavily promoted beer, Kichsel is intentionally introducing confusion. They are conditioning young people to drink the company's products without any differentiation. Kichsel's claim that this look-alike policy is based on a desire to maximize trade-name recognition is specious, to say the least. That is why NOBBY is supporting the Ludlums. Nothing can repay them for their own loss, but they hope to spare hundreds of other families a similar tragedy."

Whatever the validity of her cause, Madeleine Underwood's performance could not be faulted. She was avoiding the hectoring shrillness of so many ardent proselytizers while radiating a serene confidence that her message would, in due time, appeal to all right-thinking sensible people.

In the meantime Paul Jackson had heard enough. "That's her sermon for you," he said, heading for the doors. "*Ludlum versus Kichsel* is, in a nutshell, NOBBY claiming that little Wayne got hooked on Quax, then shifted up to Kix without ever noticing the difference. Mrs. Underwood wants governmental action to treat Quax as a dangerous substance, not because it contains alcohol—which it does not—but because of what she perceives as a psychological threat to the young."

"And with that kind of argument the main thrust of the plaintiff's case will have to be carried by psychologists as expert witnesses?"

"And how! She's got five of them she's trying to put on the stand."

No wonder Jackson was so enthusiastic about this case. While the most notorious weapon in his powerful armory was the ability to deflate any expert witness, he approached psychologists with special relish.

"For that matter, I've got a couple of my own," he added as a palpable afterthought.

"Planning to give as good as you get?"

"Planning to do a hell of a lot better," Jackson said dulcetly just before he went off to confer with his colleagues.

Searching for a seat, Thatcher spied a single vacancy in the second row and from this vantage point he turned to count the house. The usual recognizable groups were out in full force. First there were the professional observers, called forth whenever commercial interests are at stake. Then there were the hobbyists—the courthouse regulars wise in the ways of litigation tactics, versed in the laws of evidence, and familiar with the grandees of the New York bar. The size of this particular contingent was probably a personal tribute to Paul Jackson. And, last of all, occupying two full rows, was a solid phalanx. Displaying neither blasé patience nor carefree camaraderie, they all gleamed with the light of battle and conspicuously sported large NOBBY badges.

When Madeleine Underwood finally entered, she paused in her progress down the aisle to bestow a few words on her supporters before following young Cushing to the seats in front of Thatcher. They were both too preoccupied with their own exchange to notice his presence.

"It's wonderful to see so many members turning out," Mrs. Underwood remarked as she sat down.

Cushing's mind must have been elsewhere. "Yes, Iona scheduled a different bunch to show up every day," he replied, absently destroying the illusion of spontaneity while he focused a disapproving glance at the remaining empty seats. "The Ludlums are running it close again. I wish to God you had let me look for a better test plaintiff instead of settling for the first ones who approached you."

"Now, Sean, you know as well as I do that they're perfect for our purposes. The jury will be watching them all the time and just think how they look. Nancy Ludlum is too bereaved to respond to anything while Mr. Ludlum manages to project grief but also determination."

"It's the victim I'm talking about, not the parents," he countered. "I still say we could have gotten more mileage from a younger boy, say a sixteen- or seventeen-year-old."

"On an emotional level, perhaps," she said kindly. "But you have to remember we're in a courtroom now. Of course I was pleased to meet those two classmates who were Wayne's friends. Their testimony will be useful, but it's still just personal recollection and we could duplicate that with almost any victim. It was when I came across all those photographs that I realized we had, in terms of the litigation, a real treasure trove. Those snapshots and videos of Wayne drinking Quax at barbecues and beach parties are documentary evidence."

The last phrase was meant to clinch the argument, but Sean Cushing remained unconvinced.

"It's not that hard to establish some kid was in the habit of drinking Quax. The difficulty is persuading a jury it has anything to do with what happened afterward."

"You say that because you haven't been at the conferences with the attorneys. There are all sorts of peculiar rules about what constitutes proof."

"Yes, but the older the victim, the more time for other forces to—"

"Shh!" she hissed warningly. "The Ludlums are coming."

Thatcher, following their discussion, decided that Mrs. Underwood tended to carry her platform manner too far. That calm, impregnable certainty, so effective from a public spokesman, had a crushing effect on informal give-and-take.

The arrival of a rabbity-looking couple taking seats next to Mrs. Underwood coincided with the commencement of official proceedings. Preliminary motions defining the extent of expert testimony were on the tapis and a parade of psychologists began, with representatives from the Mayo Clinic, Bellevue, the Maclean Institute and Cornell Medical School following each other. These aristocrats confined themselves to a somber recognition of the knotty questions to be resolved. They were succeeded, however, by a younger man, artfully bearded, who unhesitatingly advanced directly into the minefields. Self-assured, authoritative and terribly articulate, Dr. Joseph Schumacher produced one flat declaration after another.

"To the mind of any trained psychologist, the potential perils are immediately discernible. The absence of alcohol is irrelevant. We are not dealing with a problem that can be measured in terms of physical factors but rather with . . ."

". . . the vast literature of studies on early conditioning in related areas has established that . . ."

"A paper of my own published last year considered the consequences of early exposure to . . ."

At each effusion the brown curls ahead of Thatcher bobbed in accord.

"That's the kind of testimony we want the jury to hear," she whispered to her companions. "If the judge cuts down the number of experts, we keep Dr. Schumacher, no matter what."

She was watching the wrong actors, Thatcher thought. If Madeleine Underwood had been really knowledgeable about choosing witnesses, she would have been watching the opposing counsel.

Paul Jackson was leaning back with his eyes closed, lost in an inner reverie. But every now and then, at some particularly telling point from Joseph Schumacher, his lips involuntarily twitched, like a large dog dreaming of rabbits to come.

2. Selected Beverages

T HATCHER LEFT THE courthouse largely unimpressed except for one niggling little question. So upon returning to the Sloan he sought out Miss Corsa.

"Quax?" she replied when he interrupted her. "That's some new non-alcoholic beer, isn't it?"

Her uncertainty allayed one fear. Quax, of which he had never previously heard, was not imprinted on the national consciousness. Even Thatcher had not been able to escape saturation advertising from the Kichsel Brewery, proud sponsor of the World Cup of Soccer. There was, he believed, something called the Kix Cup, but whether it applied to tennis, golf, or hockey escaped him.

". . . which suggests that Quax hasn't been getting the full treatment," he mused aloud.

Miss Corsa, eager to return to her proofreading, agreed that Quax was not yet a household name. This led Thatcher to another conclusion. Mrs. Madeleine Underwood might be training her heavy artillery on a chipmunk.

"If so, I think we'll be able to put Quax from our minds," he said, making one of those reasonable predictions that prove to be fatally flawed.

HE COULD NOT know that, at that very moment, Claudia Fentiman was working hard to enhance Quax's name recognition. Normally

10

she would have been doing so out of her office at Kichsel head-quarters, where Quax was brewed. But Claudia brought flair as well as a track record to her job, and when NOBBY began hurling charges, she knew that Quax's marketing manager had to abandon formula. So instead of sitting tight in Illinois and churning out pious rebuttals, she had flown to San Antonio, Texas, where she was currently extending her right hand across a vast conference table to meet that of the man opposite her.

"That's it. Hold it a second!"

Camcorders commemorated the traditional after-signature hand-shake. Then Elmer Rugby sauntered around to join Mrs. Fentiman.

"There's a crew waiting outside," he informed her. "Local TV's doing a feature on the contract."

"Wonderful!"

Even as they shared a triumph, they presented a striking contrast in style. Elmer Rugby, like his growing chain of hamburger franchises, was following a trajectory from modest beginnings through regional renown to national prominence. His menus were heavy on tangy sauces, and when he was touting his wares—which he did so indefatigably that all over the Southwest Rugby's *was* Elmer—he sported a Stetson and boots. His kindly weathered face and beguiling drawl conjured up the romance of the Old West even when, as today, he wore a well-cut business suit.

It was impossible to visualize Claudia Fentiman riding the range. Urban to her fingertips, she was a creature of taxis and elevators, of high-rise apartments and expensive downtown boutiques. As usual, she was making no concession to her current locale. Her beige shift under a black-and-beige jacket, her patent-leather pumps and jade earrings would have been at home on Madison Avenue. Her dark-brown hair was cut in an artful short bob while sleek eyebrows arched over warm hazel eyes.

"I thought we'd meet them out front," Rugby told her.

This came as no surprise. Rugby commercials were all filmed outdoors. The nation would soon be seeing him as Texas did . . . communing with a herd of beef cattle or hopping out of a jeep.

"That's a good idea," said Claudia.

She had every reason to cooperate. It had been Claudia Fentiman's inspiration that one way to emphasize the wholesomeness of Quax and its role in the happy family was to piggyback on an acknowledged expert in wholesomeness, value and fun. Furthermore, it was Claudia who had calculated that the fast-food giants would be too tough to crack, too cautious to take chances. After months of research she had come up with Rugby's, still in the risk-taking stage, still eager to make a splash as it conquered new worlds.

That Rugby's should also entail a rugged individualist like Elmer, she had to admit, was an unexpected stroke of luck. As she had reason to know, unabashed admirers of the bold gesture do not always practice what they preach.

Outside, Rugby positioned himself before the larger-than-life-size statue of a chuck wagon and addressed his public:

"No, hard as it is to believe, we're still improving our offerings at Rugby's. So we're pleased to tell you that Quax is going to be added to our beverages. Folks can enjoy the taste of beer with their barbecue, and we all know what a winning combination that is."

Claudia smiled supportively. She was willing to let Elmer star until the inevitable question. When it came, she was ready.

"But Elmer," cried a reporter, "a lot of your outlets are on the highways. Is it such a great idea for kids to see people downing suds while they're on the road? Won't they get the wrong idea?"

"Just the opposite," Claudia intervened briskly. "Everybody knows that lectures don't affect children while they're growing up. It's the example set for them. At Rugby's they'll see adults acting responsibly, parents who care enough about safety to stick to an alcohol-free soft drink."

Rugby promptly seconded her: "If there's one thing you see too often in my business, boys, it's people running in to grab their food—then crossing the street for a six-pack. Rugby's is going to show them a better way to go."

The questions continued and Rugby and Mrs. Fentiman alternated fielding them. Even when the television crews were collecting their gear and the print reporters took their humble turn, nobody would have guessed that the self-possessed Mrs. Fentiman was itching to be off and away.

"A man as successful as Elmer Rugby," she said, her thoughts elsewhere, "is the kind of partner that fills Quax with confidence."

For an hour she spoke, smiled and even managed a friendly wave toward the dispersing crowd. Freedom came only when she left Elmer Rugby and returned to her hotel. When at last she closed the door behind her, she kicked off her spike heels and pounced on the phone.

"Alec! We just signed, and the release has gone out to the financial press!" she announced buoyantly.

"Great! I knew you'd pull it off."

She exploded into a relieved gust of laughter. "I only wish I'd felt that confident. But we've got our deal, and I think we can work with Elmer."

For Claudia and her immediate supervisor it was an unadulterated joy to discuss joint advertising, budgets and special coupon offers. But Claudia's sense of perspective remained strong. With some regret she turned to the small cloud on the horizon.

"What's been happening with that NOBBY case?"

Headquarters remained blithe. "Oh, them. We can talk about that when you get back. And when you arrive, Claudia, baby, there's going to be a bottle of champagne waiting."

With the barest hint of a frown she said, "We'll be too busy concentrating on Quax."

EVENTS IN far-off Texas had yet to catch up with Thatcher, but before the day was out, he accidentally caught a glimpse of a related development.

Dinner at the National Association of Exporters provided it. Tedious as such functions were, they all mandated a Sloan presence. Ideally, this was provided by George Lancer, chairman of the board. But since there were limits to how many times a week Lancer could be cozened, the Sloan maintained a back-up roster. Tonight was Thatcher's turn.

Since most of Thatcher's tablemates were cut from the same drab corporate cloth, they did not provide much food for vagrant thought—with one exception. Roger Vandermeer was president of Vandermeer & Adler, a public-relations firm with offices in Washington, New York and London, and, Vandermeer implied, a client list that virtually replicated the Dow Jones Industrial Average. This evening he was representing a trade association, the Soft Drink Institute, and doing so with considerable force.

"My point is that for Americans to break into new markets like Japan and the East, they couldn't do better than to look at us," he announced confidently.

Mild opposition came from one of his companions who observed that there was a big difference between soda pop and earthmoving equipment.

"Maybe there is," Vandermeer shot back. "But I still say we should concentrate on success stories, not on all the difficulties. Take Coca-Cola. Everywhere you go, even if you can't read the signs, you'll recognize their logo. And Pepsi was ready to get into new markets long before the Soviets collapsed. That didn't just happen. It took planning . . ."

His message might be commonplace but Vandermeer delivered it with a flourish. As he spoke, he automatically shot his cuffs, revealing two heavy gold links. They were fitting adjuncts to a veneer that included Italian tailoring and an all-season tan. Vandermeer's appearance was calculated to impress and, as Thatcher discovered during the interval when plates of roast beef were cleared away, it had certainly done the job with Monroe Biggins, the president of the Soft Drink Institute.

"We're lucky to have a man like Vandermeer," he confided, "and he's doing crackerjack work for us."

Thatcher switched his attention from spokesman to warrior. Monroe Biggins, despite his timid demeanor, was mobilizing the Soft Drink Institute for domestic conflict, as well as expansion abroad.

"It's dog-eat-dog out there," he explained.

Thatcher was already familiar with the desperate battle for supermarket shelf space, but it was an ever-fresh topic to Biggins.

"Baby food, cat food, salad bars!" he said, loathing every usurper of valuable footage. "But SDI's fighting back. And if anybody can keep Quax out of our supermarket section, it's Roger. He knows how to get results."

"Quax, eh?" said Thatcher, registering its second emergence in one day and its growing band of opponents.

"Roger knows how to go for the jugular," added Biggins with thin-blooded ferocity.

Taking a second look, Thatcher decided that there probably was muscle beneath Vandermeer's expensive serge. On the other hand, he did not think he discerned any of the moral fervor that marked Madeleine Underwood.

"Tell me, are you familiar with the activities of NOBBY?" he asked.

"A valuable organization," Biggins replied vaguely. "Naturally we welcome input from the public."

Overhearing them, Vandermeer contributed his own opinion.

"At least NOBBY's on the right side. But the people we really need on our side are the supermarkets. Did I tell you Greengrocers are giving Quax thirty inches?" he told Biggins.

"For a novelty item!" Biggins protested.

"It's not selling like a novelty item," said Vandermeer dourly. "Sales are picking up all over the Northeast. I'm going to have to try twisting some arms about our two-for-one promotions."

Biggins took fright. "That's just a manner of speaking," he assured Thatcher.

But Thatcher fastened on another aspect of all this unguarded shop talk.

"I assume that the Northeast is where most of the publicity about *Ludlum versus Kichsel* is being carried. Do you think that may be contributing to this upturn in sales?"

Vandermeer's shrug was eloquent. "Who knows? People are funny."

Monroe Biggins, for one, was not amused. "We've got to do something about that!" he cried.

Thatcher suspected that Vandermeer was already working on it.

3. Six-Pack

T HIRTY-FIVE MILES northwest of Chicago, the Kichsel Brewery was still producing and shipping ten million barrels of beer each year and retaining, as it had for three generations, its share of the national market. This was quite enough to occupy the time and attention of management and staff. No one felt this more keenly than Dean Kichsel, the latest Kichsel at the helm. Today, however, he had been dragged off to inspect the corner of his empire dedicated to Quax.

Only two years old, the facility should have encouraged warm proprietorial satisfaction. Giant stainless-steel vats, white-tiled walls, hoses snaking in every direction, all gleamed with first-rate maintenance. From the lager cellars to the bottle-capping equipment, everything hummed with smooth precision.

"I just don't know," Kichsel said dubiously. "Expanding your operation again means going to the board ahead of schedule, and we've got the Teamsters' negotiations coming up. Besides, there's that Water Board hearing . . ."

"The reason we're ahead of schedule is that Quax has been a success," said Alec Moore, ignoring lesser matters.

Kichsel nodded without enthusiasm. But then nature had made it difficult for him to look enthusiastic about anything. His white receding hair exposed a broad-domed forehead that bulged over baggy eyes and drooping jowls.

"You can see for yourself," Moore continued his argument, sa-

16

voring the bustle around them. "Quax is running close to capacity now. Pretty soon we won't be able to meet demand."

It was Quax and Alec Moore that were making retirement look good to Kichsel. Like most of the young men in the family, Moore had spent two years in the brewery before concluding, again like most of his cousins, that he preferred a future elsewhere. In his case, this had been a professorship of statistics at Northwestern, until fate caught up with him. Then, just after he inherited his mother's substantial holdings in the family firm, researchers discovered that per-capita beer consumption was leveling off. Instantly Alec Moore decided that the Kichsel Brewery needed the skills he had been wasting on the young. Armed with data about beer versus light beer, the growing popularity of wine, soft-drink marketing and, above all, low-cost techniques to produce alcohol-free beer, he descended.

"But that's nothing new," Dean had objected on that black day. "All the major brewers are offering non-alcoholics, next to the basic line—"

"And that's where Kichsel's missing an opportunity," Moore had instructed. "Forget about producing, Dean. Think about marketing. None of the alcohol regulations apply, so there's no reason to stick to package stores and taverns. We'll sell it like a soft drink—right next to soda in the supermarket, in vending machines along with fruit juice!"

Kichsel had not given up the fight, but he was outgunned. He had thrown in the towel long before Alec Moore ran out of arguments.

"With beer sales declining, Kichsel has to diversify," Moore had continued, twitching his glasses professorially. "You don't want us to try selling cheese, do you? Making Quax will be just like making beer, except for that last step of cracking out the alcohol. So, we hang on to the same work force, we deal with the same suppliers. And Kichsel keeps the edge you've built up over the years."

Thus, Quax was born and Alec Moore was installed as division manager and perpetual thorn in his cousin's flesh. Brimming over with ideas, he was unshakably confident.

"You'll have to find another name," Kichsel had tried to object. "Quax sounds too much like Kix."

Kix had been, was, and always would be the flagship of the line. "But that's the whole point!" Moore pounced. "We'll package it the same way too. We're openly selling a product that looks like beer, tastes like beer, has a head—and we're proud of it."

"Oh God," said Dean Kichsel to himself as Moore swept on:

"We can't sneak onto the market, hoping nobody will notice. We can't sell in new outlets without causing talk. So what's our answer? It's: *What are you complaining about!*"

"They'll say we're teaching kids to drink beer," said Kichsel with last-ditch stubbornness.

"They can try!" Alec Moore had said gleefully.

Initially, Kichsel had hoped that Alec and Quax would just go away. But from feeble beginnings, sales grew, modestly but steadily. Now he was stuck, talking about expanded capacity and more of the selling campaign that had already wrecked his peace of mind. Self-respect, and self-respect alone, had kept Kichsel from recrimination when Madeleine Underwood and NOBBY marched into court. Sustained by loyalty to family and firm, he signed the legal papers and held his tongue.

Fortunately, he was not the lone guardian of the larger interests at Kichsel's. Theo Benda stood beside him, without family ties or family stock, but a pillar of strength.

Alec Moore had come to value Benda too.

"What's your thinking, Theo?" he demanded. "You're the guy who really knows."

"Oh, there's no doubt Quax will be needing a new plant," Benda replied almost absently. "But not necessarily here, Alec. I want to do some number crunching before I commit myself. We've got to think about regional patterns for the next few years—and that means factoring in transportation costs."

Illinois was home base for Kichsel's, the site of its largest brewery. But satellite operations had sprung up in California and New Jersey. The considerations that Benda raised were legitimate, and Moore accepted them.

"Anything you decide," he said. "I'm not really competent on that end."

"Also," Benda added, "the union contract still has to come first.

18

That's what the board's really got to wrestle with. It's where we're going to see a real impact on earnings."

If Moore was chastened by this reminder of Quax's minor role in the Kichsel scheme of things, he did not show it. Setting a brisk pace, he led the way outdoors, charging ahead until they reached the railroad siding where hops and malted wheat were delivered.

"We're running out of silo space too," he announced.

Engulfed by the semisweet, semi-arid aroma that pervades all beer making, Kichsel dispiritedly studied the towering structures.

"I suppose we could take care of that to ease some of the pressure."

"Better wait until we come up with a master plan," said Benda softly. "It's not cost-effective to do things piecemeal."

His lack of emphasis was a statement in itself. Benda's square head sat solidly atop a bull neck and massive shoulders. Unlike Moore and Kichsel, he was informally attired, a rumpled, shirt-sleeved figure who was a familiar sight as he stomped around the compound. Even the slight accent he had brought from his native Czechoslovakia contributed to the picture of a master artisan supervising an age-old art. In fact, he was Kichsel's chief financial officer, one of the first non-family executives.

"It's a shame they put the employees' rec area over there," said Dean Kichsel. "Otherwise we could use the land on the other side of the tracks, and we wouldn't even have to extend the siding."

When public tours of the brewery became popular, the dusty old baseball diamond had been replaced by immaculately groomed playing fields, a professional jogging track and tennis courts. Furthermore, in recognition of midwestern weather, a substantial structure rose in the rear, housing squash courts and weight rooms.

"Unfortunately, we can't," said Benda. "The drainage there would cost a fortune. That's why we've left it as it is."

Moore did not share his cousin's sentimental paternalism about Kichsel, or Benda's encyclopedic grasp of its reality.

"So long as we can keep Quax up to the mark," he said singlemindedly. "Speaking of which, have I told you two the latest good news?"

Benda cocked his head warily, but Kichsel gave himself away.

"That woman's dropped the court case?" he exclaimed hopefully.

Moore blinked. The heartburn Madeleine Underwood and NOBBY were causing others left him untouched.

"Not that I've heard," he replied. "No, it's Claudia. She's pulled off a big one."

This brought a subterranean twinkle to Benda's eye. His habitual reserve did not extend to Mrs. Fentiman, whose energy and ambition touched a chord. Without ever saying so, he felt that they shared a special bond. Highly paid professionals both, they were not Kichsels like Dean and Alec.

"And what has this marvelous marketing lady done now, Alec?" he inquired jovially.

"She's signed up Rugby's—the fast-food chain that is expanding east, you know. She's convinced them to carry Quax," Alec announced.

This time Kichsel groaned aloud, and when Benda and Moore both indicated curiosity, unburdened himself.

"It'll just hand that Underwood woman more grist for her mill," he lamented.

"Oh, for God's sake," Alec replied. "You're not still fussing about that nuisance suit, are you?"

In intergenerational tussles, youth has the strength and optimism. But there is one powerful weapon available to the opposition.

"You don't remember Prohibition," Kichsel accused. Actually he didn't either, but he had heard enough about it from his father and grandfather to think that he did.

So many distilleries, vineyards—and breweries—had disappeared during the Prohibition years that the survivors all got religion. Moderation, designated drivers and knowing when to say "when" became their watchwords. An industry tarred by the mark of Satan had embraced virtue in a big way.

But the history that weighed so heavily on Dean Kichsel, and haunted every serious brewer, meant little to Alec Moore.

"That was a long time ago, and things have changed," he declared. "There aren't a lot of crazies out there agitating to ban beer."

"Don't you believe it," said Kichsel darkly, but Benda was more inquisitive.

"What about Mrs. Underwood and NOBBY?" he asked.

Moore laughed aloud.

"A nuisance—but nothing more. Hell, she couldn't lay a finger on Kichsel if she tried—and all she's doing to Quax is giving us a lot of free publicity."

His insouciance goaded his cousin.

"Forget about Quax," he snapped with unwonted vehemence. "In fact, you can forget about beer—if you haven't already. Think about cars and drunken driving! Think about minors drinking! Think about substance abuse. They're all out there, waiting to clobber us if we give them a chance."

But, as Theo Benda observed with amusement, for every old argument there is a new one. Moore, ignoring Kichsel's outburst, indicated that he had no intention of forgetting Quax.

"Concentrate on health, Dean," he said kindly. "That's what sells America these days—not all these scare stories. And that's where Quax is a winner all the way."

"Health!" Kichsel snorted.

"Just think about it," Moore cajoled. "The country's into light, nutritious and natural. Well, that's exactly what Quax offers. The fact that it's brewed is irrelevant. Quax is healthy—and that's what matters. It doesn't have a lot of fat and salt. It isn't loaded with artificial additives or sugar. And it doesn't contain dangerous stimulants—like caffeine."

Then, modulating to a less hortatory tone, he added: "So instead of agonizing about all these bogeymen of yours, Dean, you should be thanking God Quax sales are growing, while everything else Kichsel produces is flat as a pancake. Isn't that right, Theo?"

"Ye-es," said Benda, withdrawing himself from the controversy.

"Quax," said Dean Kichsel thickly, "will have to grow astronomically before it makes the slightest damn difference to Kichsel!"

"And that," Alec Moore retorted, "is just exactly what it's going to do!"

4. Another Round

MADELEINE UNDERWOOD was as enthusiastic about free publicity as Alec Moore. To disseminate the NOBBY message, she seized every opportunity that came her way. For twenty minutes on talk radio, she was willing to drop everything, *Ludlum versus Kichsel* included, and rush down to Philadelphia for the night.

Congressman Harry Hull could do better than a local radio show any day in his Texas home district. But with an education convention in Philadelphia, three full hours were going to be dedicated to the child-related issues that had helped sweep him into office. That much exposure, shared with a rotating cast of near celebrities, was irresistible to an ambitious congressional freshman. Hull accepted the invitation to appear, to shine and, with any luck, to broaden his base.

And even after one hundred and forty minutes of close attention to often incoherent questions, he was still able to summon a warm welcome for Madeleine Underwood as she replaced her predecessor—a police specialist on schoolyard drug dealers—in front of the microphone.

Jack Marten, the low-keyed talkmaster, seized the commercial break to spell out the ground rules for the newcomer.

"I'll introduce you and give you a couple of minutes to outline your subject. Then the congressman, here, will briefly give us his position and we'll go directly to taking calls. Right?"

Madeleine nodded energetic agreement and they were under way.

". . . Mrs. Madeleine Underwood, executive director of NOBBY. Perhaps you'd explain to us the goals of your organization, Mrs. Underwood."

As Madeleine competently reproduced her prepared text, Hull began to relax. With lethal schoolyards behind him and newborn infants displaying withdrawal symptoms yet to come, this could be the breathing space he sorely needed.

"And Congressman Hull, what is your response to NOBBY's program?"

"I am not only familiar with the organization's work on the East Coast, I am already on record as calling for adequate research into the long-term results of Quax's promotion. Without prejudging the issue, I think it's a good example of the everyday dangers to which we could be exposing our children. Glue-sniffing alone demonstrates the need for more extensive investigation of what comes into our homes and possibly the need for regulating packaging and promotion."

It was only after the first few calls that Hull realized his relaxation might be premature. As John Thatcher had noticed before him, Madeleine's strength as a solo performer did not extend into the area of give-and-take.

She had been startled enough by a rough-hewn male voice to let herself be embroiled in an irrelevant argument.

"Listen, it all comes down to whether or not you stay on top of your kids," the basso had growled. "I told mine that if I caught them having a drink before they were eighteen, I'd beat the bejesus out of them. As long as they know you mean business, it works fine."

"And you call that communication!" she gasped indignantly. "It's a sure road to secret alcoholism. You have to make them understand the reasons for your . . ."

And they were both off and running.

"I think we may be straying from the topic," said Hull, responding to the silent plea from the talkmaster. "Mrs. Underwood's primary concern is for the innocent and parentally

23

approved use of a beverage that may lead to alcohol consumption."

That was all Jack Marten needed.

"And now for our next caller," he broke in swiftly. "Is that Barbara from Ambler?"

Barbara from Ambler was very elevated indeed and had called primarily to give the world the benefit of her own superior domestic arrangements. She and her husband regularly drank a stately glass of wine with dinner, not only as a source of personal gratification but in order to educate their children in the way they should go.

Everyone breathed a sigh of relief when the next caller evinced no desire to parade his individual excellence.

"Either it has alcohol or it doesn't. I say anything that isn't the real stuff is a godsend. You just have to look at what's floating around out there."

It should have been the perfect, foolproof call for Madeleine to handle. But within three sentences she had Harry Hull straightening in alarm.

"When you hear that Congressman Hull has joined our movement, that should convince you that opposition to Quax is justified. A responsible government official would not endorse our program unless there was a real peril."

Oh, no you don't, lady, Hull thought to himself. I haven't broken my back to create an image just to have you cast me as a spear carrier in your production. And you sure as hell aren't getting a blank check for my support.

"I certainly do sympathize with the anxieties of NOBBY's membership," he chimed in the minute Madeleine paused for breath. "What's more, I'll admit I get edgy about the resemblance between Quax and Kix. But I don't know if my alarm is justified. That's why the action that *I* advocate is a moratorium on Kichsel's whole marketing strategy until we've had adequate time to study its consequences."

He had managed not only to set limits to his identification with NOBBY but also to cue in the next caller.

"I don't think I can agree with that, Dick," Hull was able to say a few minutes later. "Just because packaging and promotion in certain areas have never been regulated doesn't mean we shouldn't do it in the future. We had this argument about the Surgeon General's warning on cigarettes. You have to realize that the sale of consumer goods gets more sophisticated every day. Ten years ago the big companies hired market researchers. Now they employ behavioral analysts, which means the messages are becoming subtler and perhaps more insidious."

While Harry Hull was delicately tap-dancing along the fine line between hysteria and callous disregard, Madeleine Underwood was thoroughly enjoying herself until a calm young woman took the field.

"I think Mrs. Underwood is overreacting," she began. "National crusades and mass protests are entirely inappropriate in this instance. Quax is not alcoholic and the problem of our children drinking beer a few years later should be treated separately."

"So many people make that mistake," Madeleine said sadly. "They don't understand the powerful influence of association, which can ultimately be just as dangerous as eighty-proof content. NOBBY's function is to create awareness of the psychological games that the Kichsel company is playing."

"No, you're the one who doesn't understand," was the crisp reply. "There are two totally different kinds of prohibited conduct that parents have to deal with. The first kind you want your children to avoid for the rest of their lives—such as taking drugs. But there are other potentially dangerous activities you expect them to engage in as adults—for example, driving a car, having sexual relations or drinking beer. You have to teach them to do those things responsibly. No parent can slough that responsibility onto a company."

Two angry red spots had appeared on Madeleine's cheeks but, to do her credit, her voice was rigidly controlled. "NOBBY is certainly not recommending that any company act as a surrogate parent. But your examples are simplistic. Parents should of course teach their youngsters to be careful crossing the street. At the same time it helps to demand safer streets, to insist on enforcing speed limits and revoking licenses of drunken drivers. NOBBY simply wants a safer street." Pleased with her felicitous response, she adopted a more discursive manner. "And now that I come to think of it, that analogy could hardly be more timely. You may not know this, Congressman

Hull, but a large fast-food chain called Rugby's has just agreed to serve Quax. In other words, they are preparing to expose young children to the notion that hamburgers and a beer look-alike are natural companions. I assure you NOBBY plans to mount protests against this transparent attempt by Kichsel to enlist allies in its campaign to increase adolescent alcoholism."

Swallowing the suggestion that the expansion of a Texas-based enterprise was an open book to Mrs. Underwood while remaining a secret to Texas legislators, Hull said mildly, "Elmer Rugby may be misguided in this decision but it was certainly not inspired by any desire to promote alcoholism."

They had both forgotten that the caller was still on the line.

"The trouble with your organization is that you're trying to turn the whole world into a child-safe play area. The first place most children see a beer next to hamburgers is in their own home."

The evening was not proving to be the banner event Madeleine Underwood had expected. Some offensive young woman called Phyllis was pretending to know more about the dangers posed by Quax than her elders and betters. And Harry Hull was proving to be a very wayward recruit into the ranks of NOBBY. On top of all that, an uneasy recollection of conditions once prevailing in the Underwood household made it impossible to refute Phyllis's last proposition out of hand. Instead, Madeleine turned her mounting ire on a less embarrassing target.

"Mr. Rugby knows exactly what he is doing and has to be held accountable for his actions just as if he were a drug dealer. The many teenage addicts caused by his willingness to profit from Quax must be laid directly at his door."

This time Jack Marten did not aim his SOS at Congressman Hull. Instead he directed a meaningful gaze at the engineers on the other side of the glass and clutched his own microphone.

"Thank you very much for joining us, Mrs. Underwood. Now it's time for another word from our sponsors, but don't go away, folks. When we return, we will hear from Dr. Olympia Arkwright."

He turned to Hull the minute the door had closed behind a still flustered Madeleine. "Sorry about that, Congressman."

"It's my fault, I was the one who suggested her," Harry admitted gloomily. "When you said you wanted some leavening in that slot, I thought she might be light relief."

In the course of any given year, more than five hundred people eager to express their views passed through Marten's studio. He was an expert.

"Mrs. Underwood doesn't see it that way. As far as she's concerned, NOBBY is right up there with stopping the war in Vietnam. She's—"

He broke off to produce a practiced smile.

"I'm Jack Marten, Dr. Arkwright. Why don't you take that seat next to Congressman Hull and I'll give you the rundown on our drill here."

"QUAX!" SAID CHARLIE Trinkam out of the blue. "All of a sudden everywhere you look, there's something popping up about Quax."

He was amusing himself with *The New York Times* while Thatcher studied the latest effusion from the Atlanta Fed. More than willing to be diverted, he looked up, mildly surprised to hear his own sentiments voiced. To the best of Thatcher's knowledge, nobody at the Sloan, apart from George Lancer, had the slightest interest in Kichsel's foray into the youth market—and emphatically not Charlie. Good gray Everett Gabler, Trinkam's counterpart and polar opposite, would have been weighing in with strictures about beer, profits and morality, but Everett was currently enjoying the Spartan pleasures of a health resort in northern Maine.

Charlie had to jog Thatcher's memory. "Rugby's just announced that it's going to sell this Quax stuff," he said helpfully. When this did not ring a bell, he added, "You haven't forgotten that Elmer Rugby's one of our clients, have you?"

"I'm not sure I ever knew," Thatcher replied. "Between George and Kichsel and now you and Rugby, why do I get the feeling that pincers are closing?"

Charlie ignored the aside and stuck to the essentials. "We just signed him up when he began expanding east. So far he's only opened two outlets here in New York, but he's planning more."

"Delighted to hear it," said Thatcher. Given the impossibility of keeping tabs on all the Sloan's commercial clients, he was always pleased to learn that one of them, unbeknownst to him, was prospering. "Just don't mention Rugby's to George or he'll have another crisis of conscience."

"Not when he sees Rugby's cash flow," said Charlie stoutly. "But that means you haven't met Elmer. You're missing an experience. Next time he comes around, I'll trot him in. He's a fellow who appreciates attention, and I think you'll get a kick out of him. He's one of a kind."

"Shoot him in," said Thatcher, returning to Atlanta.

Within the week, Charlie was doing just that.

"Glad to meet you," said Elmer Rugby, pumping Thatcher's outstretched hand. "It's a good idea to get to know the people you do business with. It would have saved me from making a lot of mistakes if I'd learned that early on."

Thatcher did not turn a hair. "And did you make a lot of mistakes, Mr. Rugby?"

"Call me Elmer. Mistakes? I've made every one in the book. Didn't get on the right track until I was damn near forty—and that's leaving it pretty late."

Thatcher was in no danger of swallowing all of this self-criticism. "Charlie here is enthusiastic about Rugby's prospects. In fact, the only reservation I've heard—"

"Reservation?" barked Rugby, raking Charlie with a cold stare.

"Not guilty!" said Charlie, hands raised in surrender. "Don't shoot!"

"I was thinking about your tie-in promotion with Quax," said Thatcher hastily. While he enjoyed watching the games people play, he himself preferred the straightforward approach. "The opposition to that appears to be growing."

"You mean those maniacs who're running around claiming that serving Quax is the devil's work?" Rugby retorted. "That's Quax's problem—not mine. And from what I saw of that little lady from Kichsel, they can take care of themselves."

"Okay," said Charlie. "And maybe the mad-mothers movement won't make waves for you, but now there's this congressman—and from Texas, too—who's making noises on the House floor."

28

"Politicians," said Rugby with robust contempt. "Listen, I wouldn't be where I am today if I was scared of those stumblebums."

This was an avenue that neither Charlie nor Thatcher cared to explore, so Rugby continued, "The way I see it, if Quax pulls in the crowds, fine! Rugby's will get an edge over the competition. If not, then we yank it and no harm done."

This pragmatism had its appeal, especially for bankers. But, as Thatcher knew, life does not always cooperate. Rugby probably knew exactly how to cope with government, local or national; most successful entrepreneurs do. But energized citizens on a single-issue rampage could be new to him, and easy to underestimate.

"So you're not seriously worried about NOBBY?" he asked.

"Hell, I haven't bothered to find out what NOBBY means," snorted Rugby. "That's how worried I am!"

"IT'S NOBBY," EXPLAINED Sean Cushing. "That's for 'No Beer-Buying Youngsters.' "

"Sounds interesting," said his companion. "Do you like it there?"

"It's a challenge," said Cushing, modestly self-confident. In this restaurant, assurance was as obligatory as a credit card, and even lunch with an old friend could not be treated as a purely social occasion.

"I was just a little surprised," said Karen Zwick artlessly. "When I heard that you were hooking up with a non-profit."

"Executive director," he replied, automatically inflating his status. Titles had mattered to him and to Karen back when they were both riding high at Crain Company. Since then their paths had diverged, and Karen, who had survived the great downsizing, could still glow naturally. Cushing had to work at it.

"Don't sell non-profits short," he said. "Plenty of them are as big-time as anybody else."

Karen nodded. "Oh, I know," she said.

Fortunately she did not know about the chaos standing between Cushing and his goal of transforming NOBBY, of replacing Madeleine Underwood and her amateurs with a large, well-heeled apparatus. But Karen had known when he got the ax at Crain and she probably guessed that months of unemployment had cost him the BMW, the condo and the time share in Aruba. So necessity had to be presented as choice.

"It's the right place and the right time for me to start over," he said, defying her to sympathize.

He had forgotten Karen's tenacity.

"The people you work with," she said, tracking his own calculations. "What about them?"

Pretending to misunderstand, he said, "A great bunch, Karen."

She pursed her lips and he unbent. "They're nothing to worry about. I can manage them with one hand tied behind my back. There's a woman named Underwood who's a royal pain in the ass. But I know how to handle her."

5. Turning on the Tap

T HE TRAIN TRIP back to New York gave Madeleine Underwood an opportunity for a grand review of programs and projects. When she swept into NOBBY's downtown office, she had a list in hand.

"Naturally, I'll be monitoring *Ludlum versus Kichsel*," she declared. "But at the same time, we've got to organize a major demonstration against Rugby's. Now, I've roughed out a draft letter to our members in the metropolitan area to encourage them to join in, but I don't have time to polish it. Can you whip it into shape by this afternoon, Sean, so we can mail it in time?"

Silently, Sean Cushing nodded. What Mrs. Underwood called a rough draft he described as a disorganized jumble.

". . . and it would be a good idea to add some numbers to show how important Rugby's is. Things like how many outlets they have, and how many people they serve. Do you think you can get that?"

"Already done," he said sturdily, illustrating how far NOBBY had come since it first saw the light of day in a corner of the Underwood living room in New Jersey. There, after thirty years of marriage, Madeleine had found herself with an empty house, substantial alimony and time to fill. One day she penned an indignant letter to the local newspaper about Quax, thereby discovering a new role in life. Soon she was writing, phoning and speaking to community groups. The response was so encouraging that it became necessary to transform NOBBY as well. Madeleine and her supporters still supplied the enthusiasm, but the acquisition of a proper office and the installation of Sean Cushing moved NOBBY's operations onto a more professional level. Inevitably, there were conflicts.

"We also have to finalize the schedule for your tour," he reminded her. "You'll be leaving in two weeks. California is no problem because we already have the makings of an organization there. So you'll start with L.A. and San Francisco."

"As well as San Diego," she said.

"Right. But the real question is the stops on the way back. There's not much point to them unless we get a good payback. I've already got you booked for Minneapolis and Atlanta."

"What about Cleveland? I thought that was on the list too."

Sean shook his head. "Not unless they get their act together. So far they've got a membership of seventy-five. It just isn't worth it."

"But my appearance will bring in new people."

"Madeleine, there are just so many hours in your day and so many days in a week. Now that we're going national, you'll have to ration your time. I think we should adopt some ground rules—say, at least two hundred members before they get a personal appearance."

She was torn and Sean added, "These barn-storming tours are very taxing. I don't want you coming back here totally exhausted."

"You know I thrive on work."

"It's not the work that bothers me. It's all the hassle in traveling—checking in at airports, dealing with bad ventilation in hotels, eating strange meals, just getting your laundry done."

Madeleine did not give up easily, but Cushing finally induced her to sacrifice Cleveland. This returned them to the present.

"I promised the Ludlums I'd talk to them today to bring them up to date," she remembered. "Schedule a call to them for about four o'clock, will you?"

"Do you want me to take care of it?" he asked, knowing she would decline.

Since instinct had led Mrs. Underwood to pluck the Ludlums from obscurity, their performance as NOBBY stars was a matter of personal pride to her.

"I'll make a point to reach them," she said quickly.

"They've been in court every day," Sean observed. "What kind of update do they need?"

"They're a little overwhelmed by all the attention," she explained. "The poor dears can use all the encouragement I give them."

A flurry of voices from the outer office caused her to glance at her watch with a squawk of dismay.

"Where has the time gone?" she exclaimed. "That must be Iona coming in, and I'll have to leave in five minutes."

When a young woman burdened with a bulging portfolio entered, Madeleine overflowed with apology.

"Oh, Iona, I'm so sorry. I know I said I'd meet with you now, but I have another appointment."

"That's all right, Madeleine. Of course you have to keep your appointment," the young woman said placidly.

"But it's not all right. This is the third time this has happened. It's not fair to ask you to take so much responsibility."

"Don't worry, I understand how busy you are. Anyway, I can work it all out with Sean."

Madeleine was shaking her head in vexation. "This will be our most important demonstration to date and I can't afford to lose contact with it. If we don't stop Rugby's in their tracks, there's no telling what the other hamburger franchises will do. Everything has to be just right."

Suddenly her face cleared and she began rooting around her capacious shoulder bag. "I've got it," she said, triumphantly producing a small recorder. "All you have to do, Sean, is tape your meeting with Iona. That way I can review all the plans tonight."

"Sure thing," he agreed.

Madeleine's unwillingness to delegate was equaled only by her enthusiasm for electronic gadgetry. Six months ago she had fallen upon the notion of a fax in her home.

"That way," she had said earnestly, "I can keep in touch even when I'm not here."

Convinced that every vagrant thought about NOBBY was of value, she had generated a flood of material. Fortunately Sean Cushing was a sensible young man who had taken the measure of his employer from the outset. Knowing full well that she lacked the self-discipline to read mountains of material, he had matched her, word for word, page for page. Within two weeks the fax had fallen silent.

Her current toy was the tape recorder and Sean confidently expected this experience to be even more disillusioning. Like many people, Madeleine had no idea that most conversations, stripped of the immediacy of participation, were unbelievably boring, repetitive and disconnected. Hours and hours of playback would soon bring her to her senses. In the meantime Sean assiduously produced tape after tape to join the growing pile in New Jersey.

So he smiled blandly as she scooped up her belongings and raced for the elevator.

"You know," he said, in the sudden calm, "I sometimes wonder what all the damned fuss is about. What difference does it make if Rugby's serves Quax?"

"That's because you don't have kids," said Iona Perez.

It was because she was the mother of two boys, aged nine and eleven, that she had joined NOBBY. As the coordinator of volunteer activities, she was a godsend to Sean Cushing. Under her guidance, envelopes were stuffed for fund-raisers and brochures were distributed at subway stations. The right number of volunteers showed up at the right place at the right time. And if they were appearing in public, they had been coached in the right answers to all predictable questions.

Now she cast an appraising eye over the hodgepodge of notes that Sean would shortly be transforming into a polished document.

"Oh, dear, Madeleine does get carried away sometimes," she said indulgently. "You will tone it down, won't you? We can't sound as if we think Quax is the only problem out there."

In addition to her other virtues, Iona managed to combine admiration for Madeleine with realism.

"Trust me," Sean murmured.

As they settled at the desk to deal with the voluminous documents Iona had presented, they could have been mistaken for brother and sister. They shared the same undistinguished physical appearance—medium height, slim build, bland coloring, neutral features. Iona had the advantage of a lilting musical voice while

Sean's only claim to fame was a gap between his front teeth that gave his infrequent smile an engagingly boyish quality. But their chief similarity was the quiet, serious determination with which they plodded through the host of preparations necessary to a successful, effective protest. The creation of shift schedules, the production of suitable posters and placards, the wording for flyers—all were dispatched on an orderly basis.

Iona, ticking off each item as they went, gave a sigh of satisfaction as they neared the end.

"One thing more. I've agreed to provide buses for the chapters in Nyack, Huntington, Tarrytown and Passaic."

"Can you take care of that?"

"No problem," she assured him as she prepared to leave.

Sean, conscious of their progress, marveled to himself at the difference between these two women. From the day she first appeared, Iona had made it clear that her sons constituted her first priority. Her stints in the office were rigidly confined to school hours, with suitable adjustments for holidays and vacations. She rarely mentioned the other demands on her time, never seemed hurried or excited, and yet, at two-thirty every afternoon, the day's assignment was invariably completed.

What a contrast with Madeleine, who rushed into NOBBY later that day like a whirlwind, stalking into her office to use the phone, demanding her messages, examining the afternoon's mail. She even, to Sean's private amusement, pounced on the tape recorder as if it were a jewel of great price.

"Now, Sean, I don't have much time," she announced, perching on a chair ready for instant flight, "but we really must discuss our approach to the Food and Drug Administration."

"That may be a little premature."

"Nonsense! A research report from NOBBY will be just the thing to wake them up."

"But that's the difficulty. NOBBY doesn't have the resources to do any research."

They were using different dictionaries. Madeleine, who resorted to her favorite word to describe any piece of writing containing a number, shook her head vigorously.

"Of course we do. It's just a matter of getting the facts together. We have over ten thousand members, and we can always circularize them to enlist the help of husbands and friends with useful expertise."

"Actually, there are no physical facts to support the claim that drinking Quax promotes beer addiction."

"Oh, physical facts," Madeleine replied with an airy wave. "I think we should concentrate on the psychological dangers. There we know we're on firm ground, and Dr. Schumacher will be an enormous help."

Silently Sean debated tactics. First he had to persuade Madeleine that the opportunity for a formal presentation to the FDA was not a matter of course. There he had some hope of success. Schumacher, however, represented more sensitive ground. It had not escaped Sean's notice that Paul Jackson welcomed Schumacher's appearance with a wolfish grin and employed every possible device to extend his stay on the stand.

"Look what a good job he's doing for us in the trial," said Madeleine, who had relished every word of Schumacher's performance.

"Of course that's the right line to take when he's addressing laymen," said Sean, sacrificing truth to expediency. "But a less dogmatic approach would probably be more useful with the FDA. It would be an acknowledgment that they're the ones who get to make the decision."

Madeleine had not been listening. "And once we've won the case, his testimony will have official sanction. By the way, did I tell you how much the Ludlums appreciate our help? They were quite touching just now."

"Well, we're paying all the bills."

"Sean, Sean, you never see the whole picture," she replied with playful censure. "Of course the money is part of it. But the Ludlums want to see that this doesn't happen to other boys. They could never get all this publicity if it weren't for NOBBY."

At last there was something he could agree with. When he was opposing Madeleine, Sean thought it wise to throw in as much approval as possible.

"How right you are. And what we need is more publicity before we approach the FDA. We can't impress them with Dr. Schumacher because they have access to their own psychologists. What they don't have available is a barometer of public dissatisfaction with Quax's marketing. If we can give them that first, then we'll have a basis on which to interest them."

"It will all work out," she replied buoyantly. "You'll see. I only wish I had more time to thrash this out, but I'm due for a conference with our attorneys. We still have to finalize our strategy for the trial."

Sean refrained from pointing out that lawyers were supposed to earn their fat fees by undertaking this task themselves. He was otherwise occupied trying to identify the flicker of apprehension that danced down his spine. It did not take long. For over a year NOBBY had risen smoothly from one plateau to another. Madeleine might not understand Sean's systems or even Iona's carefully dovetailed schedules. She was, however, a born showman and her deficiencies had not mattered.

But now Madeleine was thirsting for new worlds to conquer.

"So what?" Sean tried to reassure himself. "The lawyers will bird-dog her at the courthouse."

"And after that?" persisted an inner voice.

Sean might be able to squash the desire to tangle with the FDA, but Madeleine's end run with the Ludlums spoke for itself. He would come into the office some morning to find that she had indentured NOBBY to the service of some other unknown.

"I'm losing control," he admitted, finally putting his finger on the sore spot. "And there's no telling what she'll be up to next."

6. Hops and Skips

ITH PRIVATE CITIZENS, special-interest groups and the courts buzzing about Quax, it was inevitable that another entity should want to join the fun.

"Congress to Investigate Quax," said the handout from the office of Congressman Leon Rossi, (D.-N.Y.).

Reproduced almost verbatim in the metropolitan press, it prompted comment in New York and Washington.

"What's gotten into Leon?" wondered an assemblyman from the Bronx.

Rossi, a dapper old warhorse, represented mean streets and schools with metal detectors. In Washington he was famed for his unswerving loyalty and his absenteeism.

". . . a real party hack," ran the think-tank consensus. "Which is why they finally gave him this subcommittee on Inner City Youth."

By then, Rossi had issued the first statement he had ever made that was not a bid for more funding. Speculation mounted, at least in some circles.

"Reform Candidate Challenges Rossi!" wrote a usually well-informed columnist.

Rossi found the attention gratifying, but after ten lackluster terms in obscurity, it did not go to his head. He was still proceeding on the tried-and-true principle that the best way to keep the electorate sweet was to appear in its midst—at rallies for District C Steamfitters Local 302, at weddings in the Portoriqueño Pentecostal Chapel, or at rummage sales for the Boys' Club. Congressional hearings conducted within shouting distance of Central Park qualified, so he issued orders that set administrative assistants and staffers scurrying, then leaned back and lit an ivory-tipped cigarillo.

Ranking members of the subcommittee were less content. Enthusiasm for the hearings was concentrated at the lower end of the seniority scale, where Congressman Harry Hull sat. His only regret was that his own name figured so slightly in the coverage, and that the Rossi road company was not heading for Austin.

"But that's just plain ridiculous," he remarked, laughing at himself.

"What a spectacle Rossi would make in Texas," said his wife, passing the bag of potato chips. "He always looks as if he goes to a Mafia tailor."

The Hulls were unwinding in their modest Washington home, a furnished apartment near Capitol Hill. Harry and the realtor described it as gentrified, but Betty Jo was as down-to-earth as she was pretty. She recognized a dump when she saw one.

"Leon's not so bad, once you get to know him," said Harry.

Betty Jo, who had campaigned at his side, knew better.

"Even if that's true," she said, reaching out to rescue the few remaining chips, "I still say you played him just right, Harry."

He would have liked to agree but mistakes do happen, so instead he reviewed the record.

"Well, the leadership took some convincing," he said modestly. "But nudging Rossi—hell, that was easy as pie, Betty Jo. He'll do anything to get some ink in New York."

"In the end, you're bound to get a lot of the credit," she predicted. "After all, you're the only one who knows a damn thing about Quax."

Harry nodded, seeing rave reviews ahead. Favorable exposure could make the Hull dream a reality, if the inevitable hurdles were safely negotiated.

"Something worrying you?" Betty Jo asked, deciphering his frown.

"Nothing, really," he hedged. Even to himself, Hull was reluctant to admit that, since Philadelphia, his certainty that Quax was a vehicle sent to give him mileage had been slightly chilled.

"It's just that I hope there won't be any surprises."

"There shouldn't be," she assured him.

But then, Betty Jo had not met Madeleine Underwood.

NEITHER HAD DEAN Kichsel, and he had already passed beyond surprise. Rattled to the core by a summons from the subcommittee, he traversed Chicago's O'Hare Airport in a state of open perturbation. Captains of American industry usually radiate near divinity, even when they are part of the stream of humanity converging on a departure gate. They are not expected to halt abruptly, pile up pedestrian traffic, and glare at banners festooning a concession stand.

QUAX—AND YOU CAN FORGET JET LAG!

Kichsel drew a shaky breath. "Will you take a look at that!"

George Lancer had no alternative.

"It's tantamount to telling people not to drink beer," Kichsel fulminated. "As if Quax hasn't done enough harm, now it's turning against Kix."

Lancer made soothing noises which he amplified later in the day for John Thatcher's benefit.

"Naturally, Dean's upset," he explained, understanding as usual.

"Naturally," Thatcher agreed.

They were in the Lancer duplex, awaiting the arrival of the dinner guest. With Mrs. Lancer in the Bahamas, Dean Kichsel was being entertained *en garçon*.

"You will remember that it's been a hard day for him, won't you, John?" he said.

Lancer did not request similar forbearance for himself, but then, as Thatcher had frequently noted, George was a mild-mannered, soft-spoken man of iron. His ability to go from speech to meeting to convention—and back—was awe-inspiring. Lancer's day had been just as taxing as Kichsel's because it had been largely identical, although there had been one salient difference.

"I'm not emotionally involved," he said scrupulously as he checked his watch. Kichsel was running twenty minutes late.

"But concerned, George," Thatcher replied. "You can't deny that you're concerned."

Lancer had been in Chicago fulfilling his duties as a Kichsel director.

"I gather your meeting this morning was sheer hell," said Thatcher.

"Yes," said Lancer after some thought. "You can put it that way."

Thatcher's shorthand version was comprehensive as well as accurate. Apparently when Lancer had joined the rest of the board members, he had been primed to tackle the Teamsters, the Water Board, even, at a pinch, Alec Moore's expansion hopes. But some busybody had distributed copies of the morning *Tribune* alongside the carafes and notepads. Even without the careful yellow highlighting, the damning words leaped from the page.

". . . Quax, produced by Chicago-based Kichsel Brewery. Said New York Congressman Leon Rossi today: "This is not a witch hunt. We only want to get the facts."

As is so often the case, headlines preceded legal notification.

"And Dean went into a tailspin," Lancer commented. "That's why he put on that unseemly display at O'Hare. The last thing he wants is to be grilled in public about Quax. Frankly, he's beside himself."

Several questions immediately leaped to Thatcher's mind, but silvery chimes sounded in the distance, followed by discreet murmurs from the Lancer's newest faithful retainer. A minute later, Dean Kichsel bustled into the library, full of apologies for his tardiness.

". . . checking in and, good God! You wouldn't believe how many messages were waiting for me."

He broke off for his introduction to Thatcher, then continued his explanation.

"For one reason or another, half of Kichsel seems to be here in New York," he concluded wearily. "That's what held me up."

Thatcher suspected that the calls on Kichsel's time might have cost him a much-needed nap. But apart from fatigue, which could be attributed to any air travel these days, there was nothing immediately noteworthy about Kichsel. That he had spent many honorable years as the company's faithful steward seemed credible enough. Even in post-merger America, worthies like him abound—solid, safe and dependable.

"Until a crisis looms," said Thatcher to himself, although, as the evening progressed, he was inclined to revise this opinion.

If, as Lancer maintained, Dean Kichsel had been shattered by news of the Rossi Subcommittee, he was making a fast recovery.

"Naturally, we'll be grateful for any support the Sloan cares to give us," he said over soup. "But before I left Chicago, I spoke with our lawyers—"

"Paul Jackson?" asked Thatcher, trying to strike a livelier note.

"No, our in-house counsel," Kichsel corrected. "At any rate, they assure me that Kichsel may be subjected to a short, politically motivated media event, but nothing more serious is likely to emerge."

His dignity was undented by the prospect of notoriety and Lancer took this to mean that he was back in form. So did Thatcher.

"I'm glad to hear that you don't anticipate serious repercussions about Quax," he said to keep the conversational ball rolling. "I don't pretend to be an expert on the subject, but it happens that another Sloan client, Elmer Rugby of Rugby's, is involved. I know you must be familiar with him, but if you haven't actually met, we'd be happy to introduce you. Rugby's in town for a few days too."

"I'd like that very much," Kichsel replied. "A big customer is always a big customer."

"I'll try to get hold of him," Thatcher promised.

Kichsel smiled sourly. "You'll probably find him at the subcommittee hearings," he said. Then, bursting forth: "It's just like Alec to sign him up in time for a congressional investigation."

Lancer played the good host. "Oh, come on, Dean. Alec couldn't have foreseen that."

Recovering himself, Kichsel agreed. "I suppose not." Then, with an effort, he turned to other woes, and the Teamsters lasted them through the rest of dinner.

Kichsel lingered long enough for coffee, then departed pleading his early start the next morning.

"And what was that jab about Alec, whoever he may be?" asked Thatcher.

Lancer got up to poke the fire. "Quax is Alec Moore's brainchild," he said shortly. "Dean's gotten so that he hates the sound of the name."

With a House probe in the offing, this seemed comprehensible, but, as Thatcher remarked, Kichsel gave every indication of coming to terms with the immediate menace of Leon Rossi.

"Oh, he's doing his best to sound positive," Lancer agreed. "Unfortunately, that's difficult for him. Dean's let Quax make his life miserable for the last two years."

"Uncomfortable, yes," said Thatcher. "But miserable?"

Obligingly George supplied some background. "You see, Quax goes to the heart of things at Kichsel. Dean's been assuming that he'll go on until he's ready to step down and hand over to his next in line, who happens to be a very competent CFO named Benda. Then, out of the blue, up pops Alec Moore!"

"And Moore is . . . ?"

"Moore's a cousin, he's Quax, he's ambitious, and as far as Dean's concerned, he's trouble waiting to happen," said George, more acidly than was his habit.

"Trouble, some of which is already upon him," said Thatcher, unheard because just then Lancer exploded into a paroxysm of sneezing.

7. Bottled Up

IKE TRIALS, CONGRESSIONAL hearings attract a motley crowd. There are those whose presence is mandatory. When the Rossi Subcommittee convened in the Babcock Auditorium, the official witness list included representatives from the Kichsel Brewery, NOBBY, the Soft Drink Institute and several consumer groups. Others, however, were there of their own free will. Dr. Joseph Schumacher, for example, had not been asked to appear. But, convinced that the undetected danger of non-addictive substances was his road to fame and fortune, he arrived long before the first gavel fell and stayed late, making himself available to anybody willing to listen.

His was a special case, but as old hands know, the importance of congressional hearings is often better gauged by examining the audience than by listening to the testimony.

Roger Vandermeer, casting a professional eye over the crowd, instantly spotted one significant block of seats.

"You can see which way the wind is blowing," he whispered, leaning over to address one of his clients. "Those guys in the fifth row on the other side are McDonald's and Burger King."

Swiveling, the burly man made an even more distressing identification. "But look at the ones two rows further back," he snarled. "They're from Disney. You don't think Kichsel's had the nerve to try to sell to them, do you? I can't believe it!"

"I wouldn't put anything past that outfit," a companion said darkly. "They'll probably try to peddle their stuff at the next Boy Scout Jamboree."

Vandermeer fell back on the hard-headed approach. "We have to face facts. Kichsel's position has been the same from the start. According to them, Quax is just another soft drink. That's how they justify their aggressive marketing, and it means nothing is safe from them."

A long way off, Dean Kichsel was also spotting familiar faces. "All the other breweries have got someone here," he said, acknowledging a wave from a section toward the rear.

"Makes sense," Theo Benda grunted. "They want to see what their future holds."

Neither Alec Moore nor Claudia Fentiman was familiar with the senior management of their chief competitors. Moore, shrugging, did not bother to turn, but Claudia immediately demanded chapter and verse from Benda.

"I'll remember them," she promised after a long hard stare.

In the meantime Kichsel was lamenting the absence of George Lancer due to influenza. "But at least," he said, checking the composition of the committee, "we have some good friends on the panel."

Congressmen hailing from St. Louis and Milwaukee are just as zealous in protecting local interests as those from districts specializing in wheat farming, aircraft production and oil drilling. And if brewery employment figures alone are incapable of securing their dedication, then campaign contributions will do the job.

Sean Cushing, although not a veteran in Roger Vandermeer's class, was learning fast.

"Look," he said to Madeleine, "the MADD people have sent an observer. At least they're keeping an eye on things."

But Madeleine was too distracted to care. Leon Rossi had gotten off to a bad start in her opinion by taking over an hour to define the aims of the subcommittee. Then came a parade of speakers who occupied the rest of Thursday and all of Friday. As hour succeeded hour, as nearby spectators chatted, yawned and even opened books, her frustration grew.

She was particularly scornful of the technical people. "They talk about absence of alcohol and wholesome ingredients. Don't they realize that nobody is claiming Quax itself is poisonous? The danger lies in the entire elaborate attempt to imitate beer."

But Monday morning produced the worst shock of all. The committee had steered clear of all the participants in the Ludlum lawsuit and, instead, had invoked the aid of the nation's leading psychologist specializing in alcoholism.

His testimony was a model of common sense. When asked about the fundamental cause of alcoholism, he shook his head.

"I can't isolate one cause for you and neither can anyone else," he said bluntly. "There are almost always a host of factors involved, and the mix varies from one person to another. I am of course talking about the excessive use of alcohol."

He went on to remind the committee that in this country, as in many others, a modest consumption of alcohol was not regarded as harmful either to the individual or to his society. He cited the long-established use of beer and wine at mealtime. He tolerantly alluded to medical theories that some alcohol could be beneficial with certain disorders.

"As long as we take the position that the problem is not alcohol, but how much alcohol, we are talking about a judgment call and one that involves variables—both physical and psychological—which differ with each individual. Identical circumstances may render one person alcohol-dependent and not the other. Moreover, judgment itself is a complex process entailing almost every aspect of any given personality."

Finally returning to the question at hand, he told the microphones that contributing causes could range from lack of self-esteem to unendurable stress.

"But if you were to ask me to confine myself to those causes that can be traced back to the formative years," he said, clearly implying that they should have, "I would have to say that the two most prominent are the behavioral example set by the parents and the pressure imposed by age-peers."

He could not resist a disapproving addendum: "And these days the second is becoming more important than the first."

Madeleine could barely control her indignation. "The man is completely incompetent," she seethed. "Hasn't he read what Dr. Schumacher told the court? Doesn't he keep up-to-date?"

Shushing firmly, Sean managed to keep her quiet, but the rest of the witness's testimony was delivered to an accompaniment of silent comment from Madeleine. There were angry tosses of the head, grim pursing of lips, spirited little jerks of sotto-voce exclamations.

By the time Madeleine Underwood was finally called to center stage, she was itching to set everybody straight.

Fortunately there was the opening statement on NOBBY's position to be read. It was far too long—twenty-five pages in all—but its very length accomplished two useful purposes. The act of reading dissipated much of Madeleine's impatience, and by its conclusion she had regained her equanimity. Second, she was unable to recall its original contents in any detail. Reveling in the too-long deferred opportunity to deliver her message, she was deaf to the fact that that message had been subtly altered. Quax was not now necessarily evil incarnate. How could one tell whether or not its effects would be deleterious without long and patient research? Flat statements were rigidly confined to those areas that no politician in his right mind would contest:

"The American public is overwhelmingly concerned with the welfare of its children." And later: "We have all seen sad evidence of how impressionable youngsters can be attracted by the lure of nicotine, alcohol and drugs."

Thanks to Sean Cushing, Madeleine had successfully surmounted the first hurdle. But with a sinking heart he watched her shuffle her text together and set it aside.

Within minutes she was getting into trouble.

"The purchase and consumption of Quax should be confined to those of legal drinking age. Then these problems would be solved." Combatively she continued, "Not that there would be any. Quax would have to be withdrawn from the market because its sole purpose is to hook the younger generation."

"But Mrs. Underwood, non-alcoholic beer has been sold along with beer for years. Most breweries have been eager to pursue that market."

"I would have no objection to such a disposition of Quax," she declaimed.

She managed to induce genuine confusion in the second committee member to speak.

"Are you advocating temperance, Mrs. Underwood?"

"Certainly not. NOBBY has always taken the position that that is a decision every responsible adult must make for himself," she said thrillingly. "I repeat, that is a decision for adults. My organization has been appalled by the Kichsel Brewery's latest ploy with the Rugby chain. It is asking too much to expect small children to distinguish between the sight of an adult drinking a bottle of Quax with his hamburger and that of one drinking beer."

"But they see adults drinking in every restaurant with a liquor license."

Aware that she herself had polished off two glasses of wine with her lunch, Madeleine knew there had to be a distinction escaping the Honorable Member.

"Those are not specifically designed as family environments," she said, undermining in one sentence half the restaurant advertising of the Northeast.

Soon she was trying to elevate her opinion to the level of evidence.

"Our studies show a slow, remorseless identification between Quax and beer."

"How can there be studies of this slow, remorseless process? The stuff's only been on sale for two years."

"I was referring to our ongoing studies."

"Then they haven't shown anything yet, have they?" persisted her critic.

Sean, all too conscious that she was speaking of anecdotal contributions by two NOBBY members, cringed, but Madeleine sailed on, unruffled.

"Nonetheless their tenor is clear."

Fortunately, Harry Hull intervened at this juncture. "As your studies are incomplete, Mrs. Underwood, I think we should defer any consideration of them. Should they be completed in the near future, you will, of course, be given an opportunity to submit them to the committee."

It was not the first time he had come to her rescue. He was not doing it consistently enough to draw attention, but Sean Cushing, grateful to have a surrogate, had noticed. Frowning in thought, he decided that while Hull had no objection to Madeleine making a fool of herself, he did not intend to let her discredit the entire cause.

He certainly made no attempt to prevent her disastrous foray into NOBBY's plans with regard to the FDA.

"We shall shortly be forwarding to them our request for a hearing," she announced. "It is high time that this entire situation received the governmental attention it so urgently needs."

This brought the entire committee to life. One member wanted to know whether the FDA was backed up for the next five years or the next ten, while another was inspired to ask what the agency was supposed to do for NOBBY. With the entire issue about to dissolve into an internal discussion among members, Madeleine forgot an explicit promise to Sean Cushing.

"If you want instances, I can give you one right here in New York City," she said. "An example that resulted in the death of a young man entirely due to his exposure to Quax."

Once again Harry Hull's services were required.

"I am familiar with that case," he broke in, "but as the entire matter is still under adjudication, it would scarcely be appropriate to consider it in this forum."

MADELEINE UNDERWOOD was not the only one performing in public that afternoon. In the courtroom assigned to *Ludlum versus Kichsel*, the victim's father had been taken through his carefully rehearsed tale of the final two years of his son's life. His counsel Arthur Cleve had painted the picture of a high school boy imbibing Quax regularly, confining himself to that beverage at parties—here Po-

laroid shots of young Ludlum at his junior prom were introduced—
and then shifting to beer, with the fatal consequences already known.

Now it was Paul Jackson's turn to cross-examine. He began by
seeking clarification of certain details. He soon established that
Ludlum Senior had been well aware of his son's partiality for Quax.

"I thought it was good for him. They say so much about its being
alcohol-free, I thought that meant it was safe. You know what kids
can get into these days."

"And when did you notice your son's change in drinking habits?"

"Not right away," Ludlum Senior admitted. "That's another
thing. They look so much the same you don't notice. You're so used
to seeing your son drink out of that brown bottle, you don't think
twice about it."

Jackson's usual animation was in abeyance. As befitted the
subject, his voice was solemn and muted. He knew better than to
antagonize a single jury member by any suggestion of callous in-
sensitivity to a bereaved parent. Opposing counsel understood the
manner and was not alarmed.

"And then you say he shifted to beer?"

"That's right. I guess he didn't see that much difference between
those two brown bottles either," Ludlum said bitterly.

"But there might have been other reasons for the shift. Did he
have personal problems?"

"What kind? He was going to school to become an aeronautics
technician and he liked it. He was popular, he had a nice girlfriend."

"Then what about the pressure from his friends who drank? I assume that some of them did."

"Sure, some of them drank beer. But that had been going on for
a couple of years and he was used to it. He never would have taken
to beer if the Kichsel people hadn't put him in training for it."

Jackson had angled for exactly the formulation he wished.

"Well, now, that's not entirely accurate, is it, Mr. Ludlum?" he
asked gently.

The alteration in tone was barely perceptible but it was enough
to make Arthur Cleve raise his head, scenting menace.

"I don't know what you mean."

Jackson had drifted back to his table to consult a document. Retaining it in his hand, he returned to Mr. Ludlum.

"Is it not true that your son was arrested for drunken driving in Massachusetts when he was sixteen years old, arrested before Quax was even available?"

"I don't believe it."

Ignoring him, Jackson addressed the bench. "The defense wishes to introduce in evidence this certified copy of the arrest report, to be marked 'Exhibit D' for purposes of identification."

Cleve, cursing under his breath, was huddled with his associates. "Didn't we check the kid out?"

"We checked New Jersey, New York and Connecticut," someone said sadly.

Unlike Paul Jackson, the NOBBY attorneys had never followed the trail of Wayne Ludlum, Jr., to his summer job on Cape Cod shortly after acquiring a driver's license.

"Here is the report, Mr. Ludlum. The name is Wayne Ludlum, Jr., the address is 1247 Sycamore Avenue, Babylon, New York. That is your son, is it not? That is your address, is it not?"

"Yes," gritted Ludlum between clenched teeth. "But I never heard about this."

Inexorably Jackson continued. "But you did hear about it when he was suspended from school for three days after being found drinking beer in the schoolyard, did you not? I have here a copy of the letter notifying you of the suspension and its reason."

"Yes."

"And that occurred when your son was fifteen, did it not?"

Ludlum's voice was so low as to be almost inaudible.

"Yes."

"And that was before Quax was being sold."

"But he was over it. Wayne was dry for two years. And there was never a drop of stuff in our house."

"But your eighteen-year-old son didn't have to be introduced to beer by anyone, did he? He already knew all about it."

Barely suppressing a groan, Arthur Cleve had finally levered himself to his feet and was asking for an adjournment in order to study this new evidence. The judge courteously turned to Jackson.

"Unless you expect to conclude your examination within the half hour, I am inclined to grant the request."

The famous wolf grin suddenly illuminated Paul Jackson's face.

"The defense has no objection, Your Honor. I expect my examination of this witness to be quite lengthy."

8. One for the Road

APPILY UNAWARE OF Paul Jackson's tactics, Madeleine Underwood regarded her appearance before the Rossi Committee as an unqualified success. Moreover, she was not yet finished. Tomorrow, unfortunately, the committee would be shuttling to Washington for an important roll call, but Wednesday would once again see her in front of those microphones. Her only regret was that the feast of congratulation she had expected to share with Sean Cushing did not materialize.

"Well, that wasn't a bad start," she said, pursing her lips in a simulation of detachment. "Of course there are still a lot of points that we have to make."

Sean, however, was strangely unforthcoming. "We'll have to get together first thing tomorrow," he muttered awkwardly. "Right now I've got to run if I'm going to catch Cheryl before she leaves the office."

Left alone, Mrs. Underwood savored the surrounding atmospherics of busy people rushing off to planes, rushing off to hotels, rushing off to working dinners. She, too, she reminded herself, was now part of this intoxicating world. With NOBBY bursting out of its old format and conquering one public arena after another, the days ahead promised to be more demanding than ever. Tomorrow's recess only meant a hectic resumption of the activities necessarily put on hold since Leon Rossi hit town. There was the briefing session with the lawyers to keep abreast of *Ludlum versus Kichsel*. Then an interim report on the hearings would have to be prepared for her board of governors. And finally, lurking in the background, were the daily operations of NOBBY, with which Madeleine had lost all contact in spite of the fact that protests had started in front of the first Rugby's to grace New York City.

"So much to do, and so little time," she pretended to lament even as she was suffused by a tide of satisfaction.

Not for one moment did she consciously acknowledge her reluctance to return to that suburb where she was still known as the divorced lady in the big white house. Instead she came to a reasoned, prudent decision. It was folly for an overburdened executive director to waste precious time on daily commutes from New Jersey.

"CONGRESSMAN HULL! I didn't realize we were staying in the same hotel," she said as they stepped into the lobby from adjacent elevators.

Hull's polite, although unenthusiastic, reply gave her all the opening she needed.

"I'm so glad we bumped into each other. Now that the hearings are finally on the right track we should have a planning session for the items we want to emphasize on Wednesday morning. It's hard enough to keep some of the members to the point. I'm sure you noticed how one or two of them tend to ramble into unrelated areas."

Reminding himself that NOBBY's nationwide expansion would certainly scoop up a number of registered voters in his district, Hull forced a smile.

"Look, I was just going to get myself a quick drink. Join me and we'll see if we can put our heads together over this."

As he had expected, Madeleine was not really proposing a cooperative effort. An encouraging and supportive audience was what she had in mind. Once provided with the vodka and tonic she felt she had earned, she fished a rumpled pad of jottings from her swollen briefcase and, pencil in hand, began annotating her list to the accompaniment of murmured comments.

"Yes, we really did get quite a good deal accomplished," she summarized. "And high time, too! With the first two days spent on empty formalities, I was beginning to despair. Of course, I realize that setting out our formal position on Quax was today's major achievement. But I am pleased about the opportunity to introduce our proposed approach to the FDA. That lets the committee know we'll be tackling this question from the technical end."

Hull, unable to rouse himself beyond an appreciative grunt, wondered if this was a new formulation for the famous research with which she had peppered her testimony.

In the meantime she cast a last look at one unticked line on her list. "I'm sorry you took the position you did about *Ludlum versus Kichsel.*"

Hull's features rearranged themselves into their most portentous legislative mode. "I'm sure you understand it would be improper for the committee to embroil itself in an ongoing case."

Instantly she mirrored his gravity. "Of course, I see that we mustn't say anything prejudicial," she agreed solemnly and was then unable to prevent herself from adding wistfully, "But it's a shame, isn't it?"

"There will be plenty of opportunities to refer to the case after it's resolved," he pointed out, blandly avoiding any prediction as to the outcome.

"That's true," she said, brightening. "And who knows where NOBBY will be appearing by then?"

She was so clearly unaware that her own actions had probably barred NOBBY from ever again setting foot in a significant forum that Harry experienced a momentary twinge of compassion. One of the great things about elections, he thought, is that they define winners and losers too clearly for anyone to be in doubt as to his status. But his nascent sympathy faded when she continued:

"And while it's regrettable that we can't use the lawsuit itself, that's a minor consideration as long as we exploit all the expertise assembled for it. I just don't understand how the committee has allowed itself to be fobbed off with second-best witnesses, but I suppose it's because they aren't familiar with the whole subject. Fortunately that can be straightened out, as I happen to know Dr. Schumacher is willing to take the time to appear."

Hull was shaking his head gently. "Leon Rossi has gone to great pains in making his arrangements. The interested parties are being given time to put forth their views. That's why NOBBY is testifying and that's why Kichsel will get its turn."

"We all know they have to be given a chance to defend themselves," she said grudgingly.

Ignoring this, he continued to his main point. "But the technical testimony is something else again; it has to be strictly impartial. Leon is interested in information from them, not views."

"Surely Dr. Schumacher's credentials speak for themselves. It's not as if he's Mr. Ludlum or one of Wayne's friends. He's an expert witness, a trained scientist. You can't call him biased."

Determined to duck the entire question, Hull reached for higher ground. "Nonetheless, in order to avoid any imputation of partiality, the chairman has decided not to call any psychologist involved with the case—on either side."

"Well, if that's the only problem," she rejoined, as cheerful as could be, "then probably the best thing is for me to speak to the chairman. As a matter of fact, I have a few other suggestions for him."

"*No!*" he exploded involuntarily. Then, recovering, he achieved a more temperate tone. "No, I don't think that's a good idea at all."

Her large eyes, already emphasized by the bright-blue frills at her throat, bulged to the point of being exophthalmic. "Why in the world not? Are you afraid that we wouldn't hit it off because we're so different? That doesn't matter. I've already spoken to Leon Rossi several times," she assured him earnestly, "and we get along very well."

You should hear Leon's opinion on that, Hull thought to himself as nightmare visions of such an encounter made him want to break and run. Instead he gathered his forces to produce an explanation that would pass muster.

". . . You see, the general policy of the hearings is approved by canvassing the entire committee, and after that it's set like concrete. Any deviation from those decisions would entail another round of closed sessions, undermining all the momentum that's been gained so far."

This rapid improvisation, he hoped, sounded less like gabble than it was. At least the mutinous expression on Madeleine's face had softened slightly.

Tilting her head thoughtfully, she said in a burst of frankness, "It sounds like a very inefficient way of operating to me. But if that's the way you do things, I suppose I have to live with it. Just so long as you're not trying to tell me not to talk to Chairman Rossi."

"Of course not," he said soothingly.

But she was not through.

"If we can't have Dr. Schumacher in person, then we'll simply have to find a way to introduce the testimony he would have given. Now, it's lucky that we have a really interesting study done by one of the anti-smoking groups on the tobacco industry's program to hook teenagers. I'll just run upstairs and get it for you. I'm sure I ought to be able to do better than just introduce it into the record. It can be used to draw parallels."

Harry Hull was now anxious to end this interlude, if possible without giving offense. His career in Washington depended on how well he avoided embarrassing himself and—even more important— embarrassing the influential colleagues who could make or break him. So far Rossi was only mildly irritated, but let this woman make a laughingstock of his hearings, and he would be on the warpath. If Mrs. Underwood were allowed to reenter the bar carrying reading material, there was no way a second round of drinks could be avoided.

"Tell you what," he said, rising swiftly to his feet. "Why don't you bring that report to my suite. I have an appointment there in fifteen minutes but I'll be able to take a quick look at it."

He had pulled out her chair and was guiding her from the lounge before she knew it. It was an impromptu contrivance, but Harry Hull was beginning to think that every minute not spent in public with Madeleine was a real gain.

Now that he had set the clock ticking, he was not surprised to have her make record speed down from her quarters several flights above his. At least the report she produced had the merit of being professionally competent. Harry wasted no breath trying to persuade her there was a difference between a poisonous alkaloid well-established as habit-forming and a product irreproachable in its chemical components. Instead he killed time with a show of interest in various paragraphs until the welcome sound of a brisk tattoo on the door. By then he was so eager to end the tête-à-tête he would have hailed an orangutang.

"Sorry to be late," said Roger Vandermeer. "Hi there, Maddy!"

Until the committee hearings, Mrs. Underwood had been unaware of Vandermeer's existence. Sean Cushing had carefully described the Soft Drink Institute as an important friend, but Madeleine preferred friends who were real people. Trade associations did not register until they became personified. Unfortunately, this one had become embodied by a man she detested on sight. Everything about Vandermeer, from his sleek affability to his overpolished manners, rubbed her the wrong way.

Maddy was the last straw.

And, although she did not know it, relations were scarcely likely to improve. Three days ago Vandermeer, regarding Mrs. Underwood as potentially useful, had been on his best behavior. It was now several hours since he had written her off, and when he lowered people in his pecking order, he reverted to the natural man.

"I'd like to get started as soon as possible, Harry," he announced. "There are different ways Rossi can go."

Determinedly Madeleine thrust herself forward. "That's what we've been discussing. If you ask me, Chairman Rossi has already made some mistakes."

"That so?" Vandermeer said vaguely without bothering to look at her. "We'd better get cracking, Harry. I've only got half an hour."

Madeleine, conscious that as founder of NOBBY she *was* the anti-Quax movement, bristled at the thought of a conference on the subject from which she was excluded.

"I am not quite finished, Mr. Vandermeer," she announced in a voice calculated to depress pretension.

Hull opted for appeasement. "I'm afraid we'll have to end now, Madeleine, if I'm going to keep on schedule," he said with an apologetic smile. "In any event, I'll need more time to study this report. So, if you wouldn't mind leaving it with me . . . ?"

For one hideous moment he thought he was going to have a scene on his hands. Then Madeleine decided to underline the distinction between friend and foe by accepting his olive branch.

"A good idea," she said, adopting Vandermeer's policy of ignoring third parties. "But you'll want to take a look at the Surgeon General's estimate of the report as well."

"Oh, for God's sake—"

"Why don't you get yourself a drink, Roger," Hull said hastily. "We'll be done in a second."

Folklore insists that more flies are caught with honey than with vinegar. Mrs. Underwood took her own good time riffling through the briefcase dumped in a corner before extracting a slim folder and depositing it with Hull. Then, quite unnecessarily, she drew his attention to several underlined passages at the same leisurely pace. Finally, restored to good humor by this petty vindictiveness, she parted from Hull amiably before turning to Vandermeer with steely graciousness.

"Good-bye, Mr. Vandermeer, and I do hope that you have a productive conversation."

Then, purse in hand, she flicked out the doorway with the triumphant swagger of a woman who had accomplished what she had set out to do.

DUMPING EMPTY GLASSES in the bathroom half an hour later, Harry Hull was relieved to be rid of both his guests. Madeleine in her folly and Vandermeer in his arrogance were two of a kind. Both assumed they were the most important feature on this congressman's horizon when what he really wanted was to focus his attention on his colleagues. This evening's executive session was going to be rough enough, but some constructive suggestions at the ready would help.

The tap at the door would have signaled an unwanted interruption no matter who the caller was. But when Hull found Mrs. Underwood on his threshold he had to fight back a lowering frown.

"I'm sorry to bother you again, Harry, but I forgot my briefcase," she murmured complacently.

The bright-eyed anticipation told its own story to Hull. This damn fool of a woman had probably been waiting around the corner for Vandermeer to leave, confident that with an excuse for reentry she could extract an account of the recent meeting. It was just the kind of silly trick she would pride herself on inventing. Thankful that he had picked up his jacket and already inserted one arm, Harry was brisk and businesslike.

"You're lucky you caught me, Madeleine. I'm just on my way to dinner with Leon."

Projecting impatience and remaining glued to the doorway, he forced her to scurry in for her property and join him in a prompt exit. Disregarding her cheerful prattle, he made sure she had punched the up button on the elevator before committing himself to down.

Just as well, he reflected, that Madeleine was ignorant of what had been said. It would have been a real eye-opener for her to hear Vandermeer's brutal description of her ineptitude. But far more painful would have been his assumption that she no longer had any role to play in the great battle against Kichsel.

"We can't let that stupid broad go on lousing up," he had said.

When Vandermeer's clients got their crack at the committee, they would punch the groundswell of consumer alarm at stumbling across Quax sandwiched between root beer and ginger ale. But their description would omit any reference to NOBBY or to Mrs. Underwood.

"Not that it will do much good, considering the harm that bitch has already done," he said pessimistically. "It'll be a month or so before everyone forgets about her. Right now they're having too much fun cracking jokes."

"All that will pass," Harry had replied.

"Listen, the guy from one of those breweries out west was saying they ought to pass the hat to send her to the FDA. That way they'd be sure of getting a clean bill of health for anything they peddled."

With Roger Vandermeer, you were either with him or against him. He saw himself as the chosen champion of his clients, the one who secured victory by blasting away all impediments, by destroying enemy encampments and, of course, by discarding treacherous or incompetent allies.

Hired gun would be more like it, Hull thought contemptuously as he entered the dining room and spotted Leon Rossi's bulky form.

Fortunately, the chairman's focus was always on ways and means rather than personalities.

"We'll have to cut her short, that goes without saying. I've already had Kichsel on my neck, demanding that his people get equal time not only for the SDI presentation but for all her drivel as well."

"Absolutely, it's just a question of how," Hull said, entering into the spirit of Rossi's approach. Conscious that he was not yet being blamed for today's exhibition, he nonetheless felt it necessary to make some acknowledgment of his role. "I never thought she'd turn out to be such a loose cannon. Her printed material and speeches aren't half bad."

"Amateurs!" Rossi snorted. "You never know how they'll turn out. The main thing is to have two approaches prepared. Unless NOBBY has rocks in its head, another spokesman will turn up on Wednesday."

The words were more impersonal than those chosen by Roger Vandermeer, but the result was the same. Madeleine Underwood had been permanently removed from the game.

9. Social Drinking

T HIS DECISION WAS more than reinforced as the night wore on. It was standard operating procedure for all interested groups to retreat into strategy huddles after the day's hearings. Even before Leon Rossi and Harry Hull left the dinner table to join their colleagues, the SDI contingent and Roger Vandermeer had gathered in one hotel suite while a clutch of Kichsel competitors was ordering up bar service in another. Nothing could have demonstrated NOBBY's basic amateurism more clearly than the fact that they alone were taking the evening off.

As news of Paul Jackson's courtroom bombshell percolated into each one of these meetings, any remaining toleration for Madeleine Underwood vaporized on the spot.

Leon Rossi simply exploded into profanity at yet another blunder by one of his star witnesses.

"You say she's the one who chose the Ludlums for her test case, the case she wanted to blab about at my hearing? Christ, how dumb can you get?"

Roger Vandermeer, more constructively, immediately began to plan a future course of action.

"This settles it. It's not just Underwood who goes. We can forget about NOBBY, too."

The breweries began looking to an unclouded future.

"That should take care of Mrs. Underwood nicely," said one

CEO, reaching for a brandy. "Now, how big do you think the market for non-alcoholics sold as a soft drink will be?"

But at Paul Jackson's table at the Four Seasons it was, metaphorically speaking, champagne all the way.

"Well," he demanded, his eyes sparkling, "what did you think of my timing?"

For once Dean Kichsel had been stirred to warmth.

"It was perfect, just perfect."

This opinion was silently endorsed by Theo Benda and Claudia Fentiman on one side of the table, by John Thatcher and Elmer Rugby on the other.

But Alec Moore went further. "This should just about do it for Underwood. On top of the fiasco in court, she made an idiot of herself in the hearings. This will be the last we hear of NOBBY."

Claudia abruptly stopped nodding. "I wouldn't be too sure of that, Alec. Neither of these events will make the top news story on CBS. Probably most of NOBBY's members will never hear about them."

As the ailing Lancer's substitute, Thatcher was delighted to hear the voice of caution from Kichsel's management. Particularly as he and Rugby were supposed to be joining them not only to celebrate but to plan ahead.

"Oh, come on, Claudia. I'm not saying it will happen tomorrow. But every time the woman opens her mouth she takes mutually incompatible positions. Let her talk long enough and everyone's bound to notice."

Fifteen years in marketing had not left Claudia with a high opinion of logic. "You're not making enough allowance for emotional response."

"Congressional committees and trial judges aren't big on emotional responses," Moore retorted.

"Claudia isn't talking about them," Elmer Rugby objected. "She's talking about those ladies picketing my shop downtown. They were afraid their kids would end up like the Ludlum boy long before

Quax was ever invented, and you sure can't blame mothers for that," he said in twanging accents of sympathy. "Then some spellbinder comes along and convinces them Quax is going to make a bad situation ten times worse. So they lose their heads and panic."

Having delivered this analysis, he refreshed himself from the only stein on the table. John Thatcher, assuming that an evening spent with brewers would see a fair amount of beer consumption, had been amused earlier when Dean Kichsel had commenced the serious part of dinner by calling for a wine list.

"Have the protesters been troublesome for you?" Thatcher asked Rugby.

"Hell, no! I'll say one thing for you people here in New York. You're used to having flyers pushed into your hands. It doesn't seem to bother my customers one little bit. But that's not to say a couple of them aren't going to read the handout and believe it."

Alec Moore's jaw set. "That was yesterday. All right, so we're not making headlines. I have to go along with that. But Mrs. Underwood hasn't finished testifying. Before you know it, she'll be challenging the experts, like the one who said the real way to control teenagers drinking is by the behavior of the parents."

"I wouldn't count on it," Theo Benda said mildly. "We're not the only ones watching her. Somebody at NOBBY must have figured out by now that she's a lot better at talking to the troops than to congressmen. They'll pull her and send in a substitute."

But Paul Jackson was not ready to dismiss Alec Moore's remarks. Leaning forward alertly, he asked, "What else did that expert say?"

Dean Kichsel had practically memorized every treasured word. "He said that the two principal factors during formative years are the parents' example and peer pressure."

A smile of satisfaction appeared as Jackson sank back. "I like it," he murmured. "In fact, I may use it."

"Why bother?" said Alec. "Surely you've won the case. What jury is going to make an award to those people now?"

Jackson was reproachful. "Look, you didn't hire me just to get a jury verdict in your favor. You hired me to give Quax as much publicity as possible and to stick a spoke in the wheels of NOBBY. And I try to see that my clients get what they want."

"Well, every nail in the coffin helps," Alec said cheerfully. "And I appreciate all the publicity I can get. But as far as that woman goes, the funeral date is already set. You can talk all you want about that bunch in front of Rugby's not knowing what's going on, but you've overlooked the main point. Madeleine Underwood is a publicity hound and she wants to be the center of attention. As soon as they start criticizing over at NOBBY, as soon as they replace her at public events, she'll lose interest."

"Or," Benda mused, enlarging the possibilities, "she'll tank right over them and come swimming back to the hearings."

"Not after they've convinced her it would be bad for NOBBY, that wouldn't make sense," Moore said confidently. "Besides, even if she could come up with some twisted justification for staying in the spotlight, she'll bury herself with all those silly claims about studies and research. My God, the country is filled with AA chapters and support groups and therapists who've been dealing with alcoholism for decades. There are a lot of people who really do know what they're talking about."

To John Thatcher it was clear that Moore had settled everything in his own mind so firmly that he was surprised and impatient to find lingering qualms in others. The rest of Kichsel, while certainly optimistic, remained aware that selling a brewery product as if it were ginger ale was likely to rasp certain sensitivities. Benda and Dean Kichsel could be explained on the basis of adult lives passed in an industry open to criticism. But the fact that Claudia Fentiman had picked up the prevailing wariness, that Elmer Rugby, barely across the threshold, could comprehend his antagonists, suggested that Alec Moore, in spite of his contempt for Madeleine Underwood, might have a few king-sized blind spots himself.

Paul Jackson was simply thinking along different lines. By nature a combatant, he openly enjoyed the battlefield. With that predilection it was only natural that he tended to dismiss any theater of operations in which he was not actively engaged.

"But what it boils down to is that NOBBY, in one guise or another, will continue to present its position to the Rossi Committee," he said. "And *Ludlum versus Kichsel* still has a lot of time to run. I set off today's firecracker to coincide with Underwood's appearance at the hearings, but I'm not done by a long shot. I'm not claiming I can ever get us to page one. But by now the city editors are aware that NOBBY is bursting out in three separate New York locations. Sooner or later we'll get some ironic human-nature touch they can't resist. And then it'll be a double column on page two."

During his long successful career Jackson had learned as much about space allocation in the dailies as most of the professionals in the field. His estimate, Thatcher knew, was likely to be right on the button.

Jackson's over-the-top zeal, however, made Dean Kichsel nervous. "You've done a fine job establishing the boy's drinking patterns. So we don't really need a full-scale character assassination, do we?" he reasoned.

"Christ, no!" Jackson agreed heartily. "No matter how much trouble one of these kids is, no matter if he's a vicious, violent criminal, the minute he's dead he becomes a young life cut down too soon. That's sacred ground. From now on I'm leaving Junior strictly alone and focusing on Daddy. By the time I'm through, the jury will be ready to string him up."

"Does that mean you have few more surprises up your sleeve?" Thatcher hazarded.

"One or two little squibs," Jackson purred modestly.

Unlike Madeleine Underwood, the Kichsel management was not trying to second-guess its attorney. They had hired the best dog they could find and the barking was up to him. Nobody evinced the slightest desire for more detail. And, reflected Thatcher, they would have had a hard time getting any. Paul liked his courtroom theatrics to have just as much impact on his clients as on his adversaries.

And this evening his clients had more than enough to occupy them, as Dean Kichsel was swift to point out.

"We'll leave all that to you," he said readily. "But I would like to wrap up plans for our own presentation to the Rossi Committee and consider these demonstrations by NOBBY. I was wondering, Elmer, if it wouldn't be a good idea to print a small flyer presenting the real facts for distribution inside your outlets."

Elmer Rugby was not a time-waster.

"No way! My franchises are in the business of serving people

66

food." Remembering his company, he ducked his head apologetically. "And drink, too, of course. We don't supply reading material."

Kichsel still liked the idea. "What do you think, John? What harm could it do?"

"I imagine Elmer is talking about atmospherics," Thatcher temporized.

"Damn right I am. Outside there are people chanting and waving signs and generally making a nuisance of themselves. Then the customer comes inside and he gets to sit down and eat and be comfortable. I intend to keep it that way. My places aren't turning into some kind of schoolroom."

In Thatcher's estimation it could not have been put better. On the street you were an anonymous unit being targeted by a faceless group. But once you were within the protective embrace of Rugby's, you became an individual with whims to be catered to, someone whose decision between ketchup and barbecue sauce was of central importance. Good old Elmer had the right instincts.

Even Kichsel, now yielding the point, seemed to agree. If Paul Jackson knew how to run a trial, presumably Rugby knew how to sell hamburgers.

"That leaves us with the question of our own presentation. I think we can say that the opening statement is in satisfactory shape."

"Now that you two have practically blasted my contribution to bits," Moore grumbled.

Theo Benda tilted his head to an inquiring angle. "What's the matter, Alec? Did they tone you down?"

"Claudia damn near red-penciled me out of existence," Alec replied good-humoredly.

"I certainly did. As you know, Alec, I'm all in favor of your approach when Kichsel is marketing to customers. For them Quax is a soft drink and that's all there is to it. But when we're making speeches in the public sector, that's the time to sound more responsive than anybody else to the problems raised by drinking. That's the only way you have a hope in hell that anybody will believe what you say."

Claudia Fentiman's urgency on this subject certainly did her no disservice with Dean Kichsel.

"Yes indeed. And I particularly liked your paragraph equating Quax with our educational support for the designated-driver program."

"And exactly how did Mrs. Fentiman do that?" asked Thatcher, genuinely curious.

"She said, just as children benefit from early exposure to that program, so they cannot be introduced too soon to the concept of safe substitutes for beer," Kichsel told him proudly.

Thatcher supposed that was one way of looking at it.

"It's just another formulation," Moore scoffed. "You're still saying that Quax is a soft drink."

Claudia's perfectly arched eyebrows drew into a frown. "That's the name of the game—different ways of saying the same thing create different impressions."

Thatcher was interested to observe that Dean Kichsel, disconcerted by so many things, was indifferent to the continual sparring between Alec Moore and Claudia. Kichsel simply seized the opportunity to loft a finger for another bottle of wine before returning to his immediate subject.

"But I feel that a good deal of work remains to be done preparing answers for any questions that may be asked."

"Here's a starting list," said Claudia, efficiently producing several pages of typescript.

The next hour and a half was spent trying to forecast all possible queries—relevant or not—that might spring to the minds of the congressional panel. Kichsel and Moore could not lift themselves beyond the immediately pertinent while Thatcher and Claudia displayed considerable ingenuity in postulating wackier and wackier scenarios. But the palm undoubtedly went to Paul Jackson. Years of preparing witnesses for cross-examination had left him with an unerring instinct.

"You say it that way and this is what they'll ask," he would declare with unshakable authority.

By the time the check was being presented, Dean Kichsel was content.

"Now, that certainly takes care of every possible contingency that can arise at the hearings."

10. In a Ferment

ADELEINE UNDERWOOD was down, but she was not out. In fact, her counterattack had barely begun.

The next morning NOBBY's receptionist was startled to have the executive director arrive with a rush at nine-fifteen.

"There's a message from Mr. Cleve. He wants you to get back to him," Cheryl cried as Mrs. Underwood swept by without pause.

The call was duly placed and Cheryl, who had never allowed her interest in NOBBY to extend beyond her immediate duties, was all set for another boring day when Madeleine burst from her office demanding, with unmistakable hostility, the immediate presence of Sean Cushing.

"He's down the hall," said Cheryl, too genteel to specify further.

"Send him in the minute he gets back," Madeleine barked.

Cheryl's jaw had barely returned to normal before she was further jolted by Cushing's reception of this summons.

"So she's here, is she? Well, I've got a hell of a lot to say to her," he snarled before striding forward to stiff-arm Madeleine's door.

Tingling with pleasurable excitement, Cheryl wondered what was going on and what the lawyer had said. For the first time in her employment she regretted not having paid any attention to the burning issues supposed to preoccupy the staff. Mrs. Underwood— totally disorganized, constantly fussing and far too prone to strike high dramatic notes—was certainly not the ideal employer. But bad temper was almost unknown on NOBBY premises. Madeleine tended to forgive others for her own mistakes, Mr. Cushing could be impatient and Mrs. Perez specialized in a particularly trying form of gentle reproach, but nothing had ever approximated the rancor already exhibited.

And within minutes Cheryl could hear the two of them really going at it. Only an occasional phrase erupted with sufficient force to be comprehensible, but the background mood was self-explanatory.

". . . always think you know best when you don't know a goddamn thing," charged Sean.

And Cheryl nodded approbation. Why, she had noticed that herself.

". . . trying to keep things from me," Madeleine sang out several exchanges later.

Which was just plain silly, thought Cheryl. The whole office kept secrets from Madeleine. It was the only way to stay in operation. Cheryl herself had discarded a pile of dusty chemical reports that she knew would never be read.

The voices, both now in full spate, were combining to produce a low-throated roaring in which not only words but speakers were indistinguishable. It was like two radio stations struggling for the same spot on the dial, Cheryl decided as she eavesdropped with all her might. Finally Mrs. Underwood's transmission muscled aside the surrounding static.

". . . funds I know nothing about. I will not tolerate disloyalty and . . ."

Mildly indignant, Cheryl tut-tutted her disapproval. The nerve of her! Everybody knew that Mrs. Underwood didn't understand the first thing about the accounts. Why, Mr. Cushing had to spoon-feed her just so that she could talk to the board of governors every July.

But Mr. Cushing was not taking it lying down.

". . . responsible for the whole bloody mess and these little diversions aren't going to get you off the hook."

"How dare you!"

More rumbling. Then, cutting through the air like a knife:

". . . financial irregularities practically from the day you got here. It's stopping right now."

"The hell you say!" Cushing bellowed. "I'm going straight to the board and they won't believe their ears. But I've got you cold."

Now things would really heat up. Cheryl could have told Mr. Cushing that Madeleine hated to be reminded of the existence of an overseeing authority.

"I give the orders and you can't hide behind anybody else."

". . . silly stupid bitch throwing away the only chance you've got."

"O . . . h . . . h!"

There was at least no doubt who that startled squawk belonged to.

Finally, loud and clear: "You can pack your things right now and go!"

Good God, she's fired him, a fascinated Cheryl realized and just had time to pretend to be working as Madeleine Underwood flung open her door and stormed out of NOBBY with such vigor that her bright yellow summer dress flapped in the breeze of her passage.

Predictably Sean Cushing emerged a few moments later. Cheryl examined his face with an interest it had never inspired before, cataloging the beaky nose pushing through taut skin, the cheekbones ridged with white, the expression of boiling anger.

All innocence, she decided to fire a testing shot.

"Mrs. Underwood forgot to tell me where she could be reached."

"Who the hell cares?" he snapped, retreating to his own domain with a mighty slam of the door.

OUTSIDE THE BUILDING Madeleine Underwood, pulse still racing and temples throbbing, sucked in great healing lungfuls of the balmy spring air. One unwelcome image after another chased itself across her mind. In her present savage humor each scene assumed its darkest hues. Sean Cushing, a young man she had rescued from the unemployment line, having the effrontery to accuse her of damaging NOBBY; Harry Hull pretending that some esoteric code governed access to Chairman Rossi; and Roger Vandermeer blatantly implying there was an anti-Quax campaign above and beyond her own activities.

But along with returning calm came her unfailing ability to place herself at the center of any picture. With an impatient twitch of her shoulders she at last succeeded in shaking those elements of discomfort into a new and more acceptable pattern. Of course she had enemies and detractors. Any leader, as soon as her cause threatened to become effective, could expect nothing less. And the shabby motives of her opponents were pitifully apparent. Harry Hull stood revealed as an opportunistic politician. Sean Cushing was trying to exploit NOBBY for his own gain. And Roger Vandermeer, most contemptible of all, hoped to claim credit with his clients for her exploits.

"Pygmies, all of them!" she pronounced.

Seen in this light they were insignificant impediments to her own triumphal progress. They couldn't stop her, they couldn't undermine her credibility or steal her achievements because, quite apart from a moral integrity they were lacking, she had something else they didn't have—ten thousand devoted followers.

"It's time they learned who's in charge," she decided.

And one glance at her watch reminded her of where she would find, ready-made, a gathering of the faithful. It was ten o'clock and the starting gun of today's protest had already sounded. But there would still be only a handful of volunteers dutifully handing out flyers and circling with their placards. Iona Perez, well aware of eating patterns in the city, had busloads arriving for the noontime crowds. And that, thought Madeleine with a gleam in her eye, was the moment to strike.

"I WONDER WHAT all the fuss is about," Charlie Trinkam remarked as he and Thatcher strolled up Broadway.

Thatcher had barely spared a glance for the congestion visible down a side street. In the narrow canyons of the financial district, any object of interest that drew over five people could disrupt pedestrian and vehicular traffic.

"There's always something going on," he said indifferently.

"But that's Elmer's new franchise."

"Ah! Then it must be the NOBBY protest. Rugby said it wasn't causing him any problems."

Charlie had already veered from course.

"This wasn't what it was like yesterday. And it won't take a minute to see what's up."

It was always difficult to deflect Charlie when his mongooselike curiosity had been roused. Add legitimate concern for one of his clients and it was almost impossible.

"Just for a moment then," Thatcher surrendered.

The chief cause of the backed-up traffic soon became apparent. A large charter bus, canted half on the sidewalk, half on the street, was discharging the last of its passengers while the driver extracted fresh supplies of brochures and posters from the luggage compartment. Immediately abreast of this obstacle a patrol car had halted.

"Get that thing out of here! You're blocking the street."

Nodding, the driver slammed down the hatch and ran to his cab while the police moved off on their rounds. In the gap that now emerged, Madeleine Underwood came into view, mounted on an improvised platform and haranguing her cohorts.

"Oh, that's all it is," said Charlie, shrugging. "They've got speakers today."

Perversely, now that Charlie was willing to leave, Thatcher wished to remain.

"I want to see what she's like in action."

Today Madeleine Underwood was a far cry from the gracious matron in front of the courthouse, as Thatcher immediately pointed out to Charlie. Already in full flight, she had managed to turn her audience into a sympathetic chorus.

". . . seen it happen time and again. First it was nicotine, with the tobacco industry deliberately turning every American soldier into an addict and doing it with the Army's cooperation. Then it was marijuana and heroin. And now it's beer. The forces that traffic in these drugs are without conscience and without pity. And they are far too powerful, able to buy the police and to buy Washington. You know the result as well as I do. Cigarette smokers, hooked as teenagers, dying from cancer and heart attacks. Students overdosing at high school parties. Are we going to let it happen again?"

"No! No!"

"It's too late once the habit has started, once there are drug dealers in every schoolyard, once we have to fight our own addicted children."

The bus was finally on the move, laboring noisily through its low gears. But Madeleine, like the instinctive orator that she was, effortlessly swelled her volume to override the distraction.

"Oh, I know what you're going to tell me. They have the money and the influence and they realize we are their enemy. Already they're working night and day to crush us. Just look at what's been happening. When they learned we were taking them to court, they deliberately set up a trick situation. Oh, I admit we were taken in. We were too innocent, too trusting. And then we have this so-called investigation by Congress—an investigation where they produce phony experts to testify that Quax is not dangerous, where they plan to whitewash the Kichsel Brewery, where they hope to sweep the whole scandal under the rug. And do you know why this is happening—why I am betrayed at every turn? Because we are on the brink of becoming a national movement. They may pretend that the timing is accidental, but do they think we're fools?"

Her scornful laugh was echoed by her followers.

"Well, they may control the courts and the committees, but do they control NOBBY?"

Only one answer was possible.

"No! No!"

"Believe me, they'd like to. Believe me, they're trying to. They have tried to sweep me aside, to undermine my movement, to corrupt it! But they are not invincible. They have one glaring weak spot because they care only about money."

Now that the bus was out of earshot she was able to shift to a dramatic undertone.

"And where does that money come from? It comes from us. That's right. They are using the money we spend to destroy our children. All we have to do is make that impossible. Look at that place." She directed an imperious wave toward Rugby's facade. "They get their profits from people like you and me, people concerned about the welfare of their children. Oh, the customers aren't the enemy. They're poor gullible victims who don't realize what they're doing. But we can make it so plain that there's no hope of concealing the connection. If the sale of Quax causes Rugby's profits to fall, then Quax will disappear. And that is our strength. Every penny in the cash registers of that business is a penny directed toward turning our children into helpless alcoholics, reeling in the gutter, incapable of becoming responsible family members, citizens of their community or bread-winning employees. Now is the time to take a stand, now is the time to put every retail outlet on notice. We're not waiting until Quax has covered the countryside, until it's being sold in school vending machines and at Little League games. Rugby's is our test case and you have the power to win it. Stop everybody from entering that establishment, close the place down, send a message that will be heard from coast to coast. You have a choice, my friends. What are you going to do about it? Are you going to let them go on operating, are you going to let them fund their war chest? Or are you going to put yourselves between the customers and those doors and say along with me: *They shall not pass!*"

Her pause was recognized as a cue and she had provided a catchy phrase.

"They shall not pass! They shall not pass!"

Against this background chanting, Madeleine's voice soared into climax.

"The time to stop them is now. This day, this minute, this second, the future of our children is in your hands."

It was a nice note on which to finish. As Madeleine stepped down she was warmly congratulated by those nearby, as others maintained their war cry. Then, under Thatcher's disapproving gaze, she marched down the street where she could be seen trying to flag a taxi.

"Does that woman think she can incite to riot and then escape the consequences by trotting off?"

The student of humanity had an alternative explanation.

"She's not thinking at all. She's gone off to chow down," Charlie said wisely.

But if Madeleine had left, the fervor remained. Almost immediately an improvement on her suggestion was voiced.

"There's some construction debris around the far corner," one of the few men brandishing a placard shouted. "Let's barricade Rugby's."

The cry was taken up with gusto and within minutes sawhorses appeared as well as a motley collection of two-by-fours, pieces of plywood, pipes, and battered planks. Ignoring the protests of newly arrived customers, the NOBBY contingent set to work with a will. Eager hands clutched at swinging loose ends, encouraging yelps resounded through the air, and a large, rickety fortification began to take shape.

Bemusedly watching the frenzied efforts, Charlie murmured, "Are you thinking what I'm thinking, John?"

Thatcher nodded.

"The lady's reasoning contains a slight flaw. *They shall not pass* worked at Thermopylae because the Persians were coming from only one direction."

Aristocrats like Thatcher and Charlie could largely govern the disposition of their time. But for the vast majority of wage slaves the noontime break represented a unique period of the workday, every moment of which was precious. Some might spend a leisurely hour in their company's cafeteria, enjoying subsidized food and rampaging gossip. On a fine spring afternoon, others might carry their brown bags to the cemetery of Trinity Church to dine al fresco. But for many the location of choice was a fast-food restaurant, with the emphasis on fast. Fifteen minutes were allowed to bolt down a hamburger because they intended to squeeze in a half-hour workout at their health club, they planned to take advantage of local shopping facilities, or they were due for their semiannual dental cleaning. The group trapped inside Rugby's discovered their plight and the consequent wreckage of their rigid schedules with varying degrees of dismay until the situation was brought to the attention of a heavyset bond clerk. Only two years removed from his college football team, he cast one contemptuous look at the obstacle and unleashed a bull-like roar.

"What the hell do they think they're playing at? I've only got ten minutes to put my bets down."

It was unfortunate that at the critical moment the manager of the franchise was in the stockroom. He would probably have organized some orderly retreat through the nether regions of the store into a back alley. The bond clerk had a different solution.

"One of you open the door for me and the rest of you stand clear," he ordered, backing up to provide himself with a running start.

A young woman being denied access to a spectacular sale on panty-hose was only too ready to oblige.

The hero of the hour dropped a bulky shoulder and charged down the length of the runway, expertly adjusting his stride so that on the last step his right foot swung through an arc that brought his stout brogue crashing into the barricade, with the full weight of his powerful body behind it.

As the jerry-built superstructure began to collapse, the whole seething mass of humanity liquefied. Those inside Rugby's streamed out to freedom, those outside still desiring a bowl of chili surged forward and, sandwiched between these determined forces, were the NOBBY volunteers rushing to reerect their barricade.

Collision and conflict were inevitable. Within minutes a length of two-by-four sailed through the air above the milling throng and smashed into one of Rugby's plate-glass windows.

"Elmer is going to love this," Charlie Trinkam muttered.

Thatcher, observing the patrol car returning to check on the bus, said, "I don't think he's the only one who will be objecting. It might not be a bad idea for us to move to the other side of the street."

Matters were already well beyond the ability of two policemen to control. Summoning reinforcements on the radio, they simply turned a disenchanted gaze on the burgeoning riot and tried to identify particularly egregious offenders. But the heart of battle was hidden from their view, as it was from that of John Thatcher, in his new coign of vantage. He could hear yells of anger and screeches of indignation, he could see flailing arms appear above the struggling mass of humanity. Only on occasion, however, when a swaying group would suddenly shift position, did he catch glimpses of individual incidents.

For some reason many of the belligerents had adopted classic stances. A middle-aged woman, every inch the shot-putter, had grasped the strap of her heavy shoulder bag and was swinging it around her head. A bearded youth had tangled with a customer and the two men were squirming on the ground in a fine display of Greco-Roman wrestling. Not to be outdone, an enterprising bus boy appeared in the doorway carrying a vat, then, with fine impartiality, he heaved its load of ketchup on all and sundry. Things were at their worst when a young woman, alighting from a cab at the corner, suddenly pelted down the sidewalk and dashed into the fray, screaming "No! No!" Just as she clutched the arm of a volunteer waving a shattered piece of sawhorse, there came the sound of a second plate-glass window cracking.

Finally reinforcements arrived, complete with paddy wagon. Bullhorns brayed, police charged in, and the young woman from the taxi managed to achieve sole possession of the sawhorse at precisely the wrong moment.

The police plucked combatants from the melee and began herding them into the paddy wagon, the manager of the franchise emerged screaming curses, several women were weeping and, in the background, a late-arriving television crew scrambled for strategic spots from which to film the whole sorry spectacle.

THE DAMAGE THEY recorded included shattered windows, a scarred frontage, and construction debris littering a wide area. To heighten the graphic impact, the cameras lingered lovingly over every sinister red splotch, then panned to paramedics loading a stretcher while a policeman, blood trickling down his cheek, was led away. By the time this footage was aired over local stations, angry voices had been added.

One of the shrillest belonged to Sal Piemonte of the Piemonte Construction Company.

"Who do these people think they are?" he snarled. "That was my stuff they stole. They owe me for the material they ripped off, for all the damage they did at the site, and for my crew's down time. I intend to see that they pay."

Then there was the young woman who had been en route to a panty-hose sale. She had been hurled off her feet in the first onslaught and was caught later that day hobbling out of the emergency room on crutches.

"I'm supposed to get married next week," she wailed. "Now look at me. How am I going to get down the aisle? Somebody has to make this up to me."

But the most passionate complaint came from Elmer Rugby.

"They didn't just vandalize my premises, they sent one of my counter kids off in an ambulance."

He, too, was shown at a hospital, where he was trying to console a fragile-looking girl in a wheelchair.

"Thank God Theresa Dominguez is going to be all right," he continued in a basso profundo. "But I'll teach NOBBY a lesson they'll never forget, if I have to sue those slimeballs for every cent they've got."

The underlying theme behind all those messages was not lost on NOBBY's board of governors. Within minutes of the first bulletin they were on the phone to each other.

"My God, we'll be in court for years," one of them groaned. "And why the hell isn't Madeleine making some kind of statement?"

"Because nobody can find her," snapped Peggy Roche, chairman of the board. "I've tried the office and her home. She can't know what's going on."

But Peggy was wrong. Perched in a hotel room high above Manhattan, Madeleine Underwood had settled herself to watch the news, at first with suppressed anticipation, then with genuine astonishment and finally with unalloyed gratification. When she turned off the set she was nodding happily.

"Well, I wanted to get their attention," she murmured to herself, "and they haven't seen anything yet."

11. Full-Bodied

PREDICTABLY DEAN KICHSEL was on the phone to John Thatcher bright and early the next morning.

"In view of the appalling events at Rugby's yesterday, I intend to make a severe protest to the committee as to the advisability of permitting NOBBY to continue its testimony," he said fussily. "I know that George would ordinarily wish to be present, but his wife tells me the poor fellow is feeling worse than ever."

Once again it was time for Lancer's proxy to put his shoulder to the wheel.

"What time do the hearings start?" asked Thatcher with resignation.

"At ten-thirty."

Accordingly, two hours later Thatcher dutifully trudged into the appointed building. The energy level in the hall outside the hearing room fell short of the heat of battle, but nonetheless there was a throb of excitement rarely generated by congressional hearings. There were knots of people huddling intently, self-important staffers speeding about with self-important documents, late arrivals eagerly hailing colleagues. Undeniably the pack was closing in for the kill. While interrupting Thatcher's breakfast, Dean Kichsel had spoken in the most elevated terms, but the pro-Quax forces had scented an opportunity to finish off their opponent.

Thatcher was not surprised that the first face he recognized belonged to Elmer Rugby, hard at work on a young man he had backed into a corner.

Rugby, his eyes skewering his quarry, was conversing in the strangled, hard bursts of a big dog on a short leash. As soon as he caught sight of Thatcher, he imperatively waved him over, without interrupting his diatribe.

"What more does your bunch want?" he was demanding. "Yesterday proves that Rossi's been taken in. He's using taxpayer money to promote a bunch of goddamn lawbreakers. Hell, it's un-American, and you can tell him I'm going to make it my business to let people know."

"Leon Rossi is conducting a fair and impartial inquiry. You can't hold him responsible for a pack of weirdos."

"Oh, can't I? That's exactly what everybody is going to do. Just ask John, here."

But Thatcher, who favored more informative introductions, merely extended his hand and said, "John Thatcher from the Sloan."

"Congressman Harry Hull."

Rugby was not letting anybody duck the most significant identification of all.

"From Texas!" he snorted. "That's some state delegation we've got."

"Now look here, Elmer," Hull said crisply. "You know damn well that I was proposing some investigation of Quax long before you got involved in its sale. That didn't stop you from tying up with Kichsel. And I'm not letting the fact that you're Texas-based stop me. As far as that protest yesterday goes, I've got more to complain about than you do."

Rugby was almost gobbling.

"Trashing restaurants! Scaring customers! Calling out the riot police! And you call that a protest?"

"I call it a dangerous menace. But the point is, you've come out of this a victim. Those of us who want to approach the whole Quax issue on a reasonable, thoughtful basis are going to be smeared by this lunatic fringe group."

Before Elmer could go up in smoke, Thatcher stepped in. "Surely there are ways of disassociating yourselves from them."

"What do you think we're all talking about in the backroom? Why do you think the opening gavel's being delayed?" asked Hull with a grim smile. "The way Leon sees it, he gave that woman a chance to express her views and, in the middle of her testimony, she goes out and deliberately foments a riot. There's no way in hell he'll continue giving her a platform."

It sounded to Thatcher as if Dean Kichsel had already achieved his objective, but Rugby was a long way from satisfied.

"He ought to end the whole farce, and if he hasn't thought of it, why don't you suggest it?"

"Will you just hold your horses until you know how things work out, Elmer?" Hull said wearily. "Frankly, Leon seems to be leaning toward an indefinite adjournment right now. That way he keeps his options open. He can either let the whole thing die a slow death or he can reconvene after the smoke has settled, without any reference to NOBBY."

Before Rugby could favor them with his views on this pusillanimous strategy, Hull announced that someone was signaling him and departed with a final flap of the hand.

Still champing at the bit, Elmer Rugby soon spied another possible pressure point and stomped across the hall. Thatcher, instead of following, remained where he was in order to survey the growing assembly. As a possible source of entertainment it was far less promising than a real cross-section of humanity. Everybody present, apart from some lowlier members of the press, wore the apparel and facial expressions that obliterated distinctions of age, sex and alliance. Only the background hum of dozens of conversations enlivened the scene. And from overheard snatches Thatcher discovered that, thanks to last night's television, Madeleine Underwood and her numerous shortcomings formed the main topic of the day.

One cheerful soul was regaling his companions with a rollicking description of Paul Jackson's courtroom triumph.

"That dumb dame picked a kid who started on the hooch the minute he was out of diapers."

A more serious student was reviewing every folly Mrs. Underwood had uttered during the last hearing.

Yet another had the latest tidbit straight from the committee clerk.

". . . trying to have a letter introduced into the formal record. It was from some woman who had a sister who had a friend who'd heard of some college kid drinking beer after a year on Quax. She was insisting that was real solid evidence. It just goes to show what—"

Abruptly ruder sounds interrupted the genteel buzzing. All heads, including Thatcher's, turned as a noisy altercation approached from afar with the fanfare of a marching band.

First to come into view was Alec Moore, striding along with his eyes fixed straight ahead. Hurrying in his wake, Madeleine Underwood appeared, her red suit a flicker of flame in the sea of drabness.

"Oh, sure, try to run away now that the truth is coming out," she declaimed challengingly.

Stopping so quickly that she cannoned into him, Moore turned with a contemptuous scowl. "You wouldn't know the truth if it bit you in the face. Your idea of thinking is to fabricate facts out of thin air."

Onlookers lining the route hastily stepped aside just in time for a third arrival. Claudia Fentiman, clicking along on her high heels, ranged herself at Alec Moore's side.

"You're a fine one to talk about facts," Madeleine snapped, oblivious to her audience. "You'd say anything in order to sell Quax to kids—and you're scared to death I'm going to stop you."

"Crap!" he thundered blightingly. "You just want to play God."

"We don't have to do a damn thing to stop you," Claudia came rallying to his support. "You're doing a fine job on your own."

Madeleine's voice was now ringing through the hall. "You think I don't know all about you, but I've had you investigated. I've found out your dirty little secrets."

The most appalling aspect of the quarrel, from Thatcher's point of view, was the sheer relish Madeleine was deriving from every exchange.

"After your performance at Rugby's I wouldn't put anything past you," Alec shot back, "including manufacturing whatever seems convenient."

"You think you're going to go on the stand and give us a lot of garbage about how concerned you are for young people, how you campaign against drunken driving. Well, I can show them the kind of people Kichsel has peddling its fine product—people unfit to be near children, people ready to infect anybody with their poison."

White-faced, almost gibbering with rage, Moore snarled, "Don't try and get on some moral high horse with me. After yesterday we know all about the kind of tactics you resort to."

Madeleine's head rose proudly. "That was an expression of deep concern by my supporters. Something people as corrupt as you wouldn't understand."

By now Claudia was grasping Moore's arm to restrain him. "Cool it, Alec," she said urgently. "This woman has as much credibility as the population of Attica."

"Just wait," Madeleine said defiantly. "I've got proof positive of the kind of people trying to silence me."

Obedient to Claudia's pressure, Moore had begun to turn aside. "Why don't you take a look at your own little ego trips first?" he suggested over his shoulder.

"And at the same time I can demonstrate to the world that my campaign is moved by nothing except a genuine concern for our young people," she declared with a fervor worthy of Joan of Arc.

Then she turned on her heel and stalked magnificently away, leaving Moore free to continue his progress. Only Claudia remained on the field. Gazing coldly at the receding red-suited figure, she delivered one loud and clear syllable.

"Bitch!"

Thatcher felt the final comment was unnecessary, but his views were not shared by another bystander.

"Right on target, I'd say," he announced, turning from his companion. "We met at the tariff dinner the other night, Thatcher. Roger Vandermeer."

"Of course." Thatcher nodded. "You represent the Soft Drink Institute. I can see how you have an interest in this issue."

"We have a legitimate interest in the marketing of Quax," Vandermeer said hastily. "We have absolutely no interest in crazy broads who want to tangle with the cops."

84

The young man at Vandermeer's side groaned. "But that's the whole point of what I've been saying. Madeleine's past history now. Hell, she was on her way out even before the riot. It won't take the board more than a couple of days to bounce her."

While Cushing continued his theme, Thatcher reflected on the varying degrees of disassociation. Most of the anti-Quax elements, like Harry Hull and Vandermeer, were simply drawing away from contamination by NOBBY. Cushing had a more difficult row to hoe. He had to sound as if it were possible for NOBBY to disassociate itself from Madeleine Underwood.

"We have thousands of members, almost all of whom are parents of young children. Do you think this is what they want their kids to see? Television footage of their mothers heaving rocks and being hauled off in the paddy wagon? Absolutely not."

"Then they shouldn't have gotten involved," Vandermeer said shortly.

Soldiering on in the face of Vandermeer's repulses, Cushing redoubled his efforts at persuasion, describing the new look which NOBBY was about to assume until a young woman came hurrying by.

"Iona?" he exclaimed, breaking into his own sermon. "What are you doing here?"

Her face was very grim.

"Looking for dear Madeleine. She's got a lot of explaining to do."

As she sped off, Cushing promptly tried to exploit her obvious anger. "Now, there's a good example," he argued. "That's one of our most industrious volunteers, and you can see how she feels about Mrs. Underwood."

Thatcher, who had recognized Iona as the unfortunate arriving at Rugby's just in time to be arrested, thought that Cushing was wise not to elaborate on the grounds for her dissatisfaction.

"She is representative of the vast majority of our members and they'll make no bones about demanding that Madeleine resign. I can tell you that I myself will be advising the board to . . ."

As the hard sell was being directed exclusively at Roger Vandermeer, Thatcher seized the opportunity to drift off in search of his own party. He finally found Dean Kichsel in a secluded recess of the corridor with Chairman Rossi and the committee counsel. With Kichsel already assured about his major concern, they were all busily engaged in disparaging Madeleine Underwood.

"You've heard about that public scene she just created with Alec and Claudia?" Kichsel demanded of Thatcher.

"I saw it. Or at least some of it."

"The woman is completely bananas," Rossi declared. "The only thing to do is ignore her."

"That's easier said than done," the counsel said indignantly. "The switchboard put her through to me yesterday afternoon and you know what she had the gall to demand? Just because she didn't like the testimony of the country's biggest expert on alcoholism, she claimed we had to give equal time to her tame psychiatrist."

Rossi was smug. "She didn't get through to me but my aide says she had a list of questions I was supposed to give the committee members."

"Yesterday afternoon? Perfect!" Kichsel said with majestic irony. "Then she was trying to tell you how to run your committee at the same time her demonstrators were getting themselves arrested."

"Of course, Harry Hull is the one really taking it in the neck," the counsel continued. "He was decent enough to give her a drink after she made a fool of herself here on Monday. Then, when Roger Vandermeer showed up to see him, the woman tried to muscle in on their meeting."

"That'll teach Harry," Rossi grunted.

"Well, you know what Vandermeer's like. He got rid of her pronto, but instead of giving up, she pulled the oldest trick in the book. As soon as Roger left she turned up again, all bright-eyed and bushy-tailed. She'd left something behind to have an excuse for pumping him about what Vandermeer said. Poor Harry had to go out himself to shake her."

Kichsel immediately riposted with some gossip about Madeleine's open pride in her demonstrators' handiwork at Rugby's, and the list of Underwood atrocities might have continued indefinitely if Theo Benda had not appeared, squiring Claudia Fentiman.

"Claudia's looking for Alec," he announced. "Anybody seen him?"

"He's probably keeping out of my way after that disgraceful scene." Kichsel turned reproachful eyes on Claudia. "Surely that could have been avoided."

She was unrepentant. "I don't see how. The woman tracked us down and was hell-bent on making trouble."

"Be fair, Dean," Theo Benda urged. "What can you do if a demented woman is determined to tangle with you in a public place?"

"You cut her off short and walk away."

"Alec tried that and she simply followed him. She was ready to stalk him through the whole building. Although once his dander was up," she admitted, "he didn't seem able to stop himself."

"So we all saw," Kichsel snapped.

"Anyway, I'd better find him and make sure he's not getting into another brawl with her. Alec's been in a funny mood all morning."

Leon Rossi, scenting a family fight, said indulgently that everybody was on edge and that it was time for him to poll the committee. "You're sure to sort things out," he declared, withdrawing with his counsel.

"I wouldn't worry too much, Claudia," Benda rumbled soothingly. "If Underwood's looking for trouble, maybe it's time she found some."

"I'd rather it was with somebody else," she rejoined. "Right now our side's looking good and I'd like to keep it that way. So far, any blood on the floor's been put there by NOBBY."

As soon as she had left, Thatcher did his best to encourage Kichsel to abandon his bone of discontent. "Mrs. Fentiman seems to be doing everything possible."

"And," said Benda, checking his watch, "shouldn't we be getting inside if the committee is finally coming up with its decision? Hell, it's practically lunchtime already."

They were not the only ones on the move. Word of an approaching climax had spread and most of the crowd was drifting into the hearing room. Harry Hull, accompanied by two staffers, was struggling against the tide to make his way backstage. It was his misfortune to run into Madeleine Underwood.

"Oh, there you are," she said, planting herself firmly in his path.

"I don't care how busy you are, I have to talk to you before I go back on the stand."

Still trying to be polite, Hull said resignedly, "This isn't a good time. Can't it wait?"

"No, it can't," she said truculently. "Like it or not, you've got some listening to do."

Thatcher could no longer complain that Madeleine Underwood was enjoying the discomfort she was spreading. Her voice had sunk to a hoarse rasp and there were two angry red spots on her cheeks. Somebody, somewhere, had finally managed to pierce that self-satisfied insulation. Could Alec Moore have realized Claudia's gloomy prediction and engaged in a second round?

In the face of Madeleine's insistent discourtesy, Hull had finally lost patience. "You're wrong about that. I'm the one who has quite a lot to say," he growled, stripping off the velvet glove. "Be in the clerk's office by two. If my lunch date runs over, I may be a little late."

Unbelievably she misread this veiled threat as a concession.

"I'll be there," she said grandly. "Right on the dot."

But if she was deaf to his undertone, the rest of the audience was not. For all practical purposes her last remaining supporter had decided she was untouchable. In these circles one warning was enough. Unconsciously those seeking seats gave her a wide berth so that she was standing alone in a room that contained a milling throng on every other square foot.

Roger Vandermeer, preparing to settle himself in the row behind Thatcher, said lazily, "How dumb can you get? She must be the only person in the building who thinks they're giving her another crack at all those microphones."

If so, she was not permitted to continue in ignorant bliss for long. Almost immediately a Rossi staffer appeared in the doorway, nervously conning his notes.

"Ladies and gentlemen!" he began. "Congressman Rossi, with the unanimous—I repeat, unanimous—consent of the entire subcommittee has decided to adjourn these hearings indefinitely."

In the general babble, Thatcher involuntarily glanced toward that lonely pool of isolation. White-faced with shock, she was silent for a moment. Then:

"So they've decided on a cover-up," she announced militantly. "Well, we'll see about that!"

THE EFFECT OF her words on those near enough to hear was only momentary. With amused glances or condescending shrugs they began streaming toward the exists, already planning the disposition of time unexpectedly freed by an adjournment.

But no staged production is over when the house empties. Behind the scenes there is frenzied activity as sets are dismantled, makeup is scrubbed off, costumes returned to the wardrobe mistress. Leon Rossi's attempt at theater was no exception. Even before the public announcement, lowly members of the staff were hard at work. Striking their tents with all the virtuosity of carnival roustabouts, they began packing up one mountain of documents and shredding another.

"Will you look at this?" one of them demanded as he wrestled with some immense, flopping charts that had briefly graced the committee's easel. "I blame it all on computer graphics. If it wasn't so easy to punch these things out, the guy would simply have described the age distribution of beer drinkers."

A file clerk glanced at the display of primary colors. "It's no good anyway. All the kids lie," she said authoritatively. Then, examining the future from her youthful vantage point, she added, "For all I know, everyone else does, too."

The men breaking down the enormous committee table into its sections grumbled as usual about its weight, its inconvenience, and all those pesky wires running to individual microphones.

Two floors higher up, experts on Modern Personnel Techniques received the glad news that they would be able to move from their present cramped quarters the next morning. By then Babcock Auditorium would have returned to normalcy, with a podium boasting a row of chairs and a single lectern. With this joyful prospect before them, they thundered back from lunch shortly before two and almost obscured the brilliant dab of color that was Mrs. Underwood arriving early for her appointment.

By three o'clock, a cleaning crew was trundling its apparatus backstage to attack the clerical offices. Working systematically, they fanned through the narrow hallways, dispatching one cubicle after another.

At three-thirty the efficient process came to an abrupt halt. One of the overalled men, entering the committee clerk's office, briefly inspected its general condition. Then he opened a closet door, only to freeze into immobility, transfixed by horror.

Madeleine Underwood's body lay jammed in the narrow confines, limbs contorted and clothing twisted. As a further macabre touch, her bloodied head lolled against a red-suited shoulder with sightless eyes staring directly upward.

So, long after the stage curtains had swished closed, the Quax hearings reached their dramatic climax as the cleaning man broke free from his paralysis to run screaming into the corridor.

12. Checkpoint

OH, FOR CHRISSAKE!" growled the first detective to crouch over the closet floor. "Just take a look at this."

His partner, leaning forward cautiously in the constricted space, read the name on the driver's license.

"We'd better alert headquarters." He sighed. "This has all the makings of a circus."

Yesterday's coverage of the Rugby riot had ensured that, for this brief moment in time, Madeleine Underwood was a genuine celebrity and the New York City Police Department knew too much about the carnival atmosphere surrounding a murdered celebrity.

Within half an hour the department had mounted a full court press that would have astounded anyone dialing 911 from a housing project. Medics, detectives, photographers, and assorted specialists arrived in waves, with Inspector Timothy Reardon directing the whirlwind.

"Just our luck," he announced, creaking upright from his first inspection of the closet. "Her wallet is stuffed with cash and credit cards, her briefcase has an expensive calculator and she's wearing a diamond ring. So we can forget mugging. I'd better talk to the guy who found the body."

This unfortunate was huddled on a bench in the corridor, clutching a glass and determined to apologize for his bolt to the bathroom after raising the alarm.

"It was just so sudden, I wasn't expecting anything like that," he explained unnecessarily. "One minute everything was the same as usual, then the next minute—that!"

"But you did the right thing. You told people to stay out of the office," Reardon said soothingly. "Just take it slow and easy. I have to know if you did any cleaning before you opened the closet."

There was a shake of the head.

"No, the first thing we do after a tenant closes shop is go through the place for the Lost and Found. They're always leaving behind gloves and umbrellas and stuff like that. I took a quick look around the office, then went to the closet behind the desk."

Reardon had already noted with satisfaction that the cart containing vacuum cleaner, dusters, and other paraphernalia was still in the hall.

"Good. And everything seemed normal at first?"

"That's right. There was just the usual mountain of trash."

After taking the cleaning man over his movements, Reardon returned to the scene of the crime and said philosophically, "Well, things could be worse. At least he didn't go through the place polishing everything in sight."

"It's plain enough what happened," his assistant reported. "There's blood at the foot of the desk and on one of its legs. That's where she got clobbered, but her purse and briefcase protected the top of the desk. The killer wanted to make his getaway before anything was discovered, so he dragged the body back to the closet. Look, you can still see the marks on the rug. After that he tossed in the purse and the briefcase. Then he dumped this."

This was a heavy bronze bookend, now encased in a plastic bag, covered with stains and clumps of gummy residue that told their own tale.

"I suppose that bookend is part of the room's furnishings?" asked Reardon, gazing at several large books sprawled atop the mate to the murder weapon.

"Yes, the management provides some basic stuff—a government organization manual, a business directory, a phone book."

Thanks to the media hullabaloo, Inspector Reardon was already familiar with the basic features of the anti-Quax movement. Dispatching men to NOBBY, to Chairman Rossi, to Kichsel's New

York office and to Madeleine's hotel room, he reserved for himself the building manager—and the question that had been exercising him ever since he learned that Mrs. Underwood had been murdered on the site of a congressional hearing.

"This is ordinary commercial property, isn't it? And not a federal facility?" he asked anxiously.

"Right. This floor is reserved for short-term rentals, so we get hearings and conferences that are scheduled too suddenly to get space in a government or institutional building. The periods are anything from two to ten days."

Reardon relaxed. That meant an invasion by the FBI was not imminent. Like himself, they would be consulting lawyers to determine if one of the more obscure federal crimes was involved.

"And the committee was already gone by this afternoon?" he pressed.

"They told us at eleven-thirty that they'd be vacating the premises immediately. I gave them enough time to clear out, then sent in the cleaning crew at three-thirty. We always have a waiting list."

"Did you follow the hearings at all?"

"Are you crazy? I don't even know what they were about."

But plenty of people were willing to tell the police what the manager did not know. Reports were soon flowing back to the inspector.

Leon Rossi provided a brief résumé of the hearings, said that his clerical staff had packed up and emplaned for Washington by one o'clock, and produced the first of many character assessments.

"Underwood was a real flake, that's why I adjourned. After her stunt at Rugby's I wasn't touching her with a ten-foot pole. But why in the world would anyone kill her? She was the kind of woman you just get away from."

Rossi then turned his attention to drafting an appropriate release that deplored the tragedy and hailed Madeleine Underwood's life of public service.

Harry Hull was more concerned with his own experience.

"Yes, we had an appointment in that office. I was almost a quarter of an hour late and when the place was empty, I gave her only a couple of minutes before I left. There was no way I was hanging around for her."

"I thought she said it was important."

Hull produced a wry grimace. "That meant it was important for her, not for me. Anyway I was just going to kiss her off. But now I don't feel so good about it. I suppose if I'd waited for her she'd still be alive."

"Not likely. The elevator man took her up before two o'clock."

A look of horror dawned. "Oh my God, you mean she was already dead while I was there?"

Lesser members of the staff, unburdened by painful memories or literary composition, were more helpful. Gleefully they provided recollections not only about Madeleine's activities during the hearings but about the comments they had sparked.

"She chased two of the Kichsel people right down the hall to yell at them. She said she was going to—"

"I heard Roger Vandermeer call her a bitch."

"Mr. Kichsel was steaming. But I think he was madder at his own people than at—"

". . . there she was, claiming that the adjournment was a cover-up, and all because she was too dumb to realize—"

"Elmer Rugby said someone should strangle her."

At Kichsel, not surprisingly, there was not a good word to be said for Madeleine Underwood.

"The woman was a mischief-making nonentity," Dean Kichsel had proclaimed. "Basically she was unimportant."

"She was the one trying to start a fight. We were just trying to get away from her," protested Claudia Fentiman, unconsciously endorsing Chairman Rossi's opinion.

"She was a pain in the ass, all right," Alec Moore said bluntly. "But you couldn't take her seriously enough to want to kill her."

Madeleine's hotel confirmed that she had registered on Monday at five, explaining her intention to remain in town for the length of the hearings. A search of her room revealed nothing beyond personal possessions and some notes on Monday's testimony. The material she had intended to use on Wednesday had already been identified in her briefcase.

Amidst all this dross there were gleanings of gold. But it was at NOBBY that the police struck pay dirt. Cheryl Zimmerman, alone in the office, was caught in the middle of an elaborate makeup ritual prior to departure.

"The office is closed," she announced.

Even the production of police ID failed to impress her.

"I'm just the receptionist here. Everybody else left fifteen minutes ago. If you want to ask about the riot, you'll have to come back tomorrow."

"It's more serious than the riot. Mrs. Underwood was murdered several hours ago."

Cheryl stared, sank into a chair and burst into noisy sobs. After several minutes it developed that her shock was due more to the simple fact of Madeleine's death than to its grisly circumstances.

"I've never known anyone who actually died," she explained in awe-struck tones.

Handing her a box of tissues, the detective marveled that she was still young enough to be surprised by human mortality. But when asked about the last time she had seen Madeleine, Cheryl began putting two and two together.

"I haven't seen her since yesterday morning. Everybody's been trying to find her, but she never told me where she was going when she stormed out . . ." She straightened and her voice caught on a half-gasp. "So that's what this is all about."

"And what's that?"

"The big fight she had with Sean Cushing. They were going at it hammer and tongs."

"And I'll bet you heard what it was all about."

"Not all of it. But I could tell they were both madder than I'd ever seen them before."

The detective was struggling not to be diverted by Cheryl's clownish appearance. She was not one of those who decked out her eyes in tandem. Accordingly one side of her face, still untouched, presented to the world naked brows and lashes while the other half boasted the full array of shadow, liner and brow pencil. To make matters worse, the combined action of tears and tissues had played havoc with her mascara.

"Still, you must have heard something," he persisted.

"Of course I wasn't listening," she said perfunctorily. "But the way they were screaming at each other I couldn't help catching some of it."

Leaning forward eagerly, she began to recapitulate.

INSPECTOR REARDON WAS impressed enough to go himself to the small apartment on the Upper West Side. At the very least, NOBBY's administrator would be a fount of information about the organization. At best he might be the end of the trail. Cushing answered the third ring of the bell in a rumpled T-shirt and sweat shorts.

"Sorry," he explained after the visitor introduced himself. "I was in the middle of my workout."

Automatically Reardon assessed the figure before him. Genetics had provided Sean Cushing with a small, narrow frame, but there was nothing frail about the ropy muscles encased in that whippet body. Unfortunately, a child could have killed Madeleine Underwood with the aid of that heavy bookend.

"What can I do for you?" asked Cushing, heading into the living room where a barbell lay on the floor.

"I'm here about Madeleine Underwood."

Cushing stopped in his tracks. "Sweet Jesus, what's she done now?" he exclaimed in dismay. "Not another riot?"

"She's been murdered."

There was a moment's silence as Cushing revised his tone. "Oh my God. Was it a mugging?"

Fair-mindedly Reardon acknowledged that all New Yorkers were so concerned with random violence that a targeted murder demanded readjustment even from homicide detectives.

"No."

The bald negative had its effect. A blanket of caution descended on Cushing's face, as he took time out to mop his glistening brow.

"It's almost unbelievable," he said at last. "Madeleine exasperated a lot of people, but that's not enough to get herself killed."

"So you'd think," Reardon agreed. "But maybe something happened. When was the last time you saw her?"

"To talk to? That would have been yesterday. Of course I saw her at the hearings this morning, but we never actually spoke."

Reardon allowed himself to be mildly incredulous. "You mean you spent a couple of hours in the same place and never said a word to her?"

"Not the way she was acting. When I saw her in the middle of a set-to with the Kichsel people, I decided to steer clear."

On the principle of first extracting any information that would be volunteered, the inspector demanded more details about the encounter with Alec Moore and Claudia Fentiman. Almost without knowing it, Cushing was then led into a recital of Elmer Rugby's reaction to the riot, Madeleine's appointment with Congressman Hull, her response to the adjournment.

"That's an odd kind of public spokesman for any organization," Reardon commented.

"Oh, she was out of step with everyone at the hearings, but that's because she didn't understand the basic question. She thought the anti-Quax campaign was about good and evil, with Madeleine Underwood the symbol of virtue."

"And I suppose Kichsel and the Soft Drink Institute saw it as pure and simple competition?"

"Sure. And the committee members had still other ideas. But Madeleine didn't see it that way. If Congress was starting to investigate Quax, that meant they'd signed up as recruits in her army and she was in charge. With that twisted idea she was ready to tell Leon Rossi how he should run his hearings. Hell, she had a few words of advice for Roger Vandermeer, too."

"Who's he?"

Relaxed by now, Cushing was happy to supply general background. "He's the front man for SDI. I introduced them the first day of the hearings and right away she was suggesting ways SDI could help NOBBY, instead of the other way around. Madeleine's biggest problem was that it never occurred to her other people came with their own agendas. It was a one-way street as far as she was concerned."

"And if she didn't understand that about people outside NOBBY, I suppose the same was true for those inside."

"You mean the staff?" Cushing asked, puzzled.

But Inspector Reardon was still exploring the larger field before zeroing in on his target. His next sentence caused an explosion of protest.

"*No!* You've been listening to those morons on TV. We don't have a radical wing at NOBBY. We're not the anti-abortion movement."

"I'm not saying you people at headquarters are fanatics. But plenty of way-out types have been swept up by the anti-abortion movement. What makes you think it couldn't happen at NOBBY?"

"Use your head, Inspector," Sean urged. "This whole campaign is about a soft drink. Who's going to throw bombs or murder someone because of that?"

"Apparently they're willing to start riots and send people to the hospital."

This was so unanswerable that Sean Cushing groaned. "That was all Madeleine's idea. She'd messed up so much, she decided on a show of force, and things got out of hand."

Reardon shook his head gently. "Just listen to yourself. You're saying she was capable of making people lose their heads. Suppose some borderline freak thought she was promising more than she could deliver—like organizing bomb-throwing at Kichsel. That kind of disagreement could turn nasty."

"For Chrissake, our members aren't like that."

"How would you know?"

For the first time Cushing hesitated in his special pleading. "I don't have anything to do with them," he admitted at last. "But talk to Iona Perez, she's the woman in charge of volunteers, she'll tell you the same thing. Nobody at NOBBY was gunning for Madeleine."

"Oh yeah? That lady had a pretty short fuse and tangled with everyone in sight. But you're claiming it was all sweetness and light in the office. Like hell it was. Suppose you tell me about the fight you had with her yesterday morning."

Stiffening, Sean deliberately fortified himself with several deep breaths before launching into explanation.

"It was a real beaut," he said defiantly. "I was mad as hell and she was throwing out a lot of crazy accusations."

"*You* were mad? What did you have to be mad about?"

Cushing was impatient. "Come on, Inspector. By Monday night Madeleine had fucked up the hearings and our court case. I was getting calls from donors and members threatening to pull out. Madeleine was flushing NOBBY down the tubes."

"Sounds as if you had a grievance all right," Reardon said peaceably. "So how come she was the one throwing around accusations?"

"That was just a smoke screen. She knew she was in hot water and she was trying to change the subject."

"Funny way to do it. I hear it was all about your handling of NOBBY's finances and those funds she didn't know about. Maybe they were funds going into a separate account?"

The implication was clear and a dull stain mottled Cushing's face.

"Oh, for God's sake, you don't think . . . ? But it was nothing like that. She was trying to raise Cain about the donation from SDI!"

"Why should she go ape about that?"

"You have to understand Madeleine. She had a vision of herself leading a crusade. Large anonymous corporations didn't fit in, so she ignored them and she never understood our financials anyway. But somehow she'd found out that SDI was providing the lion's share of our funding, so she claimed that I'd sold her out, handed NOBBY over to SDI. In fact, I was surprised she had the brains to realize how much leverage they had, but I suppose she was beginning to feel vulnerable. It was all her own silly fault, but that didn't stop her trying to pretend it was mine. That's why she was yakking about disloyalty and betrayal on every side."

This was an element that had escaped Cheryl.

"And who besides you was being disloyal?"

"Everybody, according to her," Sean said sourly.

"And so she ended up by firing you. That must have made you feel great."

"It didn't mean a damn thing."

"Sure, jobs are a dime a dozen these days."

Cushing waved the comment aside. "Look, Madeleine was the one in trouble, not me. She already had two strikes against her before the riot. By yesterday night the board was fed up with her. I didn't have a thing to worry about."

"Then you won't mind telling me what you did after the adjournment."

The voice was totally devoid of inflection. "I went to that health-food place a block south and had lunch. Then I walked to the Fifty-third Street stop to catch the subway home. Once I got here I tried to call Peggy Roche—she's head of NOBBY's board of governors—but I had to leave a message."

"And when would that have been?"

"I guess it must have been between two-thirty and three."

"That's a lot of time for lunch and a short trip."

"The subway was a mess."

Reardon fell into a short reverie from which he emerged with a brisk announcement. "I'll be sending police auditors into your office. You'd better get everything ready."

"Not so fast," said Sean, summoning up a show of resistance. "I can't let you do that, not until you have permission from the board."

"Get real, Cushing," Reardon said pityingly. "I'll spell it out for you. You had a big fight with Mrs. Underwood about NOBBY's finances. It ends by her firing you and *maybe* threatening jail. Twenty-four hours later she's murdered and you don't have an alibi. I can get a court order in five minutes, so expect my people tomorrow."

Sean had risen from the sofa and thrust his jaw forward. "And you won't find a penny missing," he said pugnaciously.

"Then you don't have anything to worry about, do you?"

By the time Reardon left, Cushing's healthy glow had given way to ashen pallor.

13. Beer and Skittles

ALL THAT DAY the feeding frenzy of the press had been intensifying. On the previous evening Rugby's riot had been handled as a local feature, yet another example of the zany tribulations accompanying life in New York City. Overnight, however, the networks had decided to go national with the story. The spectacle of Americans being deprived of their God-given right to buy hamburgers would, they calculated, hit home everywhere. Besides, more than fast food was involved, as hastily summoned moralists were swift to explain on the early-morning programs.

"Once again we are confronted by a small minority determined to impose its will on the majority," pontificated the statelier opinion shapers. "Finding that educational programs work too slowly, that the public does not endorse their cause, extremists—whether they are pro-lifers, animal-rights activists or NOBBY supporters—resort to harassment and intimidation. Too often legitimate protest escalates into violence. No ends justify such means . . ."

By noon, special-interest groups were seizing the moment. MADD, DARE and a host of other acronyms gave their views on the problem of Quax. Only the Vegetarian Society of North America chose to attack the hamburger instead.

"Science proves that red meat disturbs the body's natural balance," declared a spokesman. "Flesh eaters find it impossible to maintain mental and physical harmony within themselves. We do not carry clubs like cavemen. Why are we still eating like them?"

Four hours later, when word of Madeleine Underwood's murder flashed across their desks, every news director in the business congratulated himself on his foresight.

"Thank God we started running the story this morning. We've already told them about Quax and NOBBY. Now we can concentrate on what they really want."

It went without saying that this desideratum consisted of violence and personalities. The violence was taken care of by the shrouded stretcher being wheeled across the sidewalk and the recollections of the unfortunate cleaning man. The creation of personality began, naturally enough, with the victim. The networks raided the archives of their local affiliates and even stooped to public access stations in order to provide footage of Madeleine at the hearings, Madeleine outside the courthouse, Madeleine at a parents conference in Buffalo.

At dinnertime the cast began to be enlarged. There was a tight-lipped Dean Kichsel trapped at the entrance to the Plaza and looking, in his offended hauteur, remarkably like a stag at bay. Peggy Roche was seen fighting her way grimly to a taxi while the unidentified man at her side announced that NOBBY would have no statement until morning.

Elmer Rugby chose to go a different route. Displaying that sturdy common sense approved by Charlie Trinkam, Elmer decided to get some mileage from the press dogging his steps. Accordingly he went to Spanish Harlem and was then filmed escorting the middle-aged Mrs. Dominguez into the hospital and presiding over the reunion between mother and daughter. As Theresa raised a hand from her wheelchair to pat her mother consolingly on the cheek, Elmer spoke directly into the camera.

"The doctors say she'll be fine in a couple of weeks. At least that's something for her mother to cling to."

Asked for his views about Mrs. Underwood's murder, he shook his head.

"It was a shock," he said gravely, all traces of yesterday's anger vanished. "But I don't really know anything about Madeleine Underwood, or about NOBBY, for that matter."

But the networks, in spite of their experience, were overlooking one fact. Violence and personalities do not fill the entire field of American preoccupation. As any of their sponsors could have told them, consumer products are also of general interest, and constant repetition reinforces that interest. With footage of Madeleine on public platforms, of Alec Moore announcing Kichsel's latest introduction to the market eighteen months ago, of Elmer and Rugby signaling their alliance, Quax was fast becoming a household name and public response to newscasts was turning into an informal referendum.

As EVENING SPREAD from the Atlantic to the Pacific, the East Coast was the first to react.

"There ought to be a law," said Kim Wendt in her suburban kitchen outside Boston. Kim and the kitchen being products of their time, the succulent aroma of home cooking was absent. Tonight's dinner was chicken grilled by Star Market and vegetable medley courtesy of DelMonte.

On the screen of the counter Magnavox, the personable anchorwoman had yielded to the personable sportscaster, but Bill Wendt knew that his wife was not referring to the Red Sox.

"You mean that murder?" he guessed, thinking back. "Down in New York?"

"More the riot," said Kim. "That's what got me thinking. Of course I'm opposed to their tactics, but still, Bill, making something that tastes just like beer and then advertising it on the Muppets . . . That shouldn't be allowed."

"Probably not," Bill replied, although not sure she had her facts right.

"Maybe we should write to the Governor," she mused.

Bill's enthusiasm for firing off letters in his novel role as responsible householder had waned some time ago, so he consulted his wristwatch. "Say, if you want a couple of hours at Bloomingdale's—"

"Or better still, Rugby's," she interrupted. "Just a dignified note to tell them that we won't patronize them until they stop serving Quax . . ."

She broke off suddenly. "There are Rugby's in Massachusetts, aren't there?"

"Not that I've noticed," he said. "Look, Kim, it's half past."

"Well then, what about the people who make this Quax stuff?" she persisted. "Do you know who they are?"

"One of the big breweries. They wouldn't—"

"We'll write to them!"

Subconsciously Bill Wendt was developing considerable antagonism to Quax, Rugby's, and even Madeleine Underwood.

AT PADDY'S PUB in Forest Hills, ten miles from the Babcock Auditorium, they had local knowledge and lifelong habits to shape their response. At the bar, beer drinkers sat shoulder to shoulder while couples, most of them middle-aged, occupied the tables behind them. Conversing or silent, watching or withdrawn, all of them were canted to face the giant television set spanning a corner over the cash register. Usually it delivered baseball, basketball or football. Tonight the spectator sport was different. Habitués would have preferred a play-off game but they accepted the cards they were dealt.

The report on Madeleine Underwood's murder had prompted only a few regrets that the entire congressional panel had not been targeted instead. A rehash of the Rugby riot, however, produced more variegated reactions.

"Can't blame the guy," said someone when Sal Piemonte's complaints were aired.

Without taking his eyes off the screen, one of the construction workers at the far end of the bar remarked, "I worked for the SOB over in Brooklyn last year."

The bride's plight conjured up personal testimony of another sort.

"Listen, when the hospital sent me home in a body cast, it took Marge and me about fifteen minutes to figure out how to . . ."

Those undistracted by conditions in the building trades or possibilities in the wedding bed were rewarded by Theresa Dominguez.

A mere slip of a girl, looking too fragile to support the cumbersome brace around her neck, she brought tears to many a boozy eye.

By now she was trying to smile gallantly and all the world knew that she was a straight-A student, she worked twenty hours a week and helped at home with the younger children.

"Can you figure it? Taking a two-by-four to a little thing like that!"

"She gives her paycheck to her mother," repeated the astonished father of teenagers.

"Jeez, no wonder someone brained that Underwood broad. She deserved it."

But with Theresa, the crowd began to thin. Left behind were the philosophers of Paddy's Pub, the men who relished food for thought with their tipple. Lacking an umpire's decision to critique, they at first fell back on their staples. City Hall and Bedford-Stuyvesant came in for their usual knocks, but before the evening could end with bad jokes, a laggard spoke up.

"You know one thing I don't understand?"

"What's that, Joe?"

"That woman, that bunch smashing windows. Why are they doing it?"

It was too much of a leap backward. Confusion ensued and Joe was in no shape to dispel it. Paddy was forced to lend a hand. "He's talking about Underwood, the one they showed outside the court-house, mouthing off about how this here Quax tastes just like Kix, only without the kick."

Somewhere between Sal Piemonte and Theresa Dominguez, Joe and his companions had gotten lost.

"You're kidding."

"So help me God," said Paddy with simple barkeeper authority.

"I had it once by mistake," recalled someone morosely. "Tasted like piss."

In this forum Kix without the kick did not commend itself. In fact, it led to other worries.

"I suppose they'll start messing with Kix next," said one of the group, scowling protectively at his familiar brown bottle.

"Just let them try," said Joe. "Hell, I remember how they advertised Kix twenty years ago . . ."

Nostalgia for the past, for the slogans and singing commercials of their youth engulfed him and his cronies. Both words and music eluded them but they tried an uncertain chorus anyway.

"Will you guys pipe down?" barked Paddy, rephrasing a house rule.

For a moment there was silence, then Joe began again. "Why the hell do they have to keep changing things? First it was all this crap from Germany. Then this mini-brewery garbage with beer made out of strawberries. Now they're making American beer without alcohol, for Chrissake."

"So you would have been on Underwood's side."

Joe drew himself up. "Like hell!"

"Well, if you're against Quax, you're for this NOBBY," said Paddy.

"But why take the alcohol out of Kix in the first place?" demanded Joe, turning plaintive.

After a certain hour conversations tended to go in circles at Paddy's Pub, but there was always someone with information to contribute.

"They're not making it for you or me, Joe. They're making it for kids. Or alcoholics or designated drivers."

"Oh, them!" chorused everybody with impartial dislike.

Joe, on the other hand, was inspired to sum up, reversing course as he did so.

"You know what? People are going crazy. Wars are going on, bums are sleeping on the streets. Kids shoot kids, and nobody knows how to cure cancer or AIDS. So what do these people start raising hell about? Selling non-alcoholic beer. Does that make sense?"

"Money," said someone wisely. "Somehow, somebody's making big bucks out of all this."

"The smart boys . . ."

". . . little guys never stand a chance."

Here, too, the day ended on a strong, if slightly unfocused, note of general hostility.

IN CHICAGO, AUDREY Morin represented a constant factor in all electorates. Her tub was deliciously scented by Nuit d'Amour and she had just stepped in when the phone rang.

"Damn," she muttered, grabbing her terry robe. Padding hopefully into the hall, she snatched up the receiver. But this was not the call that would transform her life.

"Ms. Audrey Morin?"

"Ye-es?"

"Ms. Morin, I represent Midwest Policy Conference. We're conducting a poll and I have a few questions."

"I don't—"

"Now, can you tell me what channel you were watching when I called?"

"I was taking a bath," said Audrey crossly.

"I see." Pause for making a note. Then, moving down the checklist: "Now, how did you feel when you saw that the instigator of yesterday's riot at Rugby's in Manhattan had been murdered?"

"I've been at work," said Audrey. "We don't have TV sets in the lab."

"Then you caught it on the evening news?"

Audrey's chin went up. "I stopped by Field's."

"Oh," said the pollster, apparently disappointed by any activity not centered on a television screen. "But you did learn what happened from another source, like radio or a newspaper?"

Audrey did not read newspapers except on Sunday morning but she had her pride.

"Radio," she snapped. "But listen, if you don't mind—"

"Just a few minutes more on another subject. Which best describes your attitude to Quax—approve, disapprove or indifferent?"

"Indifferent, I guess," said Audrey, who had never heard the name.

Further silence at the end, presumably for more data recording. Then: "How about Rugby's?"

"Their chili's terrific!"

"I'll put you down as approving on Rugby's. Thank you very much, Ms. Morin. You've been a big help."

Approbation gave Audrey a warm glow that faded fast. The tub was now ice-cold.

* * *

IN TEXAS, OF COURSE, it was no contest. There the Rugby chain had been part of daily life for over ten years and Elmer himself was a local boy who had made good. Nowhere was this more apparent than at his restaurant in downtown San Antonio when the movie next door ended. The long lines at the counter were composed of people who had relatives, friends and neighbors working at Rugby headquarters.

"Who are these NOBBY people? And what gave them the idea they could tell us what to eat and drink?" demanded a customer too far back to have any immediate hope of giving his order.

"They're a bunch of wackos in New York," said an unseen voice dismissively. "We all know what they're like."

"Well, if they'd pulled that riot here, they wouldn't have gotten off with whole skins," declared a large man in a muscle shirt.

"I don't know what you mean by whole skins. Somebody knocked off the woman in charge," his companion pointed out more in a spirit of accuracy than disapproval.

Nobody in Texas had much sympathy to spare for Madeleine Underwood.

"A crazy broad like that," exclaimed the original speaker. "She was just asking for it."

BUT THE MOST significant response of all came in California long after Paddy's customers had gone home. The regional distributor for Kichsel's had watched the late late "News" propped up in bed. After clicking off the TV he began scrabbling in his bedside table for pad and pencil. The sounds were familiar to his wife.

"Have to remind yourself of something?" she mumbled from behind closed eyes.

"I'll only be a sec, honey. It's just to jack up our inventory on Quax. The orders will start pouring in tomorrow."

And from the other side of the king-size mattress, muffled by sleepiness and a hypoallergenic pillow, came the genuine voice of the American public.

"If there's going to be all this fuss about the stuff, I suppose I'd better try it."

14. On Ice

T HE NEXT DAY found secondary witnesses being swept into the police net. Like many others, John Thatcher was obliged to describe Madeleine Underwood's confrontation with Alec Moore and Claudia Fentiman. Fortunately there was one area in which he could honestly plead ignorance.

"No, I didn't hear Rugby say she should be strangled. The only threat he made in my presence was his promise to sue NOBBY for every penny it has."

Elmer himself was less cautious.

"I said a lot of things," he agreed gruffly. "I don't remember them all now, but I know what I intended to do. Ask my lawyers."

Peggy Roche, who turned out during business hours to be Margaret Roche, Commercial Interiors, made no bones about the plans of NOBBY's governors.

"When we get calls about making bail for our members, the executive director is on her way out," she said tartly before turning to more pressing problems. "Now, how in the world am I supposed to produce a eulogy for that woman?"

There were inquiries farther afield as well. In Washington the clerical staff of the committee retailed every exorbitant demand made by Madeleine Underwood. In Philadelphia a call-in host remembered her vividly.

"I had to cut her off. She was making every mistake in the book."

And a hotel chambermaid confirmed Harry Hull's earlier suspicions.

"Mrs. Underwood was hiding around the corner until the congressman's visitor left. Then she popped over to his door, but he wasn't having any of it. He let her in to get her stuff, then, when she went on acting like little Miss Sunshine, marched her straight to the elevator."

A large law firm was able to tell the police where Madeleine Underwood had been headed when she so insouciantly taxied away from a burgeoning riot.

"She spent the afternoon here at our strategy session," Arthur Cleve explained. "The lawsuit had blown up in our faces, thanks to her."

"Then she must have been pretty upset?"

"Not half as much as we were. Her only reaction to the Ludlums was some silly remark about how people in her position had to expect to be stabbed in the back."

"Trying to weasel out from under?"

"It was more irritating than that, it was more as if she'd lost interest in the lawsuit. There she sat, all eager and excited about something else. But then," Cleve continued bitterly, "I didn't know she'd just started a riot downtown. The calls from people trying to locate her didn't start coming in until after she left."

But Roger Vandermeer took pride of place. He not only confirmed SDI contributions to NOBBY, he admitted being one of the dissatisfied supporters.

"Sure, I spoke to Cushing twice. First thing Tuesday morning I called him and said they could forget about our funding if they didn't bounce Underwood. Yesterday at the hearing I told him it didn't matter what they did. NOBBY was just a bad smell by that time."

The suggestion that SDI donations had been shrouded in secrecy elicited a snort. "Fat chance of any secrecy when it's all laid out in our books! Besides, why should there be? It's perfectly legal for SDI to support a non-profit organization whose aims they approve of."

Further questioning, however, dissipated his impatience.

"So that's the way the wind blows," he said shrewdly. "No, I don't have any idea how the money was handled over at NOBBY. Jesus Christ, I thought we were through with that bunch. All we need is to get dragged into some scandal of theirs."

But any tidbit of information was valuable in Roger Vandermeer's operation and passing it on was a recognized form of conferring favors.

"Say, Harry," he began as soon as the switchboard had tracked down the congressman. "I just had the police here. They think someone at NOBBY had his hand in the cookie jar."

There was a brief silence, followed by an appreciative whistle. "That would explain the murder all right. And I suppose embezzlement would have been easy. There was a lot of money floating around that place and Madeleine Underwood wasn't the woman to stay on top of it. But the cops didn't say anything about that to me."

"They didn't say it outright to me, either. They just had a lot of questions about our contributions to NOBBY and it wasn't hard to figure out what they had in mind."

"I didn't know you were supporting NOBBY."

"Why not?" Vandermeer asked largely. "At the time it seemed like a good idea. Now I could kick myself. But what did the police want from you?"

"It was mostly about that appointment I had with Mrs. Underwood. Naturally they wanted to know who knew about it. All I could tell them was that we talked in the middle of the room with a crowd milling around us."

"I heard you myself."

"The way she was screeching, you and everybody else," Hull replied. "At first I felt guilty I wasn't on time at the office because it might have saved her. Now I'm glad I never got to see her. I was boiling mad about that stupid riot and I could have ended up having a public row with her just before she got brained."

"Yeah, things really worked out for the best. You didn't get a chance to fight with her, but"—Vandermeer recalled happily—"the Kichsel people were doing it all over the place."

* * *

But Madeleine Underwood's argumentativeness had extended farther than Roger Vandermeer realized. Testimony from committee typists had included the description of a hot and heavy exchange in the ladies' room.

When the police appeared at the front door of Iona Perez's home in Rye, she took one look and said placidly, "I've been expecting you."

Shifting the large laundry basket braced on her hip, she ushered them into the living room, then said, "Just let me dump this into the machine and we can talk."

Nothing, it appeared, was going to disrupt the domestic schedule of the Perez household.

"I suppose you know that I was one of the demonstrators arrested at Rugby's," she began once she was settled on the sofa. "Actually I was trying to calm people down, but you don't care about that. The important thing is that I was furious at Madeleine's irresponsibility."

"You didn't approve of her tactics that day?"

"I didn't approve of a lot of things. It began with her failure to investigate the plaintiffs she had chosen for our first lawsuit. But that was nothing compared to her performance on Tuesday. NOBBY has mounted protests before and we've always been careful to keep them peaceful and genuinely informative. There was never the remotest suggestion of physical force. Madeleine, without a word to anyone, changed all that. Then, after whipping the volunteers into a frenzy, she calmly took off, leaving them to face the consequences. And finally she didn't bother to tell the office she'd disappeared into a hotel that night, so nobody was able to find her. I decided enough was enough."

Listening to this dispassionate indictment and watching the self-contained woman on the sofa, the detective found it hard to believe she had engaged in the heated altercation several witnesses had described.

"So you told Mrs. Underwood all this. What did she say?"

Iona's mouth twisted into a grimace.

"Oh, according to her, the court case was a fiasco because the Kichsel Brewery had laid a trap for her." Here there was a ladylike snort. "As if everybody couldn't see that the Ludlums were simply out to line their pockets. And when she messed up her testimony at the hearing, it was because dark forces were conspiring to take over NOBBY. But worst of all was the riot. If anything, she was triumphant over the publicity. She'd shown the world that she could cause trouble whenever she wanted."

"I don't suppose that attitude made you feel any better."

"I'll admit I was surprised. I thought she'd try to justify herself, claim that she hadn't told the protesters to start swinging. But I didn't even get that. Madeleine was different than I'd ever seen her before. All right, she was always a little flaky, but she'd turned into a real loose cannon. Not that her reaction made much difference to me. The reason I'd chased her down at the hearing was to tell her how I felt and warn her what I was going to do."

"You were going to quit?"

Iona drew herself up into a rigid, unyielding column.

"Certainly not. For over a year, I've given every spare minute I could dredge up to NOBBY. Madeleine was the one who was going to be leaving. I told her I would be asking the board of governors to remove her. That's when she went ape."

And she wasn't the only one, reflected the detective. "They tell me you were going at it pretty good yourself."

"I'm afraid so," Iona admitted with a small sigh for human frailty. "There's something very frustrating about not being able to make a dent. Madeleine, it turned out, didn't know the first thing about our charter and by-laws. To her, NOBBY was a personal possession, and it was impossible that anybody should be able to take it away from her. She told me that and then announced I was no longer working for her."

. "Then what?"

"Nothing. I was only there because I didn't want to go behind her back. Once I'd explained what I was going to do and given her my reasons, I was through. If she was too dumb to understand, that was her problem."

It all sounded very rational, very well controlled. But, the detective thought, it did not sound like the screaming exchange of insults that had been described to him. Shrugging, he went on to Iona's luncheon with Peggy Roche, then announced that would be all for the moment.

"Good," said Iona. "That leaves me time to get into the city."

SEAN CUSHING WAS delighted at Iona's arrival. He had been thinking hard about the future of NOBBY.

"I'm glad you were able to come in, Iona. There are some points I want to discuss. Without Madeleine, there will have to be some changes."

As usual on arrival, she was checking her watch.

"I still have about an hour."

"The thing is, this is an awkward time for NOBBY to be without a formal spokesperson. First off, the murder investigation is bound to require comments from us. Then the results of the riot aren't simply going to go away. We should be issuing some kind of explanation. On top of that, the Rossi hearings could start up again any day and we'll need somebody on the stand. And if all that isn't bad enough, there'll be police auditors here any minute."

Iona stiffened. "Auditors?"

"Not to worry," he reassured her with an airy wave. "It's just an insane idea that the cops have but it will disrupt the office for a while."

"Perhaps you'd better tell me about their insane idea."

"I had a fight with Madeleine on Tuesday morning. Cheryl overheard some of it and got the wrong idea. She repeated words like *financial irregularities* and mentioned *money that Madeleine didn't know about* and a lot of horseshit like that. But there's a simple explanation, really there is."

"I'm sure there is."

"I had to tell Madeleine that she'd really cooked her goose. Our major contributor was going to pull the plug unless she stepped down. When she heard that, she went crazy. Instead of seeing that she had nobody but herself to blame, she accused me of being underhanded. She claimed that I was selling out NOBBY, that I hadn't told her where the money was coming from, that nobody had the right to tell her what to do with her own organization. And so forth. Then she decided she saw a way out from under and told me I was fired."

"Who was the contributor?"

Sean was taken aback. Somewhat uneasily he said, "The Soft Drink Institute."

But Iona merely became thoughtful, then finally nodded her head. "That makes sense. Their members don't want to split the market with Quax."

"I'd like to point out this was not some under-the-table deal. The source of that money was listed in our annual report, which Madeleine was supposed to read. Hell, she could have gotten it out of the computer any day. She made enough fuss about getting the thing."

"Now Sean, we both know that Madeleine never read anything, but I wouldn't worry about it."

With a jolt, Cushing remembered that this was not the discussion he had planned. He was the one supposed to be offering support. "I just wanted to give you the general picture before getting down to specifics. Now I know public appearances aren't really your thing, Iona. But in a crisis like this we've all got to make an extra effort," he paused to smile at her encouragingly. "I'm planning to suggest to the board that you step in and pinch-hit for Madeleine during the emergency."

The flustered, self-deprecating Iona he had anticipated never materialized.

"That's exactly what I came in to tell you," she replied calmly. "I've already spoken to several of the governors about becoming director of NOBBY."

The words were out of his mouth before he could recall them. "You sure didn't waste any time."

"As you just said, this is a crisis. I told them that, while I was willing to consider the offer," she continued, "I couldn't possibly agree unless several items were settled to my satisfaction. In order for NOBBY to be successful, it has to be run on a businesslike basis, particularly as we go national. I've always thought it was absurd that Madeleine didn't take a proper salary. In any event, I couldn't possibly do a good job without appropriate compensation."

"And high time," he said warmly. "You do so much work here, you should have been paid all along."

"I explained that a substantial salary would be necessary because of the responsibilities I'd be shouldering. In addition, I'll have to employ a live-in housekeeper. That goes without saying."

"I suppose so," Cushing mumbled, beginning to understand the order of magnitude she had in mind.

Iona was ticking off her list as if it dealt with placards and charter buses. "My second requirement is that there be a NOBBY that's worth my time and attention."

Until today, Sean thought bitterly, there had never been the slightest indication that the time Iona lavished on NOBBY was worth a thin dime.

"Things aren't that bad," he protested. "The biggest problem was Madeleine. With her unable to cause trouble I'll bet I can sweet-talk Vandermeer into continuing his support."

She shook her head. "Nobody will fund us as long as we have a pile of lawsuits hanging fire. We'll just have to bite the bullet and settle the individual claims. But my husband tells me that Elmer Rugby sounded really vindictive on television. If they decide to ask for punitive damages, we can kiss good-bye to contributions. People aren't going to open their checkbooks in order to have the money simply flow through our bank account into Rugby's."

Inundated by so many other concerns, Sean had overlooked this major hurdle. Two days ago everything had seemed so simple. Get rid of Madeleine and NOBBY's future was secure. Now Madeleine was gone all right, but her legacy could prove as destructive as her presence had been.

"So Peggy Roche and I have decided on a direct approach to Elmer Rugby," Iona swept on. "She'll get the approval of the other governors and I'll agree to act as temporary director. Then we'll tackle Mr. Rugby and hope to persuade him that Madeleine's death alters the situation. Now, about this audit. How soon will the police be starting?"

"I expect them to send in their people today," said Sean, staring across the table in fascination.

"Good, the sooner the better, from my point of view. If we get a satisfactory resolution on the riot and the audit, I'll be able to give the governors my decision."

Her assurance was beginning to grate.

"What makes you think the rest of them will go along with Peggy?"

"Peggy's already sounded out three of the others. Besides, who else is there to take over?" Iona asked serenely. "The board needs somebody instantly. Unless the salvage operation begins immediately, it will be impossible. And NOBBY's image certainly won't be hurt by having a spokesman who has children still at risk."

Sean could scarcely believe his ears. Gentle, self-effacing Iona was seizing her moment with a vengeance. She had evaluated the strength of her position and was tanking right over the board. While he had still been planning his moves, she had stepped in and taken control of NOBBY.

She immediately demonstrated the strength of that control.

"So there's no point in our approaching the Soft Drink Institute until we can give them some reassurances. Now, who did you say was representing them?"

"Roger Vandermeer. He's their PR outfit."

"Fine. If Mr. Vandermeer contacts you, just tell him what we're working on. By the way, did our fund-raising extend to bottlers and distributors?"

Did she realize that she had progressed to giving direct orders?

"No, it didn't."

"Well, we might consider them for the future. It's an obvious source of support and we'll need it for going national."

Just in time Sean bit back docile agreement. Now, if ever, was the moment to establish himself as an equal. Only after consideration did he say judiciously, "You know, that's not a bad idea."

His efforts were wasted. She was still racing from one item to another.

"And, while I'm on the subject . . . don't I remember Madeleine having a meeting with the head of the San Francisco chapter to discuss penetration of the West Coast?"

God, the woman even had total recall.

"That's right, she taped it." Sean summoned up a comradely grin. "You remember, that's when Madeleine first got hooked on the thing."

"Then I'll have Cheryl dig it out. It's possible that Mrs. Hale came up with something helpful."

It went without saying that Madeleine had not.

"Listen, Iona, aren't you forgetting another little complication," he said, trying to crack that confident facade. "We're in the middle of a murder investigation. The police will be buzzing around this place like flies."

"Oh, I haven't forgotten, but there's nothing we can do about it. So I suggest that we leave the investigation to them and get on with our business."

"For Chrissake, that's easy enough for you to say. You're not the one they're after. It's bad enough that Cheryl twisted around everything she heard. On top of that, the cops don't think much of my alibi. It's just my bad luck that I was in the middle of the subway going home to—" He stopped abruptly. Somehow he could not bring himself to tell Iona that he had been plotting a meticulous approach to the governors.

"Really, Sean! You act as if you're the only suspect. The way Madeleine was carrying on, almost anybody could have become infuriated enough to lose control. I admit I came close when I was fighting with her before the adjournment."

He looked up swiftly. "I didn't know you quarreled with her there."

"Oh, yes. Fortunately in front of some witnesses who saw that I didn't give in to temptation." A small reminiscent smile played over her lips. "You know, I'm glad I had the chance to tell her what I thought. And for your information, when I finished lunch with Peggy, I spent fifteen minutes waiting for a bus on a corner only two blocks from the hearings. But I'm not letting it worry me."

Some ingrained maternal instinct always alerted Iona when her time was running out. Now, with another glance at her watch, she rose.

"Well, that covers about everything for the moment and the boys will be coming home from school." She smiled at him encouragingly. "And Sean, I want you to know that another thing that has to be regularized around here is your status. I'll talk to the board about an employment contract for you."

Sean could barely manage a casual farewell. So much for his vision of a NOBBY firmly under his own control. It was futile to delude himself that Iona would ever dance to his strings. Grimly he settled to the task of isolating his own emotions. First there was mortification at having harbored such a colossal misconception of Iona. Then there was dismay at having been so smartly outgeneraled. He had actually started their meeting on the assumption that he, the professional, would be handing good, little Iona an unexpected plum by offering to approach those eminent governors on her behalf.

There was no denying that many things would change under Iona Perez's leadership, but were they all bad? On the basis of today's performance she was far more capable than Madeleine of developing NOBBY into a powerful credit on the Cushing résumé. She would probably create a clear demarcation between her responsibilities and his own, which would make day-to-day life easier. And the brute realities of fund-raising had not sparked the slightest qualm.

So far, so good. Still sighing over lost possibilities, Sean gave himself some advice.

"My boy," he whispered, "you're going to have to watch your step."

15. Happy Hour

NSPECTOR REARDON HAD barely dispatched his auditors before his attention was directed elsewhere.

"You wanted the fingerprint results as soon as they were ready," the voice on the other end of the line said.

"Did you get anything from the weapon?"

"No, that had been really polished. But they didn't do such a good job on the telephone. The top and sides of the receiver had been wiped clean, leaving one clear thumbprint on the bottom."

"Whose?"

There was the rustle of a page turning.

"Alexander K. Moore."

"Well now, what do you know about that!"

REARDON FOUND THE entire Kichsel management assembled in their New York branch office.

"This is not a good time, Inspector," Dean Kichsel said heavily. "We're in the middle of business."

"So am I! And mine involves a woman who was murdered shortly after having a fight with two of you."

Claudia Fentiman figuratively fluttered between the combatants. "We're not denying the urgency of your work, Inspector. What Mr. Kichsel means is that we don't see how we can be of further help.

We've already told your men everything we know. Including," she said evenly, "a description of our exchange with Mrs. Underwood."

"I've been over the report. According to you two, she was a wild woman, lashing out at everybody in sight, and you just happened to be in the way."

"That's right," said Alec Moore.

"But other people in the hallway say you were giving as good as you got."

"So I was annoyed. You would have been, too. Madeleine Underwood was making up all sorts of fantastic charges, anything to put the blame for her failures on someone else. I didn't like it."

The inspector turned to Claudia Fentiman.

"And you?"

"Oh, neither did I," she said, presenting a united front. "I suppose on one level I realized there was no point in trying to reason with her. But it's just human instinct to react when someone says ridiculous things."

Nodding, Reardon abruptly changed the subject. "And when the hearings were adjourned you all went off to lunch?"

Dean Kichsel managed to invest every word with reproach. "I fail to see the value of our repeating these statements endlessly, but that is correct. Mrs. Fentiman, Mr. Benda and myself all went to the Dorchester. Mr. Moore had something else to do."

Silently the inspector cocked an eyebrow at Alec Moore.

"It's all down in the report," Moore said impatiently. "I had to check some references at the library, the one across from the Museum of Modern Art. That gobbled up most of the lunch break. So I grabbed a sandwich and a beer at a tavern, then headed to the hotel. I'd only been there a couple of minutes before the others got back."

"The waitresses at the tavern don't remember you."

"Dammit, there was a mob waiting for tables and I was alone. So I took the first free stool at the counter."

"Let's see. On the way back you would have passed within a block of the committee hearings."

Moore's jaw tilted aggressively. "That's right, but I didn't go in."

The next question came out like a bullet.

"Then how come your fingerprint is on the phone in the room where Madeleine Underwood was murdered?"

In the lengthening silence Kichsel and Claudia and Theo Benda maintained carefully blank expressions, but Alec Moore's face, screwed into thought, suddenly cleared.

"So that's where she was killed!"

"Don't give me that, Mr. Moore. You knew where she was killed, all right, or are you claiming you haven't been following the coverage?"

"Of course I have, but the papers just said she'd been found in one of the committee offices. They've got a whole rabbit warren of cubicles back there. I just ducked into one that was empty."

The inspector settled back with a grunt of satisfaction. "Well, now you know," he purred. "The office you used on your way back to the hotel was the murder room."

Moore shook his head doggedly. "You've got it all wrong. That was before I left for lunch. I have a son at Columbia and I was hoping to grab a bite with him. That's why I didn't go with the others. But when I called his apartment he wasn't there and I decided to do my library chores instead. All this happened at noon. I never went near that building afterward."

"If it was all that innocent, how come you kept so quiet?"

"For God's sake, your people asked me where I went when I left the hearings. I told them. So I didn't mention trying to make a telephone call first. Big deal!"

"All right, then let's go back to some of those charges by Mrs. Underwood. She claimed that she'd had you two investigated, that she knew where all your personal skeletons were buried, that she could prove you were morally corrupt."

Once again Claudia intervened. "Aren't you taking that out of context, Inspector?" she asked earnestly. "She also said that we'd bribed the Ludlum family to approach her, that we have Chairman Rossi in our pocket, that Quax is toxic no matter what the experts say and that we're in collusion with the networks to sabotage her program. She did everything but claim we're the Antichrist. The woman was raving, she sounded like a lunatic."

"You realize I can find out anything that she did?"

"I don't doubt that you'll dig up every nasty little bit of dirt in our backgrounds," she snapped, her temper fraying. "That doesn't make us murderers."

The inspector made a show of consulting his notes. "It says here that you left lunch early, Mrs. Fentiman. And then put in a half hour at Saks. I don't suppose anybody would remember you."

"They remember you when you make a big purchase. I didn't see anything I wanted." Her tight little smile was a long way from the tolerant superiority she was aiming at.

Before Reardon could press the issue, Theo Benda stirred in the corner where he had been quietly listening. "Seems to me you're missing the point, Inspector."

"I am?"

"This Underwood woman was screwing up every time she showed herself. Thanks to her, NOBBY was in deep trouble even before the riot. And that little effort really put the lid on things. We didn't have anything to gain by killing her, she wasn't sinking our ship. But a hell of a lot of people were being damaged by what she was doing. They must have been scared to death what she'd come up with next. No matter what they say over at NOBBY, they're breathing a lot easier with her dead. Why don't you put a little muscle into that end?"

"You mean you're claiming that Underwood's death has solved all their problems, that everything's suddenly hunky-dory for them?" demanded Reardon, projecting skepticism.

"I'm just betting that there are a whole lot of changes going on at NOBBY right now."

As always, whenever the inspector encountered resistance, he immediately shifted ground.

"And then there's the geography," he said blandly. "None of you strayed very far. The Plaza where you were all staying, the Dorchester where some of you were eating, Saks and that library. All of them in the Fifties, all of them in a tight little circle around the committee building."

Dean Kichsel was affronted. "Naturally," he said severely. "As you well know, it's much easier to walk a few blocks in New York than

123

to find a cab. And we chose our hotel to cut down on distance."

"Give us a break," Benda rumbled. "We were doing what everybody in the city does between twelve and two. We were eating, shopping and doing chores. Probably you're getting the same story from the others. There's nothing suspicious about it."

Examining his witness from beneath half-closed eyelids, Inspector Reardon was interested in the dynamics of the situation. Upon his entry Dean Kichsel had elected himself spokesman, trying to erect a defensive wall around his team with the authoritativeness that usually stood him in good stead. But insensibly leadership had passed. Kichsel was now merely a basso accompaniment in the background while Theo Benda went on the offensive, using low-keyed common sense to direct suspicion elsewhere.

And, the inspector had to admit, he wasn't doing a half-bad job.

As REARDON HAD been reminded, only one of Madeleine Underwood's recent adversaries claimed to have cleared the entire midtown area immediately upon Chairman Rossi's adjournment.

"Come on, John," Charlie Trinkam urged. "It's the least we can do for poor old Elmer. He spent the morning being grilled by the cops. It's bad enough he told some people at the hearing that someone should strangle our Madeleine, but then he comes up with this way-out alibi."

"What does he say he was doing?"

"The poor guy's story is that he went to some zoo in the Bronx. He claims he spent four hours there and nobody noticed him."

Trinkam, a confirmed bachelor with a zestful approach to life, was the Sloan's acknowledged expert on the glossy aspects of Manhattan life. But occasionally he stupefied his companions with a display of ignorance about more mundane matters.

After a moment's thought, Thatcher identified the problem. "It's not like Central Park, Charlie," he said gently. "The one in the Bronx is much larger."

Having escorted children and grandchildren to the New York Zoological Garden, he was in a position to expatiate on the vast acreage, the thousands of visitors roaming at will. It was perfectly possible, he announced, for a solitary male to spend a long time communing with the polar bears or participating in the joys of the Monkey House without attracting attention.

"If you say so," said Charlie, willing to accept but not pretending to understand. His own bottomless interest in the human animal left him no time for the consideration of lesser vertebrates.

"Never mind about that now. I still don't understand why this meeting is taking place here."

Charlie explained that Elmer Rugby did not have a New York base. When representatives of NOBBY had asked for a conference, he had arranged an appointment in Trinkam's office.

Thatcher nodded his comprehension. Rugby was unwilling to surrender the advantage gained by forcing the opposition to come to him.

"Still, I'd expect this to be a lawyer-to-lawyer meeting."

"NOBBY wants to get a few things settled first."

"And Rugby wants our advice?"

"Hell no! He wants witnesses."

Another Sloan officer might have pleaded the interests of his client. But Charlie knew a better argument.

"This is too good a chance to miss, John. One of this bunch may have knocked off Madeleine," he urged irresistibly.

The NOBBY delegation arrived within minutes of Elmer. Peggy Roche introduced herself as head of NOBBY's board of governors. She was supported by Jeremy Pfizer, another governor, and the interim director, Mrs. Iona Perez.

Peggy was eloquent about the deep regret experienced at headquarters for the totally unjustifiable conduct of the NOBBY protesters.

"Easy enough to say now that it's gotten you a lot of bad press," Elmer grunted.

Unabashed, she swept on. NOBBY realized that it was responsible for the damage caused and the hospital bills incurred.

"Damn right!"

Without a flicker of discomfiture, she soldiered on. "Court cases are notoriously expensive. We could both save a good deal of money by reaching a settlement without litigation."

Court cases also produced punitive damages, Rugby was swift to remind her. Particularly when inspired by wildly irresponsible conduct.

It was now Jeremy's turn to take up the banner.

"Very true. But let's be realistic. I checked with my lawyer this morning and he tells me there wouldn't be a hope in hell of getting this thing to trial in over two years. The publicity will have died down by then. Besides, getting an award for damages doesn't do you any good unless there are assets to pay them. Most of our members were deeply shocked by what happened. Unless we settle this quickly on the basis that it was a one-time aberration, we may go down the tubes."

John Thatcher was pleased to see that there was nothing wrong with Elmer's powers of reasoning. "Trying to have it both ways, aren't you?" he asked. "The whole thing will die down, but still you're going to bleed to death."

"It's a matter of timing," Pfizer insisted. "Our objective is to make it clear to you, as well as to the public, that this outrageous behavior was due to the sudden insanity of Mrs. Underwood."

"So you're planning to blame it all on her, while the rest of you are as pure as snow?"

So far quiet, Mrs. Perez now leaned forward. "The fact is, Mr. Rugby, you've lost your trump card for punitive damages. You don't have Mrs. Underwood anymore."

"You mean because someone knocked her off?"

Iona did not blench. "That's right. I'll admit that I was furious when Madeleine was unavailable for comment after the riot. Now I'm grateful that she never got near a microphone. If you had her on the stand she'd insist that when she did was right. But that isn't going to happen now."

"You people can't put that much distance between her and you," Rugby retorted. "If she was so crazy, why the hell didn't you yank her?"

Peggy Roche was prepared for that one. "Twenty-four hours after that riot I was having lunch with Mrs. Perez to discuss the removal of Mrs. Underwood. Before the announcement of the murder I'd already called an emergency meeting of the governors to implement her ouster. As soon as there was evidence of instability I did act."

"She'd been after Quax a long time."

Mrs. Perez seemed to prefer specific items to generalities. "Since its inception NOBBY has conducted almost a hundred protests. The record will show that, with this single exception, they were all orderly and peaceful. We can prove we had no reason to expect anything else." Pausing to take a deep breath, she plunged ahead. "That is why we feel justified in asking that the criminal charges pending against some of the demonstrators be dropped. And, in order to avoid unpleasant discoveries, you should know that I am one of those defendants."

Elmer's jaw tightened. "And this is your choice for a new director?" he said ironically to Peggy Roche. "Congratulations!"

As Rugby looked prepared to develop this theme, John Thatcher felt honor-bound to bear witness.

"I myself saw you arrive on the scene, Mrs. Perez, and try to stop the violence," he said hastily. "But, by then, disarming one protester wasn't going to stem the tide."

Surprised by this unexpected support, Iona immediately turned it to good advantage. "I had just snatched a big piece of two-by-four from one of my volunteers when the police arrived," she explained to Rugby. "The wood was heavy, I was off-balance and the two-by-four was waving around. I suppose I can't blame the police. I must have looked like the original Neanderthal woman to them."

"Bad luck for you," Elmer muttered.

On this tentative note of forgiveness the coffee tray arrived and the real talking began.

Jeremy Pfizer, disclosing that he was an accountant, immediately collared Elmer Rugby and produced a preliminary list of medical charges. "I thought we could get some idea of the order of magnitude of the property damage."

Charlie, who had been surreptitiously examining Peggy Roche for some time, swam easily to her side.

Thatcher, offering cream to Mrs. Perez, said, "It's a shame that you didn't arrive at the riot a little later. Your timing was certainly unfortunate."

"What I should have done was arrive earlier," she corrected him.

"But of course Madeleine knew I had to take my son to the doctor that morning. That's why she chose her moment."

From the tone of her voice Madeleine Underwood was not included in the general amnesty extended to the New York City Police.

"But I see you haven't let your experience dim your commitment to NOBBY."

"That could never happen. I know some people don't appreciate our work. But just think how much easier it would have been for everyone if some group had been alert to the dangers of nicotine before the entire nation became cigarette smokers."

Some quality in her voice made Thatcher glance up in time to catch the glint in her eye. No, he realized, there would be no faltering dedication here. Whatever the press might claim, it was becoming abundantly clear that Madeleine Underwood's activities at NOBBY had been restricted to those promising personal gratification. It was Iona Perez who performed the thankless tasks and, of the two, she was the true believer.

"And if there are no dangers?" he asked.

"All that NOBBY wants is to end the aggressive marketing of Quax until a proper study has been made of its possible consequences," she said soberly. "As long as it's being sold only in bars and liquor stores, I can feel that my children are reasonably safe. Once it's in vending machines and supermarkets, I can't. Nowadays, Mr. Thatcher, all mothers have to accept the fact that, from the day school starts, they don't know what their children are up to."

AMONG THOSE PARENTS who were not up-to-date on their children's activities was Alec Moore. When a detective rang the bell at an apartment several blocks from Columbia University, the door was opened by a young woman.

"I'm looking for Peter Moore," he announced, showing his credentials.

"Pete's out. And he's got a lab this afternoon, so he won't be back until after five."

"You live here, too?"

"I moved in last week."

"Then you may be able to help me."

Sighing softly, she fell back. "I hope this won't take long. I've got a real backbreaker of an exam tomorrow."

The detective was old enough to remember an earlier age, a time when college students welcomed any confrontation with the police as an opportunity to anathematize the establishment and to enlarge on the decay of society to all at endless length. But these days the problem was getting them to lift their eyes from a book long enough to answer questions. Intent on getting into business school or becoming computer wizards, they were self-absorbed and incurious. This girl was a case in point. Undeniably attractive, she possessed a glorious figure, a mass of wavy blond hair and a beautiful even tan. But she was also wearing a pair of wire-rimmed half-glasses and had obviously just risen from a table that boasted a computer, a pile of yellow pads and a collection of open tomes.

"What's this all about?" she finally asked as she sank effortlessly into a low beanbag chair.

"Nothing to worry about."

She chuckled. "I know that. Pete is as straight as they come."

"I'm just checking out somebody else's story. It's about a phone call to Peter Moore last Wednesday lunchtime."

"Last Wednesday? At noon? Then I can help you. Pete has a twelve o'clock class on Wednesday. He wasn't here." The detective had already snapped shut his notebook when she continued.

"He stayed late to talk to his professor about his term paper. I know because I'd ordered in a pizza for us and by the time he got back it was cold."

He sank back into the sofa from which he had half risen. "That means you were here at noon. So you took that call."

"There wasn't any call. I was already studying for this exam and I was doing it here to avoid interruptions. I'd remember all right."

"You're absolutely sure?"

She favored him with a blindingly sunny smile.

"Absolutely."

16. Designated Driver

A T THE SLOAN, NOBBY had looked lean, mean and in charge of its destiny. But on home territory it was otherwise. Here Sean Cushing felt as if he were under enemy occupation. Police auditors were probing every nook and cranny against a dismal obbligato of telephone calls from members ringing to express indignation, demand explanations, and threaten to resign. To make matters worse, Jeremy Pfizer had hotfooted uptown the moment Elmer Rugby's conference was over.

"We thought I could be of more use to you than Mrs. Perez," he had explained tactfully on arrival.

Clever Iona, Sean thought with gritted teeth. In her new role she was already establishing superiority and distancing herself from NOBBY's internal accounting.

Today Cushing sensed slights and suspicion on every side. For over three hours he had been manfully trying to redirect his thoughts into a more rational course. Given knowledge of Madeleine's outburst, the police were bound to look for financial skulduggery. And it was only natural that the board should want a representative on the spot. As for Iona, she would simply have been in the way.

But his good intentions crumbled under the first onslaught when Pfizer came storming out of Madeleine Underwood's office, a folder clutched in his hand.

"Did you know about this, Cushing?" he demanded, his lips twisted in distaste.

This proved to be a report from a firm of private investigators about Dean Kichsel, Alec Moore and Claudia Fentiman.

"So that's what Madeleine was yammering about at the hearings," Sean murmured. "It's news to me."

Pfizer was skimming the first letter in the file. "She was referred to them by our lawyers," he said, as if that were further cause for indignation.

"If you remember, I had objections to the whole Ludlum business."

"Dammit, we approved a lawsuit, not some personal vendetta."

They were standing toe to toe, glaring at each other.

"It's the board's job to oversee the director, not mine," Cushing snapped. "Madeleine was flying solo a lot."

"Then there could be other things we don't know about," Pfizer said, aghast.

"Damned right."

Sean was frankly enjoying his companion's anxiety while Pfizer, conscious of past laxity, was defensive. Hostilities would have escalated if they had not been interrupted by Cheryl Zimmerman. Cheryl had been in her element all day. Unbidden, she had provided coffee nonstop for the auditors, conducted Pfizer on a tour of the premises and listened with deep interest to every exchange. Now she was producing, from some hitherto untapped resource, a large supply of doughnuts.

"I thought everybody would like a nosh," she said brightly, proffering the open box. Then, eager to be a participant in all the bustle, she went on, "I've been meaning to ask you, Mr. Cushing, what I should do about Mrs. Underwood's tape. I mean, now that she's dead."

His eyes still locked on Pfizer, Sean said shortly, "What tape?"

"The one she left in my basket." Stepping over to her desk, Cheryl produced a cassette with a showman's flourish. "I've got it right here."

Three members of the police department raised their heads to look expectantly at Sean Cushing. For one sickening moment he read accusation in those shuttered eyes before realizing that it was up to him to coax further information from NOBBY's flighty receptionist.

"Uh, Cheryl," he said in the thunderous silence, "exactly when did she leave it?"

Furrowing her brow, Cheryl pondered. "Let's see . . . I found it in my basket when I came back from my lunch break. And that was . . . God, that was the day she was killed. In all the excitement yesterday I forgot about it. Do you want me to type it?"

Reflexively Sean reached out, but the police were ahead of him. Plucking the tape from Cheryl's hand, one of them said,

"That's all right, I'll take care of it. Now, Cheryl, who was covering for you while you were out to lunch?"

"THE IDIOT RELIEF girl never thought to mention it," Reardon's assistant said wearily. "Underwood grabbed a sandwich after the adjournment, then came back to the office because she wanted to dictate something before her appointment with Hull. She was only there about twenty minutes."

"And she might just as well have spared her breath, for all the use this thing is," Reardon growled. "But let's give it another try, Dave, and see if we've overlooked something."

Punching the play button, he locked his hands behind his neck and tilted back in his chair to listen once again to the shrill, tight voice Madeleine Underwood had brought to her last communication.

"Cheryl, I want this set up as the announcement of a press conference on Friday morning at ten o'clock, to be held here. Have copies sent to all the media offices on our list and, if you get any calls wanting further information, just tell them this will be a real blockbuster. Ready? Then, quote—

"*In our campaign against Quax, NOBBY has encountered continuing opposition and, over the course of time, our adversaries have persistently resorted to unethical, immoral and even illegal conduct. Our growing suspicions have recently been more than confirmed. The money-eyed interests arrayed against us have not hesitated, in their callous dis-*

132

regard for the health and well-being of future generations, to strike at the basic integrity of NOBBY itself. Paragraph.

"*As you know, on Wednesday morning Chairman Leon Rossi adjourned his hearings in the middle of my testimony. In one sense this adjournment was justified. Although I had originally planned to use that opportunity to make public a number of startling revelations, I now feel that the committee's proceedings are tainted beyond redemption. Paragraph.*

"*Naturally it is mandatory that the members of NOBBY be alerted to this peril—to the perversion of our motives and to the betrayal of the goals which we have pursued so steadily. But it is also in the interests of the American people that these activities should be revealed. Paragraph.*

"*It is therefore my intention to present you not only with our accusations, but with proof positive of the fundamental corruption which has faced us at every turn. I ask only that you give me a hearing and then, I have no doubt, you will join me in recognizing that the only possible response is to subject this entire sordid situation to the light of full publicity.*"

On his first playback Inspector Reardon had concentrated on the substance of Madeleine's message. Now he listened carefully to her delivery, but all he could discern was an electric tide of confidence that swamped what might have been meaningful changes in inflection or phrasing.

"A lot of fancy words and nothing else," he summarized when the tape ended. "God, that woman sure didn't have any use for facts."

"Or she didn't have any," suggested Dave. "From what the committee staff told us, she wasn't very clear on the difference between suspicion and proof. She thought hard evidence was something a friend of a friend of a friend said. For that matter, look at Quax. Nobody's shown there's anything wrong with it at all."

Reardon was dubious. "She may have been dumb, but she was genuinely excited. You can hear that."

"Then she wasn't giving anything away because she wanted to be the star turn at her press conference." Dave's researches had left him with a jaundiced view of Madeleine Underwood. "One thing's for sure. She can't have been talking about this junk."

He flicked a disdainful finger across the reports from the detective agency before continuing. "Even she can't have been wacky enough to think a messy divorce was hot news, and that's all she had on Fentiman. As for old man Kichsel, he's so clean it's unnatural. And even Moore is pretty dull. When he was a college student he got picked up in a raid where the kids were smoking marijuana. The only odd thing in his history is that he taught elementary school for three years."

Reardon leaned forward to check the date before saying briefly, "Vietnam."

Dave was young enough to be puzzled. "What does that have to do with anything?"

"There was a draft exemption for schoolteachers. You'd be amazed how many rich college boys rushed into teaching fourth grade right about then."

It was an aspect of Vietnam that had never been brought to Dave's attention.

"So he was a draft dodger. It's still peanuts."

"Yes, but the people at Kichsel don't know that this agency confined itself to checking public records. There could be plenty for them to be worried about. Go see how they react. At least with Moore you've got some leverage."

THE LEVERAGE DID not prove very useful.

"You can forget that garbage about calling your son," Dave began. "We can prove you didn't."

Instead of being shaken, Alec Moore was resigned. "Wouldn't you know it? I've been telling Pete to get an answering machine for over a year and now's the time he decides to do it."

Dave did not feel it necessary to explain the form that Peter Moore's answering equipment was taking.

"That means we're right back where we were. You claim you made the call before leaving the hearings. But until you tell us who you did call, it's just your word for it."

Moore's jaw set stubbornly. "Forget it! I made that call when I said I did. Who I called is none of your damn business."

And from this position he refused to budge. He was not guilty of

134

any crime, he proclaimed, and he saw no reason to expose his personal life to police scrutiny.

"No wonder you're gun-shy on the subject," Dave ventured. "Madeleine Underwood wasn't just blowing hot air about digging into your past. She'd hired a detective agency."

By now Alec Moore was so rigid with defiance it was impossible to distinguish any physical reaction.

"She could hire detectives by the carload. My past is an open book."

"Including the criminal record?"

Moore blinked but, after a moment's thought, produced a contemptuous bark of laughter. "Are you talking about the fraternity party that was busted?"

"And then there's the little matter of your illustrious war career."

The moment the words were out of his mouth Dave knew he had made a mistake. This time Alec Moore's laughter was real enough but it was propelled into the air on a gust of pent-up breath. He had been braced for some other disclosure.

"I admit it all," he said, spreading his palms in mock surrender. "Twenty-five years ago I smoked a joint and ducked going to Vietnam. You think Madeleine Underwood was going to make tabloid headlines with that?"

CLAUDIA FENTIMAN'S response was equally unhelpful.

"Private detectives," she repeated dully.

Unsure of what specters he had raised, Dave waited. When she remained silent, he finally said, "Anything Underwood dug up, we will too. Now, if it doesn't have anything to do with her death . . ."

"Oh, for God's sake!" she exploded in exasperation. "It isn't as if I'm an ax murderer. All that woman could find against me was my divorce."

In her anger she failed to notice Dave's disappointment, even when he pointed out that divorce was no longer noteworthy.

"The divorce doesn't matter," she retorted. "It's the custody case that I keep to myself. It was . . . it was about as down and dirty as they come. Five years ago . . ."

Five years ago and she remembered every degrading moment, every filthy charge leveled by the man who had become an enemy.

". . . promiscuous, picking up strangers in bars, bringing them home when Jenny was there—you name it. My God, my brother stayed overnight when he was in town on business and they tried to claim . . . Anything they could dream up, they threw at me."

There was a sheen of perspiration on her face by the time she finished.

". . . so if you'd found my ex's body about then, I could have been suspect number one. But I beat the bastard in court and he didn't get his hands on Jenny. It's just that he managed to put me through hell."

Her retreat into the past was complete and a question from Dave forced her to refocus.

"Of course I didn't talk about it when I applied for my job. Dirt sticks, you know, and Kichsel's a conservative outfit."

"Enough to fire you?" Dave asked without much enthusiasm.

Finally she relaxed. "Oh, come on. In the first place, I'm doing a great job for them. More important, they've had a chance to get to know me, enough to realize I'm not a hooker or a nympho. Actually I told Alec about it quite a while ago."

"And that's all Underwood could have on you?"

Instantly her guard returned. "Other than a couple of parking tickets."

Dave left wondering if Claudia Fentiman had used her custody case to conceal something worse buried in her past.

IONA PEREZ, HOWEVER, was looking to the future. Sean Cushing did not realize that the coolly controlled Iona who had usurped the vacant throne at NOBBY was not only playing a role, she was doing so under expert guidance. It was her sister Christine who had specified the exact salary to be demanded from the board. The amount had made Iona gasp.

"They'll never agree."

"Right now they need you more than you need them," the voice of wisdom had replied.

Twice-divorced and childless, Christine was one of New York's top theatrical agents. Today she was devoting the afternoon to creating a new look for Iona.

"I have to make a good impression on the board and look right for public appearances," Iona explained the moment she broke free from the Sloan. "But I don't want them to think I've turned myself inside out."

Christine, all business, was beginning their endeavor with a visit to the beauty salon.

"We'll do things by degrees," she said soothingly before turning to the hair stylist. "Just an inch off to get rid of that terrible in-between look. But a lot more layering on top."

To Iona's relief, the result, while a decided improvement, was not extreme. She was still lingering to admire it when Christine bustled her toward the exit.

"And now for Bendel's. Did you do what I said? Are you wearing the same thing as before?"

"Yes, I've only met the full board once."

For her previous appearance Iona had donned an inexpensive, much worn, navy-blue suit with a limp blouse featuring a large bow. When she was posed in front of the mirror at Henri Bendel's, she was torn. On the one hand she recognized the imperfections of her ensemble. Nonetheless she was wary. With the frankness that their relationship made possible, she said, "I don't want to look glitzy the way you do."

"No," Christine agreed seriously before adding, "You could never pull it off."

Christine herself favored a varnished perfection extending from top to toe. Her long, lanky frame was always perched on stiletto heels, while her face presented a near-orange glow unknown to nature. Today two sleek wings of dark hair swept back into a chignon, with giant hoop earrings almost brushing her shoulders. To her sister's surprise and disappointment, Christine ultimately chose another navy-blue suit, albeit one that cost three times as much as its predecessor.

"I'll look exactly the same."

"Not a chance. You've got to realize that most people don't notice details at all, they just get a general impression. The suit will make them think you're still the same but somehow more pulled together than they remember."

Before Iona knew what was happening, the skirt had been shortened, navy-blue panty hose replaced beige stockings and her old comfortable step-ins had given way to modish laced shoes with heels an inch higher.

Superior tailoring and significantly improved legs made all the difference. Even Iona, humbly aware that she was not blessed with an expert eye, recognized that the total effect had changed.

"Except for one thing," she pointed out. "The blouse is all wrong with this look."

"It was never right for any look," Tina replied bluntly. "But you're going to keep it for this interview, just to prove that you're the same old Iona. Then you throw it out. The next time they see you, you'll be wearing the right accessories."

Distrustful of her sister's competence, Tina went off to reappear with a scarf in a bold geometric design of blue, black and white. Draping it skillfully around Iona's throat, she stepped back.

"That's what you'll look like on a platform."

Iona was entranced. "It's perfect," she crooned, "just perfect."

But Tina, sitting with her chin propped on a braceleted fist, had fallen into a sibylline trance. "There's something off," she muttered, her critical gaze examining every inch of her sister. "Of course! Earrings!"

"Tina, I can't wear those enormous things you like."

But Christine was once again on the move. The two objects she brought back caused Iona to back away.

"They're too big and I always wear these pearls."

"Trust me. You can't use those little buttons anymore because your ears are showing now. You're out of balance."

It was not easy to coax Iona into the gold spirals with modest drops. But once rigged out, she was astonished.

"Why, they look fine."

"Of course they do," Tina said complacently.

Nonetheless, she was pleased as she saw her sister unconsciously arch her neck at the vision in the mirror. "That's enough for now. Remember, we're doing this by degrees."

"What more is coming?" Iona said apprehensively.

"The next time you have your hair trimmed, you're getting some highlights put in."

"Oh, Tina!"

CLAUDIA FENTIMAN, OF course, was already dressed for success. Nevertheless, an hour later it was hard work to turn her thoughts to Quax.

"Will you just forget about the police," Alec Moore directed as they charged up Madison Avenue. "We've got a chance to do ourselves some good. Concentrate on that—hey, watch it!"

Obediently, Claudia ducked around the Rastafarian with handouts and sprinted to keep pace with Moore. What she really craved was privacy and time to unwind. Instead she had Alec, infused with purpose.

"But Alec," she began uncertainly.

"Here we are," he said, swerving smartly into the Bryer Building. "Wetherbee's on forty-seven, isn't he?"

During the ride upward, he reviewed the script. "Now remember why we're here. We want Bernie to take over the Quax account with an advertising campaign that's as high-powered as what he's done for Kix . . ."

Claudia realized that Moore was following his own advice to forget the police. Her attempts to do likewise foundered on the problems raised by his ambitious new strategy.

Even Bernie Wetherbee saw them.

"Alec, good to see you," he burbled, greeting them in his sumptuous reception area. "And Claudia! So help me God, you get prettier every time I see you. Come in, come in."

His office offered spectacular views which Moore ignored. "Bernie," he began before they were seated, "we've got a proposition to put to you about Quax. You do know about Quax, don't you?"

Even a smooth operator can forget himself.

"Who doesn't?" Wetherbee responded. As a practitioner of the art he was well aware that there *is* such a thing as bad publicity.

He was taken aback when Moore, dismissing murder and media blitzes, presented his business plan.

"Quax has done pretty well with low-budget advertising. But now that we're ready to take off, we need a helluva lot more. Claudia's planning some major marketing moves, and no one could promote them better than you, Bernie."

For a man whose television spots were widely regarded as punchier than most scheduled programs, Wetherbee looked dumbfounded. After recovering his wits, he said, "There's just one little problem, Alec."

"What's that?" Moore demanded.

With a simulation of man-to-man candor, Wetherbee spelled out some facts of life. "Before we can begin talking, I'd have to clear it with Kichsel HQ. To be precise, with Theo Benda, who's the guy who signs my checks."

Even though those checks ran to many millions of dollars, this argument did not impress Alec Moore.

"Theo?" he said negligently. "Don't worry about Theo. I'll fix things on that end. You start thinking about a Quax campaign, something to appeal to kids as well as their parents . . ."

The conversation, noticeably one-sided, continued at some length. Nevertheless, by the time it ended, Moore had convinced himself that he had achieved something useful in New York.

"Like getting questioned by the police and spread all over TV?" snapped Claudia when he said as much.

Unmoved, he continued, "And it's lucky good old Theo's right here with the rest of us. That'll speed things up."

Claudia did not trust herself to comment.

GOOD OLD THEO, meanwhile, was cursing the luck that had scheduled his speech today. Since Kichsel Brewery was neither high-tech nor emerging market, it excited Wall Street's interest only at widely spaced intervals. But the company was duly covered and Benda, just as dutifully, reported to professional gatherings several times each year. In his capable hands Kichsel Brewery always emerged sounding like a safe pick for prudent investors from San Diego to Orlando. But, after murder and mayhem, and Madeleine Underwood jammed into a closet, that was a story sixty-five New York financial analysts were not likely to buy.

So Benda revised his prepared remarks and steeled himself for the question period.

"Yes," he told the young woman from PaineWebber. "I've been in touch with our distribution center in Laconia. Quax shipments jumped thirty percent last week."

"How's that going to impact earnings, Theo?"

For reasons of prudence as well as policy, Benda invariably downplayed Quax. Fortunately, the facts bore him out.

"As you know, Quax contributes less than two percent of Kichsel's revenues—"

"Do you expect any change there?"

"We're projecting modest but steady growth," he replied.

But with the scent of blood in the air, the financial analysts wanted more dirt.

"Let's talk management, Theo," said PaineWebber, approaching another ticklish area. "Dean Kichsel's getting on in years. Is he thinking of stepping down? And what about candidates to replace him?"

Without batting an eye, Benda unreeled the mandatory tribute to Dean and the whole management bench. ". . . but as to when Dean's going to retire, I can't tell you."

The ensuing skirmish was conducted with both sides observing the rules of engagement. No one pressed Benda for an opinion that could cost him his job. In turn, he framed replies precise enough to satisfy Price Waterhouse or any other independent investigator.

It was a process that left him feeling like one of his American literary favorites—teetering on the edge of the tureen, if not actually in the soup. The push came after he parted from the keen young intelligences from PaineWebber. As Benda trudged up Broad Street, reviewing his own performance, he heard from another critic.

"Not a bad job, all things considered. But the kids let you off easy."

Art Masling, veteran Wall Street journeyman, was one of the

more raffish figures in Benda's network. For reasons that could only be contrarian, he periodically touted Kichsel. Since he had a loyal if misguided following, his "buy" recommendations meant he had to be treated like an old friend.

"I thought it went pretty well," Benda confessed.

"Considering that you're in deep shit about a murder, you've got all hell breaking loose about Quax and the police have questioned the Kichsels themselves, you managed to finesse a lot."

"Thanks," said Benda. Brickbats from Masling were currently the least of his worries, but he felt obliged to continue. "Put like that, it sounds bad. But don't get carried away by appearances. Basically the situation at Kichsel is looking better than it has for at least the last year or two."

Masling, a hard-core cynic, smiled to indicate that in similar circumstances he too would shade the truth. He would have been stunned to learn that Theo Benda actually believed every word he uttered.

17. Empties

F OR THE NEXT forty-eight hours the burning issue of Quax made virtually no demands on John Thatcher's time. He was both gratified and suspicious. If Dean Kichsel had regarded the Rugby riot as sufficiently important to require counsel, it was certainly odd that the murder of Quax's most voluble opponent should be allowed to pass without comment. On the other hand, George Lancer, drawn and wan, had finally dragged himself back to the Sloan, so future cries for help would presumably be directed to him.

But if Thatcher was willing to accept the gift of the gods, Charlie Trinkam immediately set to work to crack the wall of silence. That afternoon he breezed into Thatcher's office with Paul Jackson in tow, only to stop short on the threshold.

"George! It's good to have you back," he cried delightedly. "You look absolutely awful."

Years ago Thatcher had noticed that Charlie Trinkam's welcome to recent flu victims was gender-linked. He told all women that they looked wonderful and all men that they looked rotten. Upon inquiry he had explained his goal was simply to give pleasure. Women required reassurance about their appearance while men, afraid of being labeled as wimps, appreciated any recognition of the severity of their ordeal.

Certainly Lancer did not seem displeased as he explained that he was bringing himself up to speed on developments during his absence.

"Then you'll be interested in this," Charlie told him. "It looks as if Madeleine Underwood's killer may be one of your buddies from the brewery."

"How can you discuss this, Paul?" Thatcher objected. "I thought you were Kichsel's lawyer."

"But not Alec Moore's," Jackson replied, answering at least one question. "Besides, this is common knowledge by now. The police have been asking too many questions of the committee staff and at the public library."

Lancer blinked in confusion. "The public library?"

Briefly Jackson outlined Alec Moore's original account of his activities after the committee adjournment.

"But the cops have blown that story sky-high. Moore never did try to call his son. What's more, the library computer he claimed to be using was down that day. To top it off, there was a regular patron in the reference section who's prepared to swear that nobody like Moore was there during the lunch break."

"So what story has Moore come up with now?" Thatcher asked.

"None. He's decided to sit pat. He says the person he called and the things he did are his personal business and he's not telling the cops one word."

George Lancer wagged his head disapprovingly. "That seems foolhardy in the extreme."

"Oh, I don't know," said the expert. "Refusing to say anything gives you a lot of flexibility later if you need it. Moore got stung once, so he's not trying again. Actually he would have been better off to keep mum from the beginning."

Thatcher was perfectly willing to accept Jackson's evaluation if a criminal trial was in the offing. Otherwise, Moore's intransigence could raise all sorts of difficulties.

"Starting with his boss," Jackson agreed. "Kichsel is hopping around like a flea. When he couldn't get a word of explanation from Moore, he called me in to recommend a criminal attorney. But Moore isn't having any of that. He says he didn't kill the woman, he's just protecting his private life."

"I can see that lying about his whereabouts would attract police attention, but how serious can things be in the absence of any motive?" Thatcher asked. "After all, Madeleine Underwood was rapidly destroying her own credibility and that of her organization. Why should Moore kill her?"

Charlie chortled merrily. "Now that is where things really get interesting. Tell them, Paul."

"The police are focusing on the quarrel with Underwood. Particularly what she said about investigating people at Kichsel."

"They've already been to see me about it," Thatcher admitted.

"How well do you remember what she said?" Jackson asked.

Obediently Thatcher parroted the memories that had been stirred to life during his interrogation.

"The real question is," Jackson pressed, "which one was she talking about? Moore? Fentiman? Or both?"

"She had been exchanging insults alternately with both of them. Then she said: 'You think I don't know all about you, but I've had you investigated. I've found out your dirty little secrets.' " After a moment's thought Thatcher shrugged. "Given the fact that *you* can be singular or plural, she could have had anything in mind. At the time Moore seemed to think it was directed at him."

"Aha! That's the puzzler. When the cops got to work they found a nasty divorce in Claudia Fentiman's past—one of those custody battles claiming she was an unfit mother. She admits she thought that's what Underwood was referring to. Now Moore says he assumed the same thing and he was defending Fentiman when he snapped back at Underwood. But a lot of witnesses beside you say, at the time, it looked as if he thought he was the target."

As always, George Lancer was scrupulously fair. "Even if he did, he could be covering something minor. Certainly the blot on Mrs. Fentiman's record is not very serious."

"Hell, no," agreed Jackson. "It sounds to me like the usual divorce wrangle where, nine times out of ten, the unfit-mother business is mostly a maneuver in the property settlement."

"Then Alec Moore may have a similar peccadillo in his past."

"Not exactly similar," Jackson countered. "First, Claudia didn't make a deep dark secret of her little trouble. Moore and some others back home already knew about it. Second, even at this stage of the game, Moore is unwilling to take Kichsel into his confidence.

He's being a lot more close-mouthed than Claudia found necessary."

"To the point of arousing police suspicion in a murder case," Thatcher chimed in.

Bright-eyed as ever, Charlie took this reasoning even further. "Which means that it has to be something that could have a serious impact on his future."

Conscious of the simmering excitement shared by Trinkam and Jackson, Thatcher murmured, "And why do I suspect that you and Paul have some notion what Moore's secret could be?"

"It was Paul's idea," Charlie said modestly.

"And that's all it is," Jackson hastened to say. "But I was thinking about all those charges the Underwood woman was slinging around. It's always possible that she hit the bull's-eye without even realizing it."

Thatcher did not bother with the list of Madeleine's wild accusations. "Which one are we talking about?"

"I haven't known Moore as long as you have," the lawyer said with a glance at George Lancer, "but I have gotten his flavor. Enough to wonder if, after all, he might have been behind the Ludlums."

"That would mean you had been gulled as well as everyone else," Thatcher remarked acutely.

"Believe me, the thought doesn't come easy," Jackson confessed.

All eyes turned to Lancer for the definitive character analysis. Thatcher was expecting an instant rebuttal but it did not come. Only after several moments of frowning thought did George speak.

"I can't say that it seems totally impossible," he said reluctantly. "There's a certain quality about Moore that's difficult to put into words, but I've seen it before in men who come to business late in life."

Thatcher had seen it, too.

"Because they succeed with one good idea, they tend to regard themselves as much cleverer than the fuddy-duddies who've been there for years," he suggested.

"Alec certainly underrates both Kichsel and Theo Benda. Furthermore, he's made a fetish of disregarding everything except the hard facts. As a result he never considers how his actions may be viewed."

146

Thatcher remembered Claudia's lecture to Moore on the difference between approaching customers and preaching in the public arena.

"So he might resort to tactics that would be regarded as imprudent or even unprincipled by others?"

All this pussyfooting was making Paul Jackson impatient. "What it boils down to," he said relentlessly, "is simple. Does he have the kind of sophomoric, dirty-tricks mentality that would think it was real smart to set up Underwood with the Ludlum family?"

Instead of answering directly, Lancer searched for practical objections. "But how would he know about the Ludlums?"

"No problem there. If you'd been following me in court, you'd know that Daddy Ludlum's form of grieving was to hike over to the liquor store where his son bought the beer and announce he was going to sue them. It never came to anything, but the store owner warned Kichsel headquarters and the letter ended up on Moore's desk. That's how I found out about it."

Lancer was looking more and more unhappy. "It scarcely seems possible but there's no denying that Moore was enthusiastic about the suit from the beginning. Dean was worried about it but Alec insisted it was a golden opportunity for free publicity."

"And he was right," Jackson pointed out quietly. "He told me that demand for Quax in the metropolitan area skyrocketed."

Now that they had reached the really delicate ground, Charlie and Jackson were signaling that the rest was up to Thatcher.

"Granting for a moment that Moore might have allowed himself to use the Ludlums, then how damaging would exposure of his role be?" he said dutifully.

"Very."

"From what you said the other day, Moore seems to have high ambitions," Thatcher continued.

"Yes, Quax has been so successful that, with Dean planning to retire in two years, Alec has begun to think of himself as a natural successor. He doesn't seem to understand that his lack of experience in the crucial part of Kichsel's operation is a barrier. Instead he sees himself as a rival to Theo Benda."

Charlie could no longer contain himself. "And if his part in some dirty tricks surfaced?"

Lancer sighed. "He could not only say good-bye to the presidency, his entire future at Kichsel would be jeopardized."

That admission was all Paul Jackson needed to enunciate the obvious.

"Now there's the kind of motive that cops can really appreciate."

IONA PEREZ HAD already begun the salvage operation NOBBY needed so desperately. But she was not receiving a warm welcome in Roger Vandermeer's office.

"Let's get one thing straight, Mrs. Perez," he said as soon as she was seated. "I wouldn't even have agreed to see you if you hadn't told me you were already coming to Washington for a meeting with Harry Hull. I could have told you over the phone that, as far as I'm concerned, NOBBY is poison."

As he spoke he was watching her warily. At the first shrill outburst he was ready to bundle her off the premises.

But Iona knew very well that all the reasoned arguments, all the cajolery must be deferred. Her first task, wherever she went, was convincing people that they were not dealing with another Madeleine Underwood.

"That's a very natural reaction," she said gravely. "We do realize at headquarters that our most important priority is eradicating the impression caused by that riot. It's not just a matter of outsiders; our own membership was deeply shocked."

"Oh, that's just great! You want me to give money to an outfit that's not only alienated the public, but its members as well."

"Reassuring our own people is the easiest part of the job. Fortunately they're well acquainted with our past record. As soon as they've recovered from their initial indignation, they'll realize that this was an aberration caused by Madeleine and one that will never happen again."

Vandermeer had begun to relax. Denying requests had never been difficult for him, and as long as he was spared a hysterical woman, he had no objection to spending ten minutes on the task.

"You've got a lot more on your plate than that," he said bluntly. "The police think somebody at your headquarters hasn't been keeping his hands in his pockets. I'm not in favor of that kind of private enterprise."

As sedate as ever she said, "We wouldn't dream of asking for further contributions until that misconception has been cleared up. The auditors are at work now and it shouldn't take them much longer to finish. But while we're on the subject of donations, I should add that we're also addressing the problem of contingent liabilities. We realize they could look like a bottomless pit."

The discussion was not going the way Vandermeer had anticipated. Usually when refusing solicitations he was punching holes in somebody's presentation. Today the suppliant was positively parading all difficulties.

"Rugby could take you for everything you've got."

"Which is why we've started with him. The chairman of our governors is quite pleased with the way things are going. Nothing's been decided yet, but Mr. Rugby is a reasonable man, not anxious for a drawn-out legal battle."

It was second nature for Vandermeer to jab at weak spots.

"Considering how that Ludlum case blew up in your face, I suppose you aren't either."

"Far from it. And of course we've already notified the attorneys that we're withdrawing from that case."

Baffled by her ready agreement, Vandermeer shrugged. "So what does it all amount to? You're trying to exercise some damage control. But a few sandbags aren't going to stop this flood."

Neatly she moved from confession of past error to future plans.

"I wouldn't be too sure of that. Given a fair settlement with Rugby's, we'll have enough funds on hand to launch our drive for national membership. With luck we can start in a few weeks."

"Planning bigger and better protests?" he asked sarcastically.

"Any public demonstrations by NOBBY are out of the question for some time. But I've always felt that we've been neglecting supermarkets. A first step would obviously be a letter-writing campaign by our members. However, in order to have a greater impact, I intend to organize wholesale canvassing so that the volunteers can present petitions signed by a big percentage of the regular customers. There are always plenty of people who endorse the goals of a movement but who don't take an active part. They're the ones who'll sign."

Suppressing an involuntary flicker of interest, he said neutrally, "It's not a bad idea."

"Ideally we would like to have Quax removed from all soft-drink sections. That's probably too much to hope for. But," she continued dulcetly, "it would be very gratifying to see Quax relocated to the beer sections where they exist."

By now Vandermeer was looking bemused. Madeleine Underwood would never have understood the basics of the war for shelf space. With this one, he was not so sure.

"I'm not saying that we don't share some of the same goals," he conceded. "But new consumer groups can be formed. Now that NOBBY's fouled its own nest it makes more sense for us to go that way. And we've got the money and the manpower to do it."

Far from being flattened, Iona shook her head almost reproachfully. "But you can't do it overnight. It will take you over a year to field the kind of effort NOBBY can make in the next three months. And Quax is gaining ground every day. Once it's established as a national favorite, it will be too late to start writing letters. If you're going to do anything effective with consumers, you have to do it now with a working operation."

Vandermeer did not enjoy conversations in which the weakness of his own position was explored. Moreover, that low, melodious voice was damn near hypnotizing him into agreeing that NOBBY's problems were of manageable dimensions.

"No way," he said decisively. "The audit and even the settlement with Rugby may come out okay. But there's still a wild card in the deck. You've got a murder investigation right in your backyard."

For this objection she had no answer. She could only protest that, as NOBBY did not house the murderer, its future usefulness would not be impaired by the result of any investigation.

"Listen, there are more motives lying around your place than any other. Maybe you'd like to pretend Underwood was so dangerous that the CEO of Kichsel bopped her. But hell! The woman was killing herself. Face it. Nobody can tell what's coming out of the woodwork on this one. And I'm sure not advising my client to buy that kind of pig in the poke."

Rising, he automatically reverted to his standard professional geniality. "Sorry I can't help you out, but it's been a real pleasure meeting you, Iona."

She was careful to produce a pleasant smile as they shook hands. "Who knows, Roger? We may yet be doing business together."

18. A Real Bash

ONA'S SECOND APPOINTMENT of the day was intended to be a replica of the first and, at the beginning, it was.

"I should explain one thing," said Harry Hull. "If you hadn't already had a meeting scheduled with Roger Vandermeer, I would have told you it was a waste of time coming down here to see me."

With all the advantages of a dress rehearsal behind her, Iona smoothly settled into her gentle *mea culpa* before proceeding to persuasion. Roger Vandermeer's refusal to continue SDI funding had neither surprised nor discouraged her. No sensible man, she felt, could possibly advise his client to write checks for NOBBY at this particular juncture. Her visit had been designed to present the organization's new director and to keep the door open. Once she had dispelled the grim specters of financial irregularity and huge damage claims, once Madeleine's murder had either been solved or faded from public awareness, then she could begin negotiations on an entirely new basis.

But, although she had not realized it at the time, Vandermeer's resistance had provided a framework for her arguments. Congressman Hull was giving her no help at all. Leaning back in his chair, playing finger games with a pencil, he remained totally unresponsive as she floundered from one point to the next. Only when she finished her set piece did he speak.

"It doesn't make any difference to me if NOBBY goes national or if it folds," he said flatly. "In my book it's finished."

Unconsciously Iona began to press harder, producing more dramatic—and less convincing—programs for the future. Like the Augean stables, the office of NOBBY's executive director would be mightily cleansed. Madeleine's files would be ransacked and all those overly ambitious plans for dealing with the FDA, for attacking Rugby at every corner, would be discarded. Rather, NOBBY would be a symbol of consumer power—enlisting the general public, penetrating PTAs, becoming the voice of parents everywhere.

Now, instead of looking bored, Hull was looking contemptuous.

"Look, Leon Rossi got fooled into going along with this once. He's not dumb enough to do it again, and neither am I."

In fact, Iona was misplaying her hand at every turn. The Raeburn Building did not boast the marbled grandeur that surrounded the luminaries of the House of Representatives, but nonetheless it still breathed the solemnity of federal authority. Hull's desk was guarded by flags of the United States and Texas. His walls were lined with signed photographs tracing his political career, from a teenaged handshake with a legendary Speaker of the House to a warm embrace from the President of Mexico last month. These were powerful indications that Harry Hull's concerns might not duplicate those of Roger Vandermeer.

"You mean you're changing your position on Quax?" she asked, unable to avoid a tinge of accusation.

"My position has always been clear," he replied impatiently. "I'd like to see its consequences investigated, although I've never been sure what the results of such an investigation would be. At the same time I've got a lot of other problems on my agenda. And the ones that don't involve me and my colleagues in a murder are the ones that get priority."

At last Iona understood. Roger Vandermeer, like it or not, was committed to the battle for supermarket shelf space. He had to be interested in anything that promised him an edge in that conflict. Congressman Hull could turn his attention to education or inner-city youth gangs.

Nonetheless she was outraged. NOBBY had police auditors poring over its books. NOBBY personnel were being interrogated about alibis and quarrels with the victim. They were the ones in the front line. Knowing it was useless, she protested that Madeleine's murder had taken place after the hearings were adjourned, after the committee had packed up and gone. Hull and the other members of the panel were merely innocent bystanders.

This piece of special pleading was not a success. Hull ended their exchange by giving her some advice.

"You've got a New York point of view," he said disapprovingly. "Try reading the *Washington Post* for a change."

Iona Perez was all too willing to broaden her outlook, but not by reading. People—what they said, how they behaved and what they believed—were her texts for self-improvement. Accordingly the next day, lunching with NOBBY's branch chairwoman for Greater Washington, she honed in on political problems.

"You can forget about that bunch on the Hill," said the chairwoman robustly. "They're too scared of scandal to come anywhere near us."

"But they were ready to form a committee and hold hearings. Some of them must be genuinely interested."

The reply was nearly libelous, ending with, "The only thing they're really interested in is their careers. Particularly the ones in the House. They have to get reelected every two years, and they start working on the next round as soon as the votes are counted. Any left-over energy is spent trying to get on the committees that will give them power and exposure. We just don't qualify."

It was a discouraging forecast but Iona was there to learn. "All right, so I forget about Congressman Hull. What about the membership?"

"Now that's what you should be concentrating on. Our people are perfectly normal. They don't give a damn about touchy feelings inside the Beltway. But they do care about riots and murders. Right now they need reassurance."

This at least was familiar ground. The same cry was coming from branches around New York.

"Any suggestions?"

The chairwoman beamed. "Actually, yes. I hope you'll agree to take a later shuttle tonight. The Falls Church members are having an emergency session at seven-thirty and the best thing would be for you to address them."

Suddenly Iona's mouth went dry. She had always assumed that her first essay in public speaking would be accompanied by support factors. There would be a kindly, knowledgeable introduction by Peggy Roche, a script that had been edited and reedited, a large showing of the volunteers she had worked with. With a refusal half-formulated, she abruptly checked herself. Conscious of the rich folds of silk swaddling her neck and the slight swaying movement at her ears, she realized that she was all dressed up and she did indeed have someplace to go. In a moment of devil-may-care abandon she reached a decision.

"Of course," she said graciously. "I'll be happy to say a few words."

AT THE SLOAN GUARANTY Trust they did read the *Washington Post*, although not perhaps in a spirit that Harry Hull would have approved.

"Just your usual hometown coverage," announced a disgruntled Charlie Trinkam. "Like when Aunt Agatha takes her vacation someplace where there's a disaster."

Thatcher, who had already read about demands for increased security at committee hearings, reminded Charlie that this particular hometown packed a powerful punch.

"If they've got so much clout, why don't they find out some details."

Charlie's complaint was not really directed toward the parochialism of the nation's capital. He had been scouring the press for information about the Underwood murder investigation and found nothing of any moment.

"And, unless the police audit is productive, I wouldn't expect to hear anything for some time," Thatcher mused.

"You mean because NOBBY's such a lightweight outfit?"

"Exactly. Madeleine Underwood was not a sufficient threat to anybody's business to provoke a murder. Even Dean Kichsel, who takes this sort of thing seriously, regarded her as an irritant."

Nodding, Charlie said, "I'll go along with that. Which leaves a personal motive."

"And that could take a long time to unearth."

"Except that you'd think anything the Underwood woman could find out, the police would be on to damn fast."

"I'm not so sure about that. If you postulate that somebody murdered Madeleine to avoid exposure, then you also have to assume that with her dead, the secret is reasonably safe."

As Charlie could not argue with this, he said, "Which brings us back to Paul Jackson's theory. While she was flailing around she hit a nerve she didn't even know about."

"Or she stumbled on something by sheer accident."

Charlie was not afraid to name names. "There's one thing you can't get away from. Alec Moore is the one she was really after and he's the one who's got something to cover."

"True, but he's also passably intelligent. It's hard to credit that, if he were the killer, he would be focusing police attention on himself this way. I'm more inclined to believe that it's something else he's hiding—and with some possibility of success."

"Well, I'll grant you the possibility of success," Charlie conceded. "From what Paul says, Moore is standing pat with absolute self-confidence."

BUT LOOKS CAN be misleading. While Iona Perez was taking her fears and frustrations onto a public platform. Alec Moore was taking his to a bar, or rather a succession of bars. For days he had prided himself on maintaining his composure. The defiant facade, however, now masked a crumbling interior. At the beginning he had been master of his own thoughts.

"What they don't know can't really hurt me," he had told himself and gained from that simple statement a comforting sense of security.

"Everything will be all right as long as I keep quiet."

Insensibly, more insidious thoughts had intruded. First there had been the inevitable spurt of exasperation.

"That damned woman. How the hell did she find out?"

To be followed, inevitably, by reassurance.

"She's dead now, so that's all right. She didn't have time to tell anyone."

But twenty-four hours ago some undisciplined corner of his mind had produced a contrary inner voice determined to paint horrifying images of the future. Tonight he had fled from his solitary hotel room to escape. By ten-thirty, however, sitting in the dimmest corner of a small establishment in the Fifties, he was learning that there is no escape from one's thoughts.

"How bad can it really be?" he asked himself, hoping to stifle any response.

"It could be the end of everything for you," the inner voice said relentlessly.

"This can't be happening to me," he insisted.

"Like hell it can't! It is."

And round and round his thoughts would squirrel, in an ever-descending spiral, until he was reduced to the ultimate childlike wail.

"It's not fair."

Immersed in private torment, he had no idea that he was the object of continuing scrutiny. The owner of the bar believed that trouble foreseen is trouble averted. And he had long since learned to categorize his clientele. At this hour, as in all midtown Manhattan bars, there were large boisterous groups of visitors determined to have a rip-roaring time in the Big Apple. With them, anything was possible. Then, thanks to the proximity of television stations and newsmagazines, there were late-shift regulars. For the most part they were social drinkers, having one or two rounds with colleagues before catching a train home.

Of course, scattered throughout the crowd were the boozers—the ones who had long since decided to maintain a blanket of insulation between themselves and full consciousness. Thankfully they were all hardened veterans, taking their nips throughout the waking day, judging to a millimeter the exact degree of desirable protection—solid enough to keep their demons at bay, permeable enough to allow continued function.

But in that distant corner with his back to the room was a member of the most troublesome tribe. These were the non-drinkers seeking refuge because of a single, shattering blow. Either their wives had left them, their bosses had fired them or their doctors had detected cancer. They were the most unpredictable because they lacked any established indicators of a flashpoint just around the corner. They were more surprised than anyone else when the inhibitions and controls of a lifetime suddenly vanished.

This one was too near his point of no return, but what form would the collapse take? An outbreak of unprovoked hostility was the worst manifestation, but after a moment's examination the barkeep rejected this possibility. The bowed head, the slumped shoulders, the immense concentration on forming perfect circles with a wet glass—all suggested that here was one of the lachrymose sort. Instead of flying fists there would be convulsive sobbing.

Inwardly the barkeep cursed. Everything else was going so nicely. The crowd perched on stools was concentrating on the Rangers' chances for the Stanley Cup. Like all such sports conversations, the discussion was heavily arithmetic.

"Now, if the L.A. Kings lose two and the Black Hawks win three . . ."

"They've got a double-header with the Maple Leafs this weekend. With a zero–two record you can't hope for better than a split . . ."

". . . out for three weeks. And they've only got eight games more in the regular season. That means you can kiss good-bye to Boston."

The most boisterous group of out-of-towners had just noisily decided to taxi down to the Village in search of excitement, while a merry group from NBC was discussing summer-vacation plans. Was this the atmosphere for a heavily sobbing customer?

At that moment a cocktail waitress drifted back to the bar with fresh orders and seized the opportunity to say in a voice of doom:

"He's begun talking to himself."

"Christ! That's all I need." Only a moment's reflection was needed before he added, "If he wants another one, call me. We won't serve him any more."

*　*　*

Iona's evening had been more decorous.

"Although I suppose I should have warned you about Avis Gellert," the chairwoman continued her congratulations as she peered through the traffic for the exit to the airport.

"I was surprised," Iona admitted.

"We're so used to her that I forgot. But you did a fine job with her."

"I didn't manage to persuade her," Iona objected.

The chairwoman chuckled. "Oh, Avis never listens to anybody, but you did get her to sit down."

Iona did not share this lightheartedness. At the conclusion of her pep talk, several members had asked routine questions. Then Avis Gellert had risen, an apparition from the past. Even though she was in her fifties, she had summoned up ancient news clips of anti-war protests and student riots. A tall, columnar woman with two straight curtains of graying hair, she had begun to harangue Iona. Most astonishing of all had been the fixed stare and the monotonic stream of disjointed phrases.

"We're fighting the Establishment . . . have to be just as ruthless . . . this is war and there have to be casualties . . . they've killed Madeleine . . . stop at nothing . . ."

This episode Iona had no intention of discussing with the chairwoman. Scrambling to board her flight, she restricted her remarks to hasty thanks and farewells. Not until the plane was in the air did she allow her attention to return to Avis Gellert. Because the final blood-chilling moment had come in the form of a casual aside.

"I warned Madeleine of the dangers when I was in New York, but she wouldn't listen."

Like Sean Cushing before her, Iona had assured the police that NOBBY was free of any radical militant element. She had done so in all sincerity. But now she was uneasily remembering the stream of visitors passing through Madeleine Underwood's office. Many far-flung members of NOBBY, coming to visit New York, arranged appointments with the director. What if Madeleine's fancy had been

159

captured by one of them—by a display of fervor for the cause or—God help us—by plans for extreme action? What if one of them lived close to a Kichsel plant? Iona could see all sorts of dire possibilities.

Hold hard, she told herself. Anybody could tell that Avis Gellert was unbalanced. Wouldn't Madeleine have recognized the symptoms?

Here the answer was unequivocal. The visitor could have been foaming at the mouth and Madeleine would have seen only what she wanted to see. Even more damning, she would have hugged any glorious discovery to herself, just as she had with the Ludlums.

Oh God, it was ironic. Iona had convinced herself that Madeleine's death spelled the end of NOBBY's problems, but she could easily have left a damning legacy behind her. Iona did not suspect that some Avis Gellert type was implicated in the murder. What she feared was that the police, in the course of their investigation, would discover a contact between Madeleine and the lunatic fringe. That's all it would take, some suspect telling the world about his God-given right to shoot anybody who disagreed with him and NOBBY would sink without a trace.

Grimly Iona decided to delay her return home and drive by NOBBY's office. At the very least there would be the file of letters arranging appointments. She was still preoccupied with her fears when she arrived at the bleak office building on Twenty-third Street.

"I'll only be a few minutes," she told the security guard as she signed in.

Emerging from the elevator on the eighth floor, she unseeingly strode past signs of life in the small accounting firm that was always busy when quarterly tax returns were in the offing.

Was there the slightest use to questioning Cheryl about visitors? she wondered, unlocking her own door. Or would Cheryl simply spread the news of this new concern?

Iona had opened the door and advanced one step over the threshold before stopping short in alarm. The dim light from the hallway made the dark figure hurtling toward her seem gigantic. With a scream of terror she tried to pivot, only to jam her portfolio in the doorway.

The figure was on her before she could move further. A garish

160

ski mask loomed to monstrous proportions, someone's breath was in her face, then an annihilating wave of pain blanketed all other sensations.

Mercifully, she pitched forward into enveloping blackness.

19. Morning After

S HE WAS LUCKY," said the young doctor.

With Iona occupying the bed between them, Christina was too exhausted to glare at him. Her vigil had begun with a distraught cry for help from Bill Perez. Rushing to the hospital in the middle of the night, she had arrived in time for an endless wait. It was hours before her anxiety began to ebb, and with daylight came new demands. Now Bill was back in Rye, making arrangements for the children while Christina stuck by the bedside.

"The fracture in her arm is a nice clean diagonal break," said the doctor. "If there's no problem with the concussion, she'll be just fine."

Looking down at a sister who was little more than a pathetic bundle beneath the white coverlet, Christina had to bite back an acid retort. Then Iona stirred, opened her eyes, and smiled weakly. "Still here, Tina? You don't have to hang around."

"I've got nothing better to do, kiddo," said Christina blithely. "How do you feel?"

Iona inventoried herself. "Okay. Just kind of woozy."

Between shock and sedatives, that sounded reasonable to Christina.

"What happened?" asked Iona, frowning unhappily.

"Somehow you busted your—"

"No, I mean at NOBBY," Iona persisted. "I remember opening the door, then there was this dark figure in a mask, then—blank!"

"Don't worry about that now," said the doctor, beaming heavy calm at his patient while he motioned Christina from the room.

Five minutes later he joined her at the nurse's station, pen already uncapped to supplement the paperwork. "I don't want her exciting herself," he explained. "And you look as if you could use some rest too."

"It'll take more than rest," said Christina. Grateful as she was that Iona's injuries were not life-threatening, she remained haunted by the vision of a brutal attack in a darkened building. If one of NOBBY's fellow tenants had not been using his Manhattan office for purposes other than accounting . . . if . . .

Then came another reminder of the dangers outside the controlled certainty of the hospital corridor as the elevator door hissed open, disgorging two large men. One wore policeman's blue, and Christina bristled protectively.

"Oh, no," she cried. "You're not going to pester—"

"It wouldn't do you any good anyway," said the doctor. "I've already explained to Reardon that it isn't a question of jogging Mrs. Perez's memory. There's no memory to come back. She got banged on the head and after that she doesn't remember a thing."

Their spontaneous indignation made the detective blink. "That figures," he said mildly. "We were just double-checking down in Emergency to see if anybody caught anything when they brought her in. But it was a no-show. And as long as we were here, I thought we'd drop by to see how she's doing."

This disingenuous explanation made Christina narrow her eyes, but the doctor merely shrugged. "Whatever," he said, returning to his records, "but I'm not letting you guys in to disturb the patient now. If more details come back to her, we'll call you."

"Anything you say, Doc."

ORDERS TO TREAD warily extended only as far as Iona Perez. At NOBBY, the police were back in force. This time, besides the auditors, a full technical crew had moved in, dusting every surface for fingerprints, photographing the jimmied lock on the hall door. Two specialists, on hands and knees, were collecting the contents of a cabinet that had been tumbled to the floor, marking and bagging each item.

"He must have been going through that cabinet when Iona interrupted him," said Sean Cushing dully.

The yellow tape that sealed NOBBY from the idly curious kept him imprisoned, under instructions to remain available and to avoid getting underfoot. This limbo left him huddled at his desk, nervously playing with the coffee cup that Cheryl insisted on refilling. She had been allowed in because of the common sense that real people bring to real-life situations. Who else would keep the percolator bubbling?

Peggy Roche, on the other hand, had brazened her way into NOBBY under the false colors of moral responsibility and inside information. Both of them were put to the test.

"But what was there in that cabinet that anybody would want?" she asked.

"Mostly, it was the tapes that Madeleine made last week," said Cushing, clearly wishing she would leave him alone.

Peggy struggled with irritation. The attack on Iona was horrifying, but the aftermath still had to be dealt with. Relapsing into morose silence, as Cushing showed every sign of doing, struck her as counterproductive.

"What kind of tapes?" she continued.

But Cushing was preoccupied, not defeated.

"How should I know?"

"But surely they were classified somehow."

"You know how Madeleine operated," he replied. "She taped everything under the sun, then dumped it on the girls. All they could do was file by date."

"Maybe we should ask Cheryl if she remembers . . ."

Realizing that Peggy would continue to probe; Sean reluctantly explained. "The guy was probably looking for the tape the cops already took, the one about the press conference."

"What press conference?" she asked sharply. "Nobody told me about anything like that."

Wearily he said, "Look, all I know is that Madeleine told the relief girl she was planning to call a press conference because the hearings had been adjourned."

"But that means Madeleine made a tape just before she was murdered," said Peggy with a sinking heart.

"You got it," he said, silencing her.

"Want some more?" asked Cheryl, materializing with coffeepot in hand.

"No, thank you," said Peggy.

Cushing shook his head.

Cheryl prepared to withdraw, then caught herself. "Has there been any more news about Iona?"

"Her husband called me just before the cops did. He says they think she's going to be okay."

The sour aftertaste of those early-morning calls made him stop short, but Peggy took up the slack.

"I talked to the sister," she said. "She told me they're keeping Iona in the hospital for observation, but she'll be out sooner rather than later."

"Great," said Cheryl. "I mean, she could have got herself killed or something."

"Just like Madeleine," Sean agreed somberly.

This was enough to return Peggy to the attack. "What was Madeleine planning to say at this conference?" she demanded.

Before Sean could reply, Cheryl paused in the doorway. "I'll bet it was a real blockbuster. Rita says Madeleine was breathing fire."

Whisking herself away, she left Peggy staring at Cushing with horror.

"My God, she could have said anything. I'd better ask the police."

"You can ask," Cushing retorted. "But they're not telling us one word."

"Do you want to send flowers, Mr. Thatcher?" asked Miss Corsa, depositing his morning mail.

"To whom?" he inquired, eyeing the in-pile askance. For reasons he appreciated and deplored, topping the heap was a garish brochure touting the latest wonder of commerce. This one was called Mohawk Crossing, a megamall and theme park scheduled to open over the weekend in upstate New York. Since the ceremony figured in Thatcher's future, he was eager to defer historically accurate log cabins and Iroquois encampments, but the flowers eluded him.

"To Mrs. Perez," Miss Corsa explained.

Thatcher was still lost. "A pleasant woman and a capable one too, I suspect, but I don't feel that I'm on candy-and-flower terms with her."

Miss Corsa's morning commute often equipped her with tabloid tidbits that Thatcher had missed.

". . . said it looked as if she interrupted a robbery," she explained. "I don't think they would have covered it, except that it happened at NOBBY."

"Good Lord," said Thatcher, with more than automatic sympathy for Iona Perez. The poor woman seemed to take a lot of physical punishment for her devotion to NOBBY.

"Flowers by all means," he agreed, reflecting that he was not the only one to have missed the item. Given all the parties currently resonating to NOBBY, it was significant that he was not already fielding squawks from George Lancer's tower suite. This had to mean that the Kichsels were still in the dark.

"I don't know if they're in the dark," said Charlie once he had been brought up-to-date, "but they're back in Chicago. Elmer happened to mention it last night."

"Good," said Thatcher, with real pleasure. It was the Kichsels and their proximity to crime—and George—who posed the greatest threat to his peace of mind.

Then Charlie added, "That's Dean and Theo Benda. They went back a couple of days ago. For all I know, Moore and the Fentiman babe are still hanging around New York."

"I sincerely hope not," said Thatcher.

Reading his thoughts, Charlie supplied some comfort. "Oh, I don't know," he said. "This time around the police are going to have trouble with alibis. They probably don't know how much time to cover. And you know that kind of building. I'll bet their security's a joke."

All over Manhattan there are guards at the door with sign-in sheets. But, absent vaults stuffed with gold and diamonds, most of these precautions are designed to control the traffic flow. Inevitably there are gaps that let the occasional odd fish slip through. People tape latches to basement garages, they hide in bathrooms . . .

"So somebody broke into NOBBY at a time unspecified, then waited until nightfall to get to work. Mrs. Perez had the bad luck to interrupt him. It's a plausible hypothesis," Charlie continued.

Thatcher agreed. "But there must have been a reason for the burglary. Breaking into Mrs. Underwood's office and searching it implies that she left some sort of damning record, doesn't it?"

"A nice scenario," said Charlie cheerfully. "Something damning enough to murder for, and somebody desperate to get his hands on it. We may be in for more fun and games, John, while the police go through the motions."

CLAUDIA FENTIMAN, WHO had been on the receiving end of those motions, was less carefree.

"Thank God, I had dinner with some friends. Then we went to a concert. We came back here for drinks," she said to the phone. "Some detective dragged all that out of me before he told me there had been a break-in at NOBBY. Honest to God, Theo, I was ready to scream."

"That means you don't have anything to worry about," he replied, knowing full well that her relief was razor-thin. This call was not a casual exchange but a pooling of anxiety. "What about Alec?"

"He's been avoiding me," she said, still brittle. "I haven't seen him to talk to for the past few days."

Swiftly, Benda made his calculations. "I won't tell Dean about this," he decided. "There's no use troubling him until it's absolutely necessary."

"I think that's wise," she said, tacitly joining a conspiracy.

Without saying so, they were in total agreement that what happened at NOBBY mattered. "Another installment," Benda had complained when Claudia told him about the attack on Iona.

"I wish I knew what Alec thinks he's doing," he rumbled ambiguously.

"I can't imagine," said Claudia.

This was as close as either of them dared come to admitting that Alec Moore's behavior was cause for alarm.

The chain of events that had originated with the introduction of Quax had led to murder. In every link, Alec Moore—and by extension Kichsel Brewery—was deeply involved.

"I've invested a lot of hard work in Quax," Claudia said. "I hope to God Alec isn't throwing it away."

"That's a reasonable point of view," said Benda. His own was somewhat different. "Look, Claudia, I'm glad you told me. I'm coming back east for this Mohawk Crossing shindig. We'd better get together and do some more talking about all this."

But she had sensed his withdrawal. "Fine," she said crisply. "In the meantime, I'll try tracking Alec down. And if I can get anything out of him, I'll let you know."

"You do that," he murmured.

INDULGING IN SPECULATION and surmise was a luxury denied to the police. Even though Inspector Reardon was hampered by Iona's inability to describe her assailant, he had to mount a credible search for the criminal. With other options limited, this left him retracing his own steps. Almost immediately he discovered that the roster of suspects left over from the Underwood murder was shorter than it had been.

"So half of the Kichsel crowd went back to Chicago," he summed up as he scanned an early report.

"They could have hired somebody."

"In which case we're up a river without a paddle," said Reardon. Until technical opinion could prove that NOBBY had been penetrated by a professional, not an amateur, he was sticking to his own gut instinct. By the time he quit NOBBY he had Claudia Fentiman, Dean Kichsel and Theo Benda firmly and blamelessly located elsewhere on the night of the break-in.

Even Sean Cushing had a witness to flaunt. "Sure, she'll tell you I spent the night," he said. "Why shouldn't she?"

Armed with a cast-iron alibi, he had lost some of his defensiveness, but even so his contribution was minimal. Invited to guess the object of the search, he shrugged.

"Beats me," he said. "Unless it was that tape you've been keeping up your sleeve."

Cooperation on other fronts was just as limited.

"Okay, so who got close enough to Underwood to know what she was planning?" Reardon asked aloud.

His staff was already compiling lists of names, but before they finished, one leaped to mind. Here too, Reardon drew a blank. Alec Moore was not immediately available.

"HONEST TO GOD, Dad, you've got to clean up your act."

Moore winced. Lectures from this source always galled; on top of a monster hangover, they were intolerable. Hand shaking, he popped another tablet. With his stomach heaving he did not need Pete to tell him that he looked as rotten as he felt.

"This is a helluva time for you to tie one on," said Pete priggishly.

"I've got a lot on my mind," Moore muttered, wondering what evil inspiration had induced him to land up in his son's apartment, where his welcome had not been warm. Not that he remembered any details. His recall of last night, and of last night's bars, was so hazy as to be virtually nonexistent. Unfortunately, the same forgetfulness did not encompass the tormenting tension that had set him drinking in the first place. The lesson of every morning after, that the victim had been a damned fool, was unnecessary. Alec Moore already knew it.

"Claudia called while you were still sleeping it off," said his severest critic.

"You already told me."

"I wasn't sure you took it in. It seems that the cops want to talk to you again. Something happened at NOBBY last night."

In his current state, Moore could barely focus on NOBBY. "As for last night, there's not a lot I can tell them," he said with a self-deprecating laugh.

Pete took this badly. "Well, you'd better try."

"I will, I will," said Moore. "I just need a little time to pull myself together before I face Reardon. A going-over from the police isn't a lot of fun, you know. And for God's sake, will you take that long look off your face?"

He had seen that expression before. Alec Moore's son bore a strong resemblance to Alec Moore's cousin, Dean Kichsel.

"It would help," said Moore, trying to regain lost ground, "if instead of standing there, you'd get off the dime and make me some coffee."

"HE'LL PROBABLY DITCH this story the way he did last time," said Reardon, after Moore cleared the door that afternoon.

"Give him a break. After a guy's hit all the bars in the Fifties, he's not going to be real coherent."

"*If* he hit the bars," said the skeptical Reardon. "He'd better remember some names next time around."

"Next time around, he'll arrive with a lawyer," predicted Dave.

"Not unless he's cracking up on his own," said Reardon, succumbing to pessimism. "God knows, we're not making enough progress to charge anybody. So far, we've got the world's biggest collection of loose ends."

Either the problem was intractable, or they were trying to solve it the wrong way. Reardon made himself concentrate on the second alternative. "Maybe that's because we've asked just a few people the wrong questions. Underwood didn't decide to call a press conference until the adjournment. I want to see every damned person who could have talked to her afterward. Organize teams to track them down. God knows what kind of results we'll turn up, but anything's better than spinning our wheels like this."

The setback surfaced before his program began.

"Those interviews you wanted?" said Dave later in the day. "They'll have to wait. Half the people you want are going out of town over the weekend. In fact, a lot of them have already left for upstate."

Reardon's face creased irritably. "Don't tell me, let me guess.

NOBBY's holding a convention that nobody bothered to tell me about."

But even policemen are consumers. "This has nothing to do with NOBBY," protested Dave. "It's Mohawk Crossing."

"You mean the tourist trap that's opening in the Finger Lakes?" asked Reardon.

"Sounds pretty nice to me. I've been watching the ads on TV and I thought I'd take the kids up over the Fourth, if I get time off."

Since water rides and shopping courts held no appeal for Reardon, he neglected to ask why they should attract so many individuals who had figured prominently in Madeleine Underwood's life and death.

20. Firewater

OHAWK CROSSING HAD not sprung, full-grown, from the imagination of one creator. The gigantic complex occupying a stunned corner of upper New York State was the result of spontaneous accretion. It had begun, simply enough, when a small Indian reservation decided to petition the authorities for permission to erect a gambling casino. At the same time a group of investors planning a new theme park finally reached agreement on its underlying concept. The land of James Fenimore Cooper provided exactly what they wanted—history, scenic surroundings, larger-than-life characters. The two forces, encountering each other in Albany, naturally fell into alliance. But the fat was really put into the fire by an entrepreneur dreaming of the world's largest shopping center. Through some weird process of divination he spied a correlation between acquiring consumer goods and touring the land of Natty Bumppo.

After that things simply snowballed out of control. Two hotel chains scrapped their modest plans in favor of full-blown resorts. Fans of the nearby Baseball Hall of Fame proposed a sports facility housing a Triple-A team. Before they could get to their drawing boards, representatives of Culture surfaced, suggesting a multi-purpose arena complete with a summer-stock company. Soon gourmet restaurants, first-run cinemas and art galleries were swelling the tide.

In view of the funding required, John Thatcher was not surprised to find the plane ferrying him to the gala opening filled with familiar faces. At the front of the cabin, the Chase Manhattan was chatting amiably with Manny Hanover. Behind them, brokerage houses spoke to investment bankers. But, as bad luck would have it, his own seatmate was cantankerous old Bartlett Sims.

"Damned piece of foolishness!" Having corralled his victim early, Sims was well-launched into his usual denunciation. "People don't need these frills for a vacation. I always sent my wife and children to the beach and they never objected."

Thatcher could readily believe it. The only mystery was how Waymark & Sims ever managed to invest in anything, given their senior partner's blanket disapproval of the post-war world.

"At least they have good weather for their opening," Thatcher remarked after a solid half hour of doomsday predictions.

Sims cast a disenchanted gaze at the clear blue sky.

"Probably broil everybody alive."

Enough is enough. Thatcher's presence was a salute to the Sloan's muscular endorsement of the shopping center. But after determining that this would be his companion's first stop, he decided to defer his own inspection until after a luncheon engagement with Charlie Trinkam.

"Then this is where we part," he said firmly as soon as they were debouched at the entrance.

With several hours in hand he headed into the theme park and was soon watching, with rapt absorption, the hand-fashioning of a bow and its complement of brightly feathered arrows. Then the craftsman, to prove the quality of his work, plunked an arrow dead into the bull's-eye of a distant target.

"Wonderful," cried the woman next to Thatcher.

"Yes, indeed," he agreed, joining in the spontaneous applause that was not so much tribute to marksmanship as to a perfectly rounded experience.

After that he strolled to the dock, from which boats were setting forth to visit the sites of famous Cooper scenes. Claiming the last seat in a giant war canoe, he inserted himself amidst two family parties. As their vessel emerged from the inlet and swung around a promontory into the wide waters of the lake, the festive sights and sounds on shore were left behind. The commentary began with the floating house from *The Deerslayer* and even the children became spellbound by tales of battle and siege, of silent flights and self-sacrificing diversions. With a grunt of satisfaction Thatcher leaned back and closed his eyes. How wise of the promoters to reject motorized transport! Basking in the sunshine, he could hear the rhythmic sweep of paddles, the wind rustling in the trees of nearby landfalls, the call of birds overhead. He could almost imagine himself in the Finger Lakes of Cooper's saga. By the end of their tour Thatcher was conceitedly proud of having discovered the perfect antidote to a commercial carnival.

But as he disembarked he saw that he was not alone in this superior choice. Fresh from his own canoe, Theo Benda was standing at a stall, buying audiotapes of the "Leatherstocking Tales."

"Hello, Thatcher," he said placidly. "I suppose over here you read these books as children, but I never have. They'll be great for commuting."

For years Thatcher had realized that his commitment to New York's subways and taxis debarred him from a great American experience. It seemed he was in danger of missing a literary phenomenon as well. The pace of nineteenth-century fiction, too slow for most modern purposes, was ideally suited to traffic jams. If the congestion became any worse, Sir Walter Scott would be staging an unlikely comeback.

"I'm planning to reread *The Last of the Mohicans* myself," he said, hastening to keep abreast. "But what are you doing up here anyway?"

The Mohawk Crossing theme park was strictly teetotal, Benda informed him, but its owners had agreed to sell Quax.

"Then today is a triumph for you on every front," Thatcher reasoned. "Elmer Rugby managed to beat out McDonald's and Burger King."

"I know. He was at the ribbon cutting this morning with someone from the Sloan. Claudia and I got sucked into the ceremony too. But now, while she's doing the pretty with management, I'm free for a couple of hours."

"Then why not join us for lunch? I'm due to pick up Charlie Trinkam."

"Fine," said Benda, falling into step and accompanying Thatcher to the Sports Arena, where Charlie Trinkam was discovered reading the announcement of forthcoming events.

"You've got to hand it to them. They sure know how to mix and match," he announced. "Tonight its *The Mikado*, tomorrow a rock concert, and then a production of *Who's Afraid of Virginia Woolf?*"

"Something for everyone," Thatcher agreed, beginning to realize that his silent canoe had been part of a larger design. Changes of pace were available everywhere, from gambling to golf courses, from shopping to 'Titwillow' under the stars. "But why are we meeting here?"

"There's a French restaurant a block further along, but I wanted you to see something," said Charlie with a wave across the street at a large, gleaming Rugby's. "How's that for location?"

Still expanding on Elmer's horse sense, Charlie led them to L'Aiglon, where the lounge was crowded with patrons waiting for the hostess to seat them.

"Isn't that the guy from NOBBY?" asked Benda in an undertone. "Christ, do you think they're planning trouble here? They can't be that dumb."

"And if they were, they couldn't get a congressman to eat with them," Thatcher began as Harry Hull sighted their party and edged forward with a cheerful greeting.

Sean Cushing, unwillingly trailing in his wake, was swift to disavow any threat.

"I'm just here as an observer," he blurted, then added, "Actually Iona was the one supposed to come."

This practically forced everybody to inquire about Mrs. Perez's well-being.

"She's getting out of the hospital tomorrow. The only injury is to her arm, but she was badly shaken up."

Hull meanwhile had identified Charlie Trinkam. "You're Rugby's banker, aren't you? I was just asking Sean if there's been any progress on that settlement."

"Elmer's playing his cards close to his chest on this one," Charlie replied. "He did say something about coming up with a proposal he wants to lay out."

"Well, if he wants to suggest something, he's got to tell us what it is," Cushing grumbled.

Charlie was a big believer in tit for tat. "He thinks he should wait until Iona Perez is on her feet," he said reproachfully as the harried hostess came swimming to Hull's side.

"Table for five," she said in a voice that brooked no argument, then swung around and headed briskly for the dining room.

Hull's mouth was half open to protest when he was overridden by Charlie Trinkam, already following the hostess.

"You don't mind if we piggyback on your reservation, do you, Hull?" he asked over his shoulder.

With little choice left, the congressman urged the others along, but as soon as they were seated, he apologized.

"Sorry about this," he said, more to Theo Benda than to Cushing. "I didn't mean to force Kichsel and NOBBY to break bread together."

From behind his enormous menu, Benda was amiable. "Why not? Besides, I'm as nosy as the next guy. This gives me a chance to find out why burglars are ransacking NOBBY in the dead of night."

A reluctant chuckle escaped Hull. "At least you're up front about it. I'm curious too. That's why I was glad to run into you, Sean."

"Yeah, Cushing. What the hell is going on at your place? Dealing in a little Russian uranium on the side?" Charlie asked jovially.

"There's nothing going on at NOBBY!"

Cushing stopped abruptly. To Thatcher the young man looked as if he had been losing weight steadily since Madeleine Underwood's murder. Today his face was beakier than ever.

"Well, something must be up for this guy to break in and attack your director," Charlie said as the voice of common sense.

"It's nothing mysterious," Cushing retorted. "They're pretty sure he was after Madeleine's last tape. He didn't realize that the cops already have it."

For a moment there was a dead silence. Then Harry Hull, caught with a water glass to his lips, sputtered, "Last tape?" before retreating into a spasm of coughing.

Sean grudgingly elaborated. "After the adjournment Madeleine ducked into the office to dictate a tape. And there's no point in looking at me that way. The cops grabbed it before we could play it."

"But that could be a real treasure trove." Charlie was enthusiastic. "She was burned up enough to tell all."

"And she claimed she knew everyone's personal dirt," Theo Benda chimed in.

Thatcher was remembering Madeleine Underwood's loquacity. "I'll wager that, even if you didn't hear the tape, she spoke about it to someone in the office," he said invitingly.

"She did tell one of the girls that she was calling a press conference as an alternative platform."

Unlike the others, Harry Hull had been thinking instead of giving instant tongue. Now he shook his head. "Look, if she laid it out, chapter and verse, for the cops, they'd be all over someone. It stands to reason she wasn't specific. I mean, I haven't heard anything. Have any of you?"

Thatcher cleared his throat discreetly. "You did say that Moore was unable to come, didn't you?" he asked Benda.

"The cops have been after Alec ever since his alibi for the murder blew up. This is just the same old thing," Benda replied.

"Nothing's changed at all," Cushing insisted.

"Oh, I wouldn't say that," Thatcher said reflectively. "If everybody at NOBBY knew the tape was already gone, then presumably suspicion has shifted elsewhere."

Charlie beamed at Sean. "So now you people are on easy street."

"Like hell!" Throughout the discussion Sean Cushing had been crumbling a bread stick. Now he irritably broke off the last piece. "You think it's fun having a bunch of police auditors poking into every corner and asking a lot of damn-fool questions? When they don't understand how I had to operate?"

It was Cushing's formal opponent who produced a gust of sympathy. "God, I'd hate that," Theo Benda confessed. "I'm not crazy about having the outside accountants in for the annual report."

Within minutes the two financial men were united by fellow feeling. Corporate accounts are called books for a very good reason. Like all books they tell a story, and their authors do not appreciate ham-handed, literal-minded intruders. When Sean Cushing unbent enough to describe, in tones of burning resentment, some of the methods he had been forced to justify, Benda immediately matched him with some outlandish requirement imposed by his own auditors.

As the technicalities mounted, Harry Hull's attention strayed. "If Mrs. Perez is going to be back in harness, I may stop off in New York and see what's going on," he said. "Leon Rossi would appreciate it and I hate to make this trip just for five minutes on a platform."

"I thought this was a long way from your beat," Thatcher commented.

Hull was rueful. "The developers are due for a federal commendation on their energy-efficiency program, and no one else wanted to come. As I'm in everybody's black book at the moment, I thought I'd score a few brownie points. All it entails is handing over a plaque and saying a few words."

"You boys can do that sort of thing in your sleep," Charlie reminded him.

"Yes, but only the second-termers can do it without being conscious at all."

By the time the conversation once again became general, Sean Cushing had finally relaxed. Pushing aside the remains of his poached salmon, he turned to the congressman.

"Say, I've been meaning to ask you. You remember that call-in program in Pennsylvania that you got Madeleine on? When she came back she said it went great. But since seeing her at the hearings I've been wondering if she fouled that one up too."

"It sure wasn't a triumph. The host had to cut her off at the pass," Hull said frankly. "But you can't really blame her. These call-in shows are unpredictable and people come up with the damnedest things. I remember when I was in the state legislature . . ."

The young Harry Hull had come primed to discuss cuts in athletic budgets for high schools and ended up arguing about the Texas Rangers' need for a new starting pitcher. This leisurely anecdote took them through the remains of their coffee and, with the arrival of the check, to the need to pursue their various responsibilities.

Charlie Trinkam was not only accompanying Thatcher on a tour of the shopping complex, he was acting as guide.

"Elmer went through it last night and he says most of it is what you'd expect—Gucci, Hermès, Burberry. But the place we shouldn't miss is the Native American Hall."

"They were selling souvenirs at Mohawk Crossing and I've already been there," Thatcher protested.

"This is something different."

The hall was certainly impressive. The decor was in muted tans and grays, the greenery was thick with cacti and sagebrush, the sunken seating areas boasted rustic benches set in sand, the boutiques nestled inside adobe walls. Overhead, the ceiling soared to a lofty glass roof. There was no way the profusion of upscale merchandise could be confused with gimcrack souvenirs. Expensive rugs, handsome blankets, intricate baskets, pottery, leatherwork, jewelry—all could be classed as works of art.

"And they haven't restricted themselves to the Iroquois Nations, have they?" observed Thatcher as he noticed that the well-heeled customer, unintimidated by transport difficulties, could buy a towering totem pole from the Northwest, a full-size tepee from the Plains or a birchbark canoe from Maine.

"They plan to make this a single entrepôt for the quality stuff from the whole country."

And their tactics were working with at least one buyer. When Thatcher led the way into a promising blanket shop, he found Claudia Fentiman in her element. She was inspecting two offerings with critical assistance from Elmer Rugby.

"Aren't they beautiful?" she cried, inviting admiration. "And just what I need to hang from the balcony over my living room."

"You couldn't do better than buy here," Elmer said gravely. "Both of them beat anything I've seen in New Mexico, but if I were you, this is the one I'd go for."

She accepted his counsel, and after arranging for delivery, agreed to join the others as they continued through the hall.

"Let's hope we can avoid Roger Vandermeer," she said. "He's doing the PR work for one of the resorts and an hour ago he tried to grill me about that settlement with NOBBY. I told him it was nobody's business but yours, Elmer."

Rugby, whose good opinion of Claudia seemed to increase with every encounter, beamed at her.

"I wish you could tell your boss the same thing. I'm sick and tired of his calls. Kichsel," he explained to Charlie sarcastically, "thinks it's my duty to bankrupt NOBBY. I keep telling him it's my duty to get something out of this for my chain."

In an instant Claudia was transformed from careful shopper to irritated company employee.

"Dean should stick to minding the store," she said impatiently. "He just can't leave anything alone. He's not only nagging you, he's driving Alec into a nervous breakdown."

"Moore is feeling the pressure?" Thatcher asked cautiously.

"He's going completely to pieces. And it doesn't help that he's told the police he was bar-hopping during that break-in."

Charlie was openly derisive. "Paul Jackson is right. Your man would do better to keep his mouth shut."

"It's probably true," she countered. "I myself can testify that he had a king-size hangover the next morning."

"And all this because of some dark, personal secret? That's some secret."

"Exactly. You'd think Dean would realize that, if Alec won't tell the police, he's certainly not going to open up to us," she said, reverting to her grievance. "But no. He just goes on trying to pressure Alec. So Alec becomes half-hysterical, and when Theo finally produces some sensible advice, he just makes things worse. I can't tell you how glad I was to get away for the day."

"That's some happy ship you've got there," Charlie snorted.

Elmer Rugby was more helpful. "Tell you what, Claudia. Why don't you take the morning flight back and stay to do the casino with me tonight? I've been meaning to give it a look."

"Tut, tut," Charlie chided. "Back to your bad old ways, Elmer?"

"Not on your life. Once I started gambling my whole future on Rugby's, the blackjack table became pretty flat. I'm just curious."

Claudia chuckled. "It sounds great to me. I'd love to come."

With harmony restored, Thatcher and Trinkam peeled off for their obligatory inspection of other mall areas. Charlie, however, was unusually silent during the first few minutes of their parade past designer goods. When he finally emerged from his reverie he was not thinking about their most recent companions.

"Theo Benda is an interesting guy. That gruff shirt-sleeved style of his hides a lot. Did you notice how uptight Cushing was with me and Hull? But Benda had the kid eating out of his hand without any trouble."

"A very adroit performance, I thought."

"Yeah, but then Claudia Fentiman tells us that, when things are rocky between Moore and Kichsel, somehow Theo Benda just makes a bad situation worse."

"So either his conciliatory skills don't work in the office," Thatcher said punctiliously, "or he isn't deploying them."

Again Charlie approached on a tangent. "Benda's been in the brewery business all his life, and according to George Lancer, was everybody's pick for Kichsel's next CEO. Then Alec Moore comes sashaying along and within two years wants to muscle Benda out. If anybody pulled that on me, I'd let him stew in his own juice."

Thatcher went further.

"Or possibly," he suggested, "even turn up the heat?"

21. Under the Influence

THE GROWTH OF ANXIETY is a familiar phenomenon to police interrogators. Inspector Reardon had seen hardened criminals progress from arrogance to blubbering terror, wife murderers from simulated grief to shocked foreboding, youthful gang members from macho confidence to tearful cries for their mothers. Alexander Moore's emotional course should have followed a well-charted path. Initially he had been unconcerned. The first dents in his alibi for Madeleine Underwood's murder had produced only stubborn stonewalling. With the break-in at NOBBY, mounting tension had begun taking its toll. By now, with a whole night for an active mind to squirrel frenziedly from one fear to another, he should have hit bottom and become a mass of exposed nerve endings screaming for relief. It was at moments like this that confessions were often forthcoming.

As soon as Moore entered the office Reardon knew that something had gone amiss. True, the assumption of superiority and the air of impregnable confidence had vanished. But so had the incipient twitching and the brittle hostility. Alec slumped in the chair facing the desk, totally motionless, his hands hanging from limp wrists, his rib cage collapsed onto his hips. He looked as if he had not only lost all hope, but half his skeletal structure as well.

"This time we're covering everything," Reardon began menacingly. "Underwood's threat to expose you, her murder, the break-in."

"Why not?"

It was more a sigh than a verbal comment. Alec Moore had hit bottom all right, but not in any form anticipated by Reardon. At first the inspector cursed his timing. Had he missed the critical moment? Had the delay been a mistake?

The expert in Reardon knew better. This dull animal acceptance was undeniably one way of relieving pressure. But it only surfaced with the born losers. The clever successful types didn't go this route, not when it meant admitting defeat by a dumb cop.

"Let's get one thing straight, Moore. You're in deep trouble. And," continued Reardon, punching a button sure to work, "you thought you were so smart."

"Smart?" Moore repeated tentatively, as if he had never heard the word before. "What does that have to do with anything?"

"It means you were too stupid to clean the phone right. You left a fingerprint, something a fourteen-year-old punk wouldn't do."

The gibe made no impression.

"I didn't clean the phone. I used it before I left the hearings."

"Oh, sure. You made a call to someone but you can't tell us to who. Then you went off for two hours but you can't tell us where. You're wide open."

Moore's gaze had drifted away from the inspector and seemed fixed on some distant prospect beyond the grimy window.

"But there's one easy explanation," Reardon went on, trying to wrench back Moore's attention by brute force. "You called Underwood and she hustled back early to meet you. Hell, she could even have taped your call, which is why you had to break into NOBBY."

Slowly the gaze refocused.

"Why would anyone want to talk to Madeleine Underwood?" Moore asked blankly. "She wasn't important."

"So I suppose it's all just a big coincidence. She threatens you, she gets knocked off, her office is rifled for tapes."

"What does any of it matter? Some things just happen."

"Like hell they do." Then, abandoning shock tactics, Reardon became persuasive. "Why don't you try doing yourself some good? If you told us who you called, if you had some verification of the time, that would take the heat off."

"No."

Moore did not even have the energy for a physical display of resistance. There was no shaking head, no set jaw, no clenched lips—only the same slack inertia.

Once again Reardon changed tactics. Deliberately he prolonged the silence, suggesting that he and Moore were joined on some dreamy voyage through outer space. Then he suddenly barked:

"What did she have on you that she was ready to spill?"

He had hoped to jerk their exchange into a faster tempo but once again there was that slow, laborious reply, as if Moore were internally translating a foreign language.

"I'm sorry but I won't tell you that."

My God, now the guy was even turning polite. For one dizzy moment Reardon thought he understood this strange unresponsiveness. Moore had stuffed himself to the gills with downers. But a sharp inspection was enough to dispel this theory. The eyes were clear, the pupils normal, the respiration well above tranquilizer pace. With rising exasperation the inspector acknowledged that Alec Moore had simply taken up residence on another planet. Maybe this was some new form of yoga.

"Look, Moore, I've got motive and opportunity for you, and everybody had means. You're right at the top of the list, you're our number-one suspect."

"I can't help that," Moore said apathetically. "I can't help anything."

If changing the tempo was impossible, then perhaps changing the subject would do some good.

"I told you to think about that bar crawl you claim you took."

"That's right. You did."

Trying to spark some emotion—any emotion—Reardon reverted to his harsh, demanding tone. "So? What have you come up with? This time?"

Almost to his surprise, he did not receive another flat negative.

"I don't remember any names. But after I left the hotel I went someplace a couple of blocks south that had a bright-green awning."

Moore's subsequent recollections were equally vague. All his wanderings had been on foot. At one point he had become entangled with an unusually large group leaving a restaurant.

"A party, I guess," Alec said indifferently. "But they were talking German and they were all over the sidewalk. I was heading for the bar just past them, a place with red stools." Then he actually frowned in concentration, as if he were listening to some inner ear. "There was a guy with a guitar making like Conway Twitty."

Everything else was just as fragmentary, a confused jumble of colors and sounds and people.

"Green awnings and red stools are a dime a dozen in that neighborhood. I suppose all these places were so crowded they didn't notice you."

"I don't see why they should."

Again and again Reardon tried to smash through that dank cocoon without success. The session lasted for an hour and a half, and by its conclusion Reardon himself was a good deal closer to twitching than Alec Moore.

"I'm done with you for now," he finally snapped.

And still the man remained huddled in his chair, as if conserving his strength for some ordeal to which police inspectors were irrelevant.

"YOU CAN GO!"

As soon as Moore finally shuffled out, Reardon exploded.

"I don't understand it," he burst out to Dave. "He would have sat here all day without complaining. He just doesn't seem to care."

Dave was having troubles of his own trying to collate reports flowing in from his men in the field.

"It seems to be working," he said unsympathetically. "You didn't get anything out of Moore."

"But it's not natural."

"What's natural with a geek like that? Maybe he's just paralyzed by the idea of jail. Anyway, things are narrowing down. The audit's done and the accountant's waiting outside."

"DAMN," REARDON WAS saying ungratefully five minutes later.

"If that's the way you feel about it, I'm sorry," the accountant chirped. "But facts are facts. Besides, with everything hunky-dory, you've got one suspect less."

"I know. The trouble is that embezzlement was the only solid motive at NOBBY big enough to explain a killing. Cushing might have clobbered Underwood to stay out of prison."

The newspapers had not been far behind the police in uncovering Madeleine Underwood's combativeness.

"I thought she went to the mat with everybody in sight."

"Yeah, but she was the only one who got really excited about it. She was involved with a lot of big institutions who could shrug her off. So we're left with a personal motive, and without leads, that could mean anybody or anything."

The accountant cocked his head intelligently, then decided on an oblique approach. "Everything was in turmoil over at NOBBY while my boys were ransacking the place. The people on the board were rushing in and out, the staff was gabbing its head off. And one thing came through loud and clear. The governors kept saying they were lucky to have Iona Perez available during the crisis."

He fell silent, as if he had said everything important.

"Now wait a minute. The crisis didn't make any difference to her availability. She was there all along."

"And doing most of the work," the accountant agreed. "But I'm not sure Perez would even have been considered if the board hadn't had to act fast. She was a volunteer and you know how things work. If the governors had forced Underwood to resign, they would have had a month or so to decide on a replacement. There are people making fat careers in non-profit outfits. That's what the Cushing kid is planning. The normal procedure would have been to look for a professional, particularly after they'd just been burned because Underwood was so amateurish."

Reardon had never considered this possibility. To him NOBBY was right up there with the PTA or a local bowling league, something that could inspire people to gather together for an occasional evening. He was ready to admit that Iona Perez believed in the cause and felt it was being imperiled by Madeleine Underwood. But would she kill to secure leadership of NOBBY?

"All because she doesn't want Quax sold in supermarkets?" he exclaimed incredulously. "She'd have to be crazy."

"Maybe that's not all. I admit I'm biased in favor of dollars and cents, but she's gone from making nothing to making a damn good salary. And she negotiated for it, knowing the board had no choice."

No one knew better than Reardon that some people murder for ridiculously insignificant reasons. Usually, however, they were people who accepted violence as part of their daily pattern.

"Besides," he continued his objections aloud, "Perez is the one who got hurt in the break-in. Are you suggesting that she staged the whole thing and accidentally did too much damage to herself?"

But the auditor refused to stray beyond the limits of his own province. "I'm not suggesting a damn thing," he replied jovially. "Just passing along my observations."

"Thanks a whole lot."

"By the way, I told Cushing we'd let him know our results. That okay with you?"

"Why not?" said Reardon, sounding almost as fatalistic as Alec Moore.

Incredulous or not, as soon as he was alone he riffled through the files searching for testimony about the quarrel in the ladies' room. Iona Perez's participation had been neither as coolly controlled nor as brief as she wanted the police to believe. She had sworn to see Madeleine Underwood removed by any means necessary. What if Iona had later returned to the committee room in all innocence? Feelings could have escalated during a second encounter.

Reardon shook his head impatiently. This was idle speculation that could be applied to every single suspect. The mountain of material on his desk established Madeleine Underwood as capable of whipping almost anybody into manic hostility. The miracle was that she had survived as long as she had. She seemed to have been incapable of recognizing that other people had interests just as valid and compelling as her own: that Iona Perez had not structured peaceful protests in order to land in jail; that Leon Rossi was not holding hearings simply to provide NOBBY with an audience; that the Ludlums were not in court to make legal history but to make money. That kind of blinkered vision could be inherently dangerous to its owner.

"What I need are some facts," he announced when Dave entered with the first tabulation of reports filtering in from the field.

"Well, you're not going to find any in here. Nobody heard any reference to calling a press conference."

"What about those clerks in the ladies' room? Have they been covered yet?"

"Yes, and the net result is zilch. They were all busy backstage after Rossi adjourned the hearings. Our basic problem is going to be time. If she decided on a press conference after the adjournment, we're talking about a very short interval. It's not as if she hung around for very long."

Reardon shook his head stubbornly. "But while she was there you can't tell me she was quiet. That doesn't sound like our Madeleine."

"Hell, no. A lot of people heard her claim the reason for the adjournment was to shut her up. And she said it wasn't going to work, she was going to blow things sky-high. She was big on windy threats but short on details."

"Which doesn't do us any good."

"Right!"

Having established his own claim to dissatisfaction, Dave tried to be more helpful. "The boys are still out there, running down the list. But if you ask me, the real possibility is the gang you're reserving for yourself. If she was naming names she'd do it with somebody who was part of the action, somebody who already knew the score."

"Yeah, but a passerby who overheard is more likely to tell us the truth."

"Particularly . . ."

Reardon spelled it out.

"Particularly if she was talking to the one who killed her."

WHEN ROGER VANDERMEER inflicted himself on his firm's New York office, the secretarial pool rotated responsibility for catering to his needs. It was widely felt that once a year was more than enough. In addition to being curt and demanding, he was impersonal to the point of offensiveness. To him secretaries were so many identical pieces of furniture, lacking all distinguishing characteristics. The same quality that made him blind to the rotational policy led him to assume that every clerical employee was as familiar with his clients, his contacts, his personal foibles as his permanent hand-maiden back in Washington.

Bernice Marsh knew it was going to be a bad day the minute Vandermeer came striding into the office, issuing directives and omitting any form of greeting.

"I've got some notes here from the Mohawk opening, but you'll have to get them typed up between other things. I'm already running late. First off, get ahold of Ted Pfeiffer and see if he's free for lunch. If he is, make a reservation for one o'clock at that place I always take him near his office. Then I'll need you to pull the feedback on the New England campaign for clean nuclear energy. Get out some kind of rough draft for me and I'll polish it off. But don't let me work past ten forty-five. I've got an eleven o'clock at Wade and Sullivan. Better confirm that with Paul . . ."

The beeping of the telephone came as a relief. After sedately announcing Mr. Cushing from NOBBY, Bernice was too busy scribbling notes to herself to pay attention to the conversation. Find out where Ted Pfeiffer worked. Then ask his secretary if she knew the restaurant this jackass was talking about. And maybe the last girl on the rotation had some idea about Paul's last name.

In the meantime Vandermeer, receiver in hand, had transformed himself from Simon Legree to lending officer.

"Hello, Sean. Any new developments?"

"You wanted to know the latest, Roger," Cushing reminded him happily. "Well, the police just called. Their audit is done and we're in the clear, right down to the last penny."

"That's good news."

For once Vandermeer was sincere. The financial contributions to NOBBY might be completely legal, but having them figure prominently in a murder investigation could be embarrassing to the Soft Drink Institute and to himself. These transactions always suffered in the light of day.

". . . no longer any doubt we have the resources to go national," Sean was continuing. "And with increased membership we can become more effective in our campaign."

"You don't know what your resources are until you settle with Rugby," Vandermeer said bluntly.

"Iona's working on that right now and she says things look good."

"As soon as you get something definite on that front or from the police I'd like to hear about it. Until then, as far as I'm concerned, everything's still up in the air."

Sean was too exhilarated by the auditor's report to be anything but optimistic.

"All right, so there's one problem left. It'll be taken care of before you know it."

Normally Roger Vandermeer would have brought the younger man to earth with a thud. One problem? What about an unresolved murder? What about that break-in? But this line to NOBBY was intended as a one-way street, providing a flow of information from Sean Cushing and absolutely nothing, not even speculation, from Roger Vandermeer.

"Let's keep in touch, shall we?" he said briskly.

He was then at liberty to return his attention to the unfortunate Bernice, piling on enough work to keep her long after closing time. And, she thought despairingly, it wasn't even ten o'clock.

As she half expected when she opened the door at ten forty-five to remind him, in a clear treble, of his appointment with Mr. Paul Thibault, he had a fresh list of instructions.

"You'd better come downstairs with me," he snapped. "I'll want some of this stuff ready by the time I come back."

He talked himself across the reception area and into the corridor. Even when the packed elevator received them, he continued in full spate, ignoring the other passengers and oblivious to the fact that Bernice's arms and notepad were so compacted she could barely insert a pen to write. Throughout their downward journey he continually flexed himself on his toes, as if grudging every second in transit. The lobby provided an opportunity to discharge his pent-up energy and he stalked toward the revolving doors with Bernice scuttling in his wake.

Outside, things were even worse. It was not actually raining, but there was a chilly mist being propelled along the narrow street by a breeze off the water. It was no inconvenience to Vandermeer, clad in a suit topped by a raincoat and waving his arms vigorously at every taxi in sight. Bernice, however, was wearing a thin blouse and debarred from physical exercise.

"There's a message from police headquarters on my desk," he said disapprovingly. "Call them back and say I can give their man fifteen minutes at four this afternoon. If that won't do it, then he'll have to be here first thing tomorrow so as not to interfere with my briefing on Mohawk Crossing. And nail them down. If it's tomorrow, I'll have to bump at least one appointment to the next day."

She stifled a groan. So much for her hope that this unscheduled stopover would be short and sweet. The man was going to hang around for days.

When he was finally stepping into a cab he turned for the most insulting command of all. There were many causes for resentment against Roger Vandermeer in the pool but none was felt so keenly as his sedulous courtship of other people's secretaries, at least when the other people were powerful and not readily available.

"I've been trying to get some time with the CEO at Bruckner Software. Find out his girl's name and order flowers for her. Get them to send my usual."

Like hell I will, Bernice thought mutinously. She would not waste precious time tracking down some elusive *them*. She'd send what she damn well pleased.

But even as she breathed in the fumes of the departing taxi, she was reminded of more pressing concerns.

"Brrr!" she said.

22. Case Price

UNLIKE ROGER VANDERMEER, Iona Perez was greeted at her New York office like a returning hero. There were flowers and balloons, there was a large banner reading: WELCOME BACK, IONA. Nothing was missing except the ticker-tape parade.

"It's wonderful to be back," she said, eyeing all these festive preparations. "And everything is so different now."

"If you're talking about the last time you were here, I should hope so," Peggy Roche exclaimed indignantly. "Nobody's going to attack you."

Instead of a darkened office with a masked intruder, there was daylight streaming through the windows and a bustling, cheerful staff. As the ultimate sign of normalcy there was even a serviceman trying to bring the balky copier to its senses. But these were not the thoughts absorbing Iona.

"I mean, NOBBY's future is so much brighter. It was all so discouraging then and I was really worried that the police would find we had some lunatic member."

While still in the hospital she had confided this fear to Peggy, who had instantly examined the file.

"And you didn't find anything," Iona continued happily. "Even Mrs. Gellert's letter was harmless."

"What's more, the audit is over and we've come out of it squeaky-clean," Sean pointed out.

Peggy expanded the list of triumphs. "And now we know we don't have to worry about any claims except Rugby's. I was amazed at how much insurance we have."

"You can thank Sean for that," Iona said promptly. "He's the one who managed to sneak the increased coverage past Madeleine."

"You get a lot of people milling around at a demonstration and there's always the possibility of an accident," he explained. "But there was no point trying to reason with Madeleine. She had her own ideas about what she was willing to spend money on."

Peggy had the grace to be embarrassed. "Jeremy told me what you said about its being the board's job to control our director, Sean. I want you to know that he realizes now you were perfectly right and I agree with him. We simply didn't understand how much difficulty her . . . her peculiarities . . . were causing."

"It made a lot of problems," Sean said forthrightly.

Iona listened with the air of a polite bystander. In fact, she had been dropping casual reminders, little by little, of the burdens under which she and Sean had labored. From her point of view it was all to the good if the director began her reign while the board struggled with guilty consciences.

Now, ignoring the previous exchange, she said to Sean, "I know the audit was a worry and an embarrassment to you. I'm so sorry you had all that trouble because of a few hasty words by Madeleine."

"I sure as hell didn't like it, but the results couldn't come at a better time. I don't know what you did to those guys in D.C., but at least now they're showing a little interest in us. I thought it would take months. You're a real miracle worker."

Iona failed to muffle a delighted giggle. "You wouldn't say that if you'd heard them in Washington. I think my big contribution was getting flattened and sent to the hospital. It made them all curious."

"It did a lot more than that, Iona," said Sean earnestly. "Don't you see? We all knew the police already had that tape. An outsider breaking in to get it means the killer wasn't someone from NOBBY."

Peggy Roche sucked in her breath sharply. Safe in her decorating office, she had been insulated from police suspicions. From that distance, even quarrels with the deceased has assumed a pedestrian character. Ready to accept the possibility of embezzlement, she had never pursued that thought to its logical conclusion.

"There was never any question of that," she said tartly. "Iona probably did a much better job in Washington than she realized, and having some of the other clouds roll away has helped, too."

"I really don't care why this is happening so long as things start clearing up. And look, we even have Mr. Rugby coming here," Iona diverted them.

"Now that one's a real surprise," Sean enthused. "Yesterday even his banker didn't know what he had in mind."

"When he called, Mr. Rugby said he'd come up with a wonderful idea," Iona chimed in.

Peggy did not share the prevailing euphoria. "That probably means a wonderful way for him to shaft us," she sniffed. "He thinks he has us over a barrel."

Deftly Iona refused to join issue. "Are you sure it doesn't bother you, Peggy, that we can't have Jeremy Pfizer here?"

"No, of course not. He's out of town, and anyway, Sean is just as capable of handling the financial end."

Sean ducked his head in silent acknowledgment. He was well aware that this was recognition of his confirmed probity. Before the audit results, there would have been no question of his participating in this meeting. Instead, he directed his companions' attention to considerations of turf.

"Whatever he's come up with, Rugby thinks he's got a strong hand. He didn't make any fuss about coming here."

Elmer Rugby was not only willing to negotiate on NOBBY territory, he did not even object to being outnumbered. When he arrived he was accompanied only by Charlie Trinkam.

"What I've got to suggest is really quite simple," he began. "But first I'd like to make sure that all the underbrush is cleared away. Pfizer said he was going to get a rundown of all the other claims and check out your coverage."

"He's done all that," Peggy reported. "And I want to make it clear that we're not trying to evade our responsibilities. What we're worried about is a protracted legal battle caused by unreasonable demands. I'm sure I don't have to elaborate again on the monumental legal costs we could both sustain."

"Nobody wants to make a bunch of lawyers rich," Elmer agreed placidly. "Instead I say we should put the money to better use."

His proposal was indeed simple. NOBBY would set up a fund to provide Theresa Dominguez with a college education.

Taken off guard, Peggy Roche did too much of her thinking out loud. "We could do that easily enough. She's already working for you part-time. If she goes on doing that . . ."

Elmer shattered this daydream ruthlessly. "Oh, no, I'm talking about sending her to any college she can get into and meeting her real expenses, not just tuition. That means travel, a proper allowance, provision for summer vacation. Sure, she can work for me anytime she wants, but she'll be flying a lot higher than that."

With a seventeen-year-old son and college catalogs flowing endlessly into the Roche home, Peggy knew exactly what he meant.

"You're talking about a blank check," she objected.

Expecting a chorus of support from her staff, she was taken aback when Iona, after exchanging one swift glance with Sean, set off in a different direction entirely.

"If we came to any agreement on this, there would have to be a joint announcement by NOBBY and Rugby's."

Under shaggy eyebrows Elmer was regarding her approvingly. "If we agree on terms, it's a possibility. But we have to do this right. Our little girl gets tip-top treatment."

"That would be the whole idea, wouldn't it?" she murmured.

To Peggy's dismay, Cushing came rattling in right behind Iona. "And NOBBY would be cleared of all liability whatsoever?"

Before Rugby could reply, Iona was once again in action. "Not just civil liability," she said firmly. "Those criminal charges would be dropped, too."

"Now wait just one minute here." Peggy finally managed to make herself heard. "These details don't matter. It's the basic idea we have to consider."

But, having sown dissension in the ranks of NOBBY, Elmer was far too sagacious to linger. Nodding to Charlie, who had been a fascinated observer, he rose.

"I can see you people will want to discuss this among yourselves. Why don't you do just that and get back to me?"

Peggy's indignation exploded the moment the visitors were gone.

"What got into the two of you? We're supposed to be negotiating. You do realize he's not talking about some subway college. With all the publicity that girl will get, she could go anywhere in the country."

"Don't you see? The more publicity, the better from our point of view," Iona exclaimed jubilantly. "You haven't been talking to our members, Peggy. They're not feeling very happy about NOBBY right now."

"I know that must be the case, it's inevitable. All we can hope for is that people forget the details of Madeleine's behavior as time goes on."

"That's just what I'm worried about. The details they'll forget but not the overriding bad taste. This is a golden opportunity to replace that with a good feeling, and it's cheap at the price."

In his new confidence Sean also had something to add. "This would erase an enormous contingent liability from our books—which is the first thing any potential donor is going to notice."

Peggy Roche had been braced for the usual protracted struggle over a settlement. The last thing she had expected was a pitched battle with her allies.

"Rugby's just doing this so he can get a lot of wonderful publicity while he's expanding into our area."

"Who cares?" Iona said grandly. "He's going to open restaurants in the Northeast no matter what. The point is that we can get on that bandwagon too."

"And start our own campaign to go national on a real high," Sean drove the point home.

Feeling beleaguered, Peggy cast around for additional objections. "What about the insurers? They're not going to get a tidal wave of publicity out of this."

Iona had the answer for that, too. "Why don't we ask them? Sean has an appointment there in half an hour. Go with him and find out. But if they've got a brain in their heads they'll love this. It beats punitive damages any day."

Having raised the issue herself, Peggy found it impossible to maintain lengthy resistance. Thirty minutes later, after a silent, thoughtful descent in the elevator, she was in the lobby with Sean Cushing.

"You know," she said at last, "I'm still shocked at Iona's attitude. Not so much her position, but the manner in which she pushes it. In some ways she's even more assertive than Madeleine."

Politely holding the door open, Sean was expressionless. "That's not so surprising. You see, Iona really believes in what she's doing."

THE CHILL BREEZES of yesterday had been banished by a warm front moving up the coast. Peggy and Sean emerged onto the street to find the city basking in soaring temperatures. But Congressman Harry Hull was in an airless cave at Rockefeller Center, bathed in the glow of fluorescent lighting. Lunch had been a soft pretzel snatched from a street vendor, followed by instant coffee courtesy of Municipal TV. And his discomforts did not stop there.

"Close your eyes," directed a small, dark gamine wielding a powder puff.

Hitherto, Hull had taken care of his public image himself, but preparing for cameras in Texas and Washington had toughened him. Within limits, he was willing to be appearance-enhanced. But this young woman did not inspire confidence and he had no intention of appearing, even before a local community-access audience, painted like a clown.

Not that it bothered Leon Rossi, who was now sporting makeup that made his eyes look like raisins in a bowl of dough.

"Just a light dusting," said Hull firmly.

"The lady knows what to do," said Rossi, automatically glad-handing anybody resembling a voter.

With a mulish expression, the makeup girl squinted at Hull's features, while Rossi looked on with bland disregard.

"There!" she said, whipping off the towel and whisking Hull's shoulders vigorously.

"Thanks!" he said just as briefly.

Rossi beamed at both of them. Then another fresh-faced member of the production team appeared to escort them to the green-room, where they were to await their call. Either they were today's lone performers or they were finishing the bill; they were the only occupants.

This Leon-and-Harry act, while hurriedly concocted, was designed along blitzkrieg lines. Breakfast with lay and clerical eminences from Catholic Charities of Manhattan had been followed by a tour of the Riverside Day Care Center. Once they finished with the Municipal Channel, they were booked to give a joint interview to *The New York Times*. Then, topping off the schedule, they were joining a large and distinguished reception—at Gracie Mansion—for a visiting delegation of Swedish parliamentarians and family advocates.

"Why?" Hull had demanded when Rossi sprang this grueling program on him. "I've spent too much time up here already. Hell, Leon, when I'm not in Washington, the place for me to press the flesh is back home."

Rossi removed a discreditable cigar from the corner of his mouth and studied it contemplatively.

"Opening shopping malls doesn't do much good anywhere," he pronounced.

Hull winced inwardly. True, according to all initial reports, murder in New York City was not a hot topic back in Texas. Neither were congressional hearings, whether they droned on or halted abruptly. Hull was beginning to believe that he could scrape through a bad patch without lasting damage. But, as Rossi reminded him, opening shopping malls was a feeble way to reestablish control over one's destiny.

"Okay," he retorted, "but I don't see how running around New York with you is such a great improvement."

"You won't be running around New York with me," said Rossi with weary patience. "You'll be covering up that black eye we took— you, me, the whole damned committee."

Hull's thoughts, naturally enough, turned to murder, Madeleine Underwood and Quax. But Rossi was more single-minded.

"They say we don't care about the welfare of little kids," he continued. "Well, we turn ourselves into the biggest boosters of low-cost day care this side of the Atlantic. That'll shut them up. We start here, in the media center of the world, then run with it. When you take a hit, Harry, you don't just stand there and bleed. You've got to turn it to an advantage."

Harry distrusted many of the nuggets of wisdom that circulated around Washington, but this one had appeal for him. Recapturing the high ground was worth special effort. Unfortunately he was beginning to notice he was no longer a tireless young campaigner. Too much turmoil, too many plans backfiring were taking their toll. So his compliment to the unflagging Rossi as they awaited their allotted time on camera was sincere.

Rossi mistook his meaning. "You've got to keep your eye on the ball," he said complacently. "Concentration—that's what it's all about."

In all honesty Hull doubted if he would ever rival Rossi's fearsome capacity to view everything under the sun in terms of votes. Putting politics on a par with life and death was beyond him. This weakness, if it could be so called, was not something he was prepared to discuss. So to avoid more dicta on the subject, he rose and idly inspected the surroundings.

The Municipal Channel was an essentially volunteer operation, with a heavy diet of public-service features padding its own production of council meetings, interviews with candidates and live performances by neighborhood groups. The staff was enthusiastic, if not highly skilled, and had managed somehow to acquire equipment worthy of NBC. Hull had yet to see the state-of-the-art cameras, but here, just outside the waiting area, stood a news service printer spilling white spools onto the floor—unread items from city, state, nation and world.

What the Commissioner of Parks had to say about playground rehabilitation did not rivet Hull. The next piece did.

". . . executive director Iona Perez announced outside auditors report no discrepancy or improprieties in NOBBY finances. The public, declared Perez, can have confidence that every penny donated to NOBBY has been spent properly. In addition, overhead costs . . ."

"Dammit, why didn't someone tell me?" muttered Hull.

"Tell you what?" asked Rossi, who had joined him.

The cornucopia of uncorrelated information that flows to editors and news directors had thrust NOBBY closer to the floor, so Hull could deflect this curiosity.

"Just some crazy new USDA ruling about grazing rights," he said casually.

If Rossi knew what grazing rights were, Hull would be surprised. On the other hand, Rossi's opinions about NOBBY were all too familiar. A ten-foot pole was not long enough.

Until very recently, Hull had had every reason to agree with him. But situations change, and wise men change with them. As soon as the Municipal Channel was behind him, Hull managed to snatch a few private moments on the phone. His first call was to NOBBY.

". . . glad I caught you," he said, pleasant and relaxed. "Say, congratulations on the audit . . . yeah, that's sure putting the bad news behind. Listen, I'm tied up for the rest of the day, but I was wondering if we could get together soon. Maybe sometime tomorrow . . . great."

With Sean Cushing, reestablishing contact was as easy as that. Only time would tell about Iona Perez.

23. Prosit!

T HAT EVENING DETECTIVE Francis Perenna plodded from bar
to bar in the East Fifties. Keeping a weather eye out for green
awnings and red stools, he had a sheaf of photographs that had
thus far failed to evoke any sign of recognition. Perenna, as the
newest recruit to Homicide, expected to be assigned the really
thankless tasks and this one certainly qualified. It had been an ex-
ceptionally warm day, a foretaste of heat waves to come, and now
the vast bulks of masonry were radiating their heat into the night
air. Running a finger around his sticky collar, Perenna entered his
ninth establishment without high hopes. But if he was inexperi-
enced in murder investigations, he was a longtime devotee of country music. No sooner was his foot over the threshold than he halted,
listening intently to the bearded guitarist in a cowboy hat. After a
moment's hesitation he reversed in his tracks to regain the sidewalk
and survey the immediate area. There, two doors down, was a restaurant.

Locating the maître d'hôtel was easy; questioning him was not.

"And do you know if you had a bunch of Germans in here that
night?" Perenna asked after specifying the date.

The maître d', who seemed to have eyes in the back of his head,
had swung around to hiss something in Spanish at a harried waiter.
The ensuing exchange featured an agitated justification from the
waiter terminated by a crisp command. Then, a minatory gaze still
fixed on his victim, the maître d' said over his shoulder:

"Are you talking about the Bradley party?"

"Bradley?" queried the detective.

Not until the luckless waiter had retreated to the kitchen did the maître d' explain. It had been a wedding reception and, as long as the bride's father was picking up the tab, it was firmly defined as a Bradley event. The groom, however, had been a German graduate student at Princeton.

"And some of his family and friends flew over from Munich— about fifteen of them. Mr. Bradley asked for our only German-speaking waiter to be assigned to the function room."

Suddenly the night was pleasantly balmy, the air clear and all personal discomfort a thing of the past. With the giddy feeling that he had won a trifecta, Perenna formulated his next question. But this time it was a delinquent busboy drawing the maître d' to a far corner.

It was several minutes before the detective could finally ask, "And do you remember when the wedding reception broke up?"

"Of course," was the contemptuous reply. A cleaning crew had been waiting in the wings, its meter ticking, ready to charge into the banquet room the minute the last guest cleared the door.

Now that luck was running in his favor, Perenna reentered the adjacent bar with his photographs already arranged in an inviting fan.

"AND YOU MEAN they recognized him?" Reardon asked unbelievingly the next morning.

"That's right."

"How solid was the identification?"

Perenna confined himself to facts. "The barkeep chose Alec Moore's picture without a blink."

"Was Moore drawing attention to himself?" demanded his suspicious superior.

"Nope. He was just slumped in a corner quietly getting blotto. The barkeep was worried enough about his condition to offer to get him a cab. But Moore said he was walking and managed to stagger out on his own."

Reardon nodded grudgingly. With families like the Ludlums starting lawsuits all over the place, bartenders these days were more aware of their obviously drunken customers.

"So what if Moore is clear for the break-in? Maybe he hired a pro," objected Dave.

"If anybody bought himself outside help, he'd make sure he had a gold-plated alibi. Not one like this. It was nine out of ten Perenna, here, wouldn't find the right place. What put you on to it anyway?"

"The guitarist."

Reardon, notoriously unmusical, blinked. "My God, what did he sound like?"

Before their eyes Francis Perenna, diffident novice, became the voice of authority.

"An incredibly bad Conway Twitty."

Waving Perenna irritably out the door, Reardon scowled.

"A music critic, yet."

"The whole thing is too pat. It could be a put-up job."

Reardon examined his assistant curiously. "Why are you so hell-bent on Moore?"

The flow of frustration boiled over. "Because whenever we come near him, everything goes haywire. First we find a clear print on the phone and bust his story about the library. That should have been the beginning of the end. But, instead of coming up with something we can punch holes in, he decides to keep his mouth shut. Then, when you really start putting on the pressure, he falls into a trance. Now this one-in-a-million chance about the bar pays off. It's all so weird that I was honest to God seriously wondering if he'd decided to protect someone."

"Don't you believe it! The most important person in Alec Moore's world is himself."

Dave agreed too much to mount an argument. Changing the subject, he said, "From your lousy mood I guess the witnesses you saw this morning didn't come up with anything."

"Not a damn thing. And I got to more of them than I expected. After I saw Rugby and the Kichsel people, I had some luck. It turned out that Vandermeer and a couple of the committee members are in town on business. But they all sing the same tune. They heard

Underwood explode when the adjournment was announced and that was it. The only one I've got left on my list is that banker who was with the Kichsel crowd."

"He's got less at stake than the others. Maybe he'll cough up more details."

"Fat chance. But since I'm due at his place in half an hour I'd better have a sandwich sent in. You want anything?"

Reardon whiled away the interval by remarking bitterly that it was just like Madeleine Underwood. On the one occasion in her life when her mouthings might have been of some value, she had chosen to become tight-lipped. He was rolling along nicely in his condemnation when a patrolman appeared with two brown bags.

"The corned beef is mine and the pastrami is his," Reardon directed, still intending to unleash one or two more choice comments.

But the patrolman had a message as well as food. Alexander Moore was outside, supported by Paul Jackson. They wanted a few minutes of the inspector's time.

Wordlessly the two men looked at each other.

"He's brought along some protection this time," Dave advanced cautiously. "You think he's trying for a deal?"

Reardon shook his head gloomily. "It won't be that simple. Probably he's dropped by to tell us he's entering a Trappist monastery. That way he'll never have to say another word for the rest of his life."

But the Alec Moore who came bounding through the doorway did not look ready to renounce the pleasures of this earth. He was brimming with energy, his face was split by a broad smile and he began proceedings by wringing Reardon's hand. To the rear Paul Jackson padded along, his dark eyes alight with mischievous appreciation. Before anybody else could utter a word, he raised a placatory hand and said,

"Relax, Inspector. My client has an alibi for the Underwood killing and wishes to apologize for any inconvenience his silence may have caused."

"Absolutely," burbled Moore, unable to contain his exuberance.

Reardon's disenchanted gaze swept over his guests. "There are alibis and then there are alibis," he breathed softly.

"This one is the Rock of Gibraltar. In fact," Jackson continued breezily, "it's a real doozy."

EVEN THOUGH INSPECTOR Reardon was a quarter of an hour late for his appointment at the Sloan, he had to wait a few minutes until the light on Miss Corsa's phone went out.

"That was Paul Jackson calling," Thatcher explained at once. "He tells me that Alec Moore has satisfactorily explained his movements at the time of Madeleine Underwood's murder."

Reardon had long since become hardened to the way news of every wrinkle in a major investigation speeds to the interested parties.

"His story involves six independent witnesses, so it should hold up," he admitted.

"That is welcome news for everyone at Kichsel," said Thatcher, tacitly conceding that it might be otherwise for a hard-pressed investigator.

Shrugging, Reardon got down to business with his standard query about a proposed press conference.

"No, I didn't hear anything of that sort," Thatcher replied. "I can see how it would be a logical development for Mrs. Underwood. If she was planning any startling revelation, she would have had to look for another forum. But, you know, I not only didn't hear any such reference, I doubt if there was one."

"How so?"

"She must have been the only person in the room who didn't realize that Rossi would stop the proceedings. There's no doubt she was totally taken aback by the adjournment. And if she instantly determined to take countermeasures, I assume that it would have been some time before she decided on their exact nature."

Reardon sighed. With no further prospects on his list, this sounded all too probable.

"And now that Moore's been cleared, I'm right back to the Quax mess."

"Fundamentally it's a simple battle," Thatcher said encouragingly. "Kichsel wants to invade the soft-drink market. Those in possession want to keep Kichsel out. That's a very commonplace situation."

"Yeah, except for one thing. In this fight we've got a crazy woman who doesn't follow the rules. Hell, she doesn't even know the rules, and she's been tearing the place apart for a couple of years."

"Oh, I wouldn't say that."

Reardon's eyebrows climbed so high they almost disappeared into his hairline. "You don't think trying to wreck Rugby's and having brawls with everyone in sight at a congressional hearing is crazy?"

Thatcher hastened to shore up his own reputation for sanity. "Certainly I do. My quarrel is with your implication that she'd been doing it for years. My very first reaction when I saw her whipping those protesters into a frenzy was that she'd undergone an astonishing change. I remember saying as much to Trinkam."

"You were at the riot?"

"Yes, I was there with Charlie Trinkam, a colleague of mine from the bank. He handles the funding for Rugby and he was curious when we spotted a disturbance in front of the restaurant."

"And you'd had dealings with Underwood before?"

"Not dealings. I only saw her three times in all. The first occasion was at the Ludlum trial, where Paul Jackson introduced me to her."

"And doesn't he get around?" Reardon murmured resentfully, still smarting from the great alibi clarification.

Thatcher suppressed a smile. "It is certainly one of his skills," he agreed. "But my point is that Madeleine Underwood, at the courthouse, was dealing with the opposing attorney, the press, and an unknown banker. And she was normalcy itself. Oh, she was clearly a rather silly woman basking in the limelight, but her approach was perfectly reasonable. She did not expect everyone to agree with her—far from it. Time and effort would be required to alert the public to a peril which she, in her superior wisdom, had already recognized. In fact, nothing would have disappointed her more than a universal agreement that made NOBBY's proselytizing unnecessary."

First Sean Cushing and Alec Moore had collapsed as suspects. Now the victim was painted in different colors. The inspector did not sound happy.

"You know, you're the first person who's claimed she was anything but a loony. Part of that, I suppose, is because I've been concentrating on the time immediately before her murder."

"And part could be due to the vested interest of the new management at NOBBY," Thatcher pointed out. "They're trying to restore their image by blaming everything on Madeleine Underwood. But even they have to fall back on a sudden transformation. As they keep telling Elmer Rugby, NOBBY mounted many protests without any physical confrontation."

Plucking his earlobe thoughtfully, Reardon said, "Maybe she did flake out. Is that so surprising? She'd made a lot of mistakes and she must have been wondering if she was up to the job."

"No. Charlie Trinkam has been seeing a good deal of the NOBBY people during their settlement negotiations, and according to them, Mrs. Underwood did not acknowledge any mistakes. Besides, the quality that woman projected at the Rugby riot and, indeed, at the hearings, was certainly not self-doubt."

Inspector Reardon was less impressed by Thatcher's argument than by the availability of a new source of information.

"This guy Trinkam seems to be picking up tidbits here and there. I'd better schedule an appointment with him."

It was easier to reach for the intercom than to explain Charlie's zest for the human comedy.

"Like Paul Jackson, he gets around," Thatcher murmured, his finger on the buzzer. "But if you want him, I'll see if he's free."

Upon learning that Trinkam would join them shortly, Reardon returned to the witness at hand.

"So what quality was she projecting?" he asked patiently.

Dutifully Thatcher closed his eyes and tried to summon his three sightings of Madeleine Underwood. It was as if scraps of film footage had been stored away waiting to be retrieved. There she was swimming from her limousine at the courthouse, a gracious suburban matron dressed for the occasion, confident and secure, even approaching playfulness with her suggestion that she would convert Paul Jackson. At Rugby's, of course, she had been operating on a much more dramatic level. Her voice had risen and fallen to accommodate off-stage noises; her gestures had discreetly underlined her message until the peroration, when she had flung her arms up in challenge. And finally came the hearings, where she had assumed a more compact form, buzzing around in her red suit like some stinging insect determined to draw blood.

"She was certainly combustible with everybody at the hearings," he muttered more to himself than to his guest.

"Not just them," Reardon corrected. "She took on Cushing because he accepted funding from the Soft Drink Institute and she was ready to throw out Perez."

But Thatcher was not listening. Letting his mind run free, he was presented again and again with the scene at Rugby's.

"I know what the major difference was. She wasn't enjoying herself anymore," he finally exclaimed. "At Rugby's she was appealing to the protesters to bar the doors primarily as a show of support in the face of nameless threats. If the woman at the courthouse had discovered something discreditable about Alec Moore she would have been smug and complacent. But at the hearings she wasn't. In fact, you could almost say there was a diffused paranoia about her accusations there. As if she herself were being threatened and was lashing out in self-defense. When I come to think of it, the change is very curious."

By the time Charlie Trinkam sauntered in five minutes later, Thatcher had almost as many questions for him as Inspector Reardon did. But, as usual, Charlie beat everybody to the punch.

"Something new on the Underwood murder?" he asked hopefully.

"Alec Moore has come up with an alibi," Thatcher relayed, "but Paul Jackson says the details are confidential."

Unabashed, Charlie immediately swiveled toward Reardon.

"That's what I say, too."

"My God, don't tell me he's the last flower of chivalry and he's protecting a lady's fair name," Charlie protested.

This innocent suggestion produced an astonishing result. The inspector engaged in some internal struggle for a full minute before the first strangled guffaw erupted.

"Not exactly," he managed to gasp in the midst of his spasms.

With Reardon temporarily out of commission, Thatcher sought confirmation of his own theory. "You've been seeing the people at

NOBBY, Charlie. Haven't they said anything about a sudden change in Mrs. Underwood?"

"They can barely talk about anything else. Peggy Roche called her at home on Sunday to wish her luck at the hearings and to discuss the Rugby demonstration starting the next day. Peggy swears that Underwood wasn't planning anything unusual. In fact, Madeleine was so excited about the hearings, she said she probably wouldn't have time for the protest but she was sure Iona Perez could handle everything."

Like Thatcher, Reardon saw the possibility for support of a hypothesis. "But then she fouled up. Don't they think that's what upset her? Maybe made her try for extra mileage out of something she was good at—whipping up her members?"

"Hell, no!" Charlie said genially. "She didn't think she was messing things up. Cushing says after her stint on the stand, she thought she'd done a first-class job."

"That's right," said Reardon in exasperated recollection. "Congressman Hull said the same thing. She was proud of her testimony and looking forward to more of it."

Thatcher had equipped himself with a notepad. "Let's get these times down and see exactly when she changed."

"Some of it is easy enough," said Reardon, tolerant of amateur enthusiasm. "On Monday she testified. After she split from Cushing she checked into a hotel around the corner."

"Unexpectedly?" asked Thatcher. "That might mean something."

"I don't think so. She explained to the desk clerk that she'd almost been late that morning because of a traffic jam. So she decided to stay in town until the hearings were over."

"And," caroled Charlie, "she didn't tell the people at NOBBY. That's one of the things that made Perez sore. After the riot nobody could find Underwood."

Thatcher frowned reproachfully. "We'll come to that, Charlie. Right now we're establishing a sequence."

"Well, she was still at the top of her form then," Reardon amplified. "When she ran into Congressman Hull, they had a drink together. She thought she should have a meeting with the chairman so she could tell him how to run the hearings."

"Still the same old Madeleine," Charlie said irrepressibly.

Reardon grinned in approval. He was finding Trinkam a welcome antidote to the ordinary run of witnesses.

"It gets better," he promised. "Hull took her up to his room to show her some report and listen to her idiot suggestions. When Roger Vandermeer turned up for an appointment, she had to be levered out of the place."

"I'll bet she did," Charlie agreed. "Peggy says Underwood hated the idea of anybody discussing the anti-Quax campaign when she wasn't there. At one point she tried to get the governors to tape their talks among themselves."

"How awkward for Hull and Vandermeer," Thatcher remarked. "They could scarcely tell her that their session was about containing the damage caused by her silliness on the stand."

This time it was Reardon sternly returning them to duty. "I thought you wanted to do this as a time sequence. She even left her briefcase in Hull's room so she could come back and pump him after Vandermeer left. Of course as soon as Hull saw who was at the door he said he was on his way out. But get this. The brush-off didn't bother her. Both Hull and the chambermaid in the hall agree that Underwood was still chipper as hell. Even while she ducked in to get her case she was telling Hull that they'd have to get together some other time. Unfortunately we lose her after that. All we know is that she didn't eat in the hotel. She could have met anybody that night."

"It must have been a wingdinger of a meeting," said Charlie, nodding in appreciation. "Because, bright and early on Tuesday morning, she raises Cain with Sean Cushing, then rushes off to start a riot."

At last Reardon was prepared to release new information. "Yeah, but she was still feeling her oats because after Rugby's she went to the law firm handling the Ludlum case. They were still reeling from Jackson's firecracker and none too pleased to see her."

"Ha!" Charlie snorted. "Just think how they would have felt if they'd known what was going on across town. Her people were being carted off to the hoosegow about then."

"They didn't find that out until after she'd left and calls started coming in from people trying to locate her. But they were annoyed enough anyhow. Seems she was shrugging off the case, saying it was just another betrayal."

Until now Charlie had been a neutral bystander, deriving what pleasure he could from the recital of Madeleine Underwood's antics. Now he announced his allegiance.

"In other words, she was making the same pitch as at Rugby's—all that business about dark forces ganging up on her."

Reardon was prepared to set out facts; he was not enthusiastic about character analysis. "She left the lawyers about a quarter to five and went back to her hotel. After she had dinner there at six-thirty we lose sight of her briefly. But we know she was in her room at nine o'clock when she called her son in California. That, incidentally, was the only charge for an outgoing call."

"And of course you've checked with the son," Thatcher said perfunctorily.

"Sure, but she just talked about some trip to the coast she was planning. Nothing about what she was up to that evening."

Thatcher dismissed not only the son, but the entire evening. "The more I think, the surer I am that the damage was done on Monday night."

"Why? She was still steamed on Wednesday. She turned up at the hearings ready to take on everybody in sight."

"Because the most important thing in the world to Madeleine Underwood was NOBBY. And it was on Tuesday morning that she reversed its central policy. Also, on that day, both at Rugby's and at the attorneys', she was seeing herself as the victim of some sort of conspiracy."

Reluctantly Reardon nodded. "I admit you've got a point. My boys have been going through all the junk stacked at NOBBY. It's useless as far as a murder motive goes, but one thing comes through loud and clear. Underwood was leading the fight against Quax and enjoying every minute of it."

Charlie had risen to drift behind Thatcher and peer at the notepad.

"Well, if John's right, look how things have narrowed down. All you have to do is find out what Underwood was doing on Monday night and who she was doing it with."

"That's not so easy. We've already tried getting at it from the other end, but it's no go. News about the courtroom boo-boo had been spreading and almost everybody was busy. Rossi had called a meeting of the committee members that didn't break up until after eleven. The soft-drink people were huddled with Vandermeer a couple of blocks away. And as for the Kichsel bunch . . ."

He allowed his voice to trail away and looked expectantly across the desk. With a start Thatcher realized that he was being asked for corroboration. "Good heavens, I'd forgotten. We were all, including Elmer Rugby, at Paul Jackson's victory celebration."

Reardon was now a monument to long-suffering patience. "With Cushing out on a date and Perez home with her family, you see where that leaves me. Madeleine Underwood simply stepped out into a city of nine million people and disappeared."

"Taxis?" Thatcher suggested without much hope.

"She didn't take one, at least not from the hotel. Face it, we may never know what she was doing."

But Charlie Trinkam, who had withdrawn again into a study of the notepad, now lifted his face with a broad grin.

"Dummies, both of you," he said amiably.

"What's that supposed to mean?" growled Reardon.

"You did say she checked into a hotel on the spur of the moment, didn't you? The woman had to go home to get some clothes."

And, swifter than conscious thought, Thatcher's mind produced the twin images of Madeleine in her summer dress at the riot and Madeleine in her pool of isolation after the adjournment was announced.

"Lord, of course! She was in red on Wednesday."

Faced with an avalanche of wardrobe detail, Reardon slowly nodded. "You're probably right. We'll check with the hotel. But she could have seen anybody in New Jersey."

"Not with all your witnesses tied up," Thatcher reminded him.

Reardon's face brightened. "And if she called anybody in New York, it will have been a long-distance call. I think I'll get busy on this."

* * *

"IT'S A GOOD THING you joined us, Charlie," Thatcher remarked as soon as Reardon left. "The woman's clothing was staring me in the face and I never thought of it."

But Charlie had recovered from his first flush of triumph. "Where does it really get us? We would have done better to have a psychiatrist sitting in here. The place is lousy with people having mood swings."

"But scarcely the kind that calls for deep analysis. Moore, for some reason, refused to explain his alibi. That made him enough of a murder suspect to worry him. When he could clear himself he was relieved. Cushing, suspected of embezzlement, remained edgy until he was proved innocent. Iona Perez was nervous at the beginning of her promotion and is now settling down."

"That's one way of describing these people," Charlie retorted. "Now here's another. Moore was verging on clinical depression and has swung into wild euphoria. If he knew all along he could clear himself, why go into a fugue? And the same holds true for Cushing. As for Perez, she isn't settling in, she's tanking over everybody. And then we come to the really batty one, Madeleine herself."

Thatcher was not going to fight this last illustration. "No one is claiming her last three days were an exercise in common sense."

"Oh, it started before then. She didn't have the sense to know when to be depressed. There she was, bombing all over the place, and instead of being down she was up."

He could have expanded this indictment but Thatcher, stiffening, suddenly snapped, "Repeat that!"

Obediently Charlie recited, "Instead of being down when things weren't going her way, she was up. Everyone at the hearings agreed she'd made a fool of herself, but she never noticed. She thought . . ."

He let his voice trail away when it became apparent that he had lost his audience. John Thatcher had once again seized his notepad and was staring at one line, transfixed. When he broke free from his reverie he produced a non sequitur.

"Everyone says that Madeleine Underwood behaved badly."

Charlie Trinkam was well established at the Sloan as an admirer of the opposite sex. But he was also a financial conservative. His broad tolerance did not extend to feminine disruption of standard business practices.

"The woman was a menace. She hires experienced lawyers and tries to second-guess them. She thinks a congressional chairman is her junior staff. She unleashes private detectives to dig up personal dirt. That's a woman who thinks she's so important the rules don't apply to her."

"The question is, just how badly would she behave?"

"She'd pull anything she could get away with and think she was perfectly justified."

Thatcher nodded, a grim smile creasing his face. "I think you've just solved a murder."

Charlie was piqued. "That would be more gratifying, John, if I knew what the hell you were talking about."

When Thatcher told him, however, Trinkam instantly transformed himself into a devil's advocate. The volley of objections he produced merely increased Thatcher's conviction. With every sentence another compelling vignette sprang to life in support of his theory. There was the committee staff outdoing each other in a recital of Madeleine Underwood's exorbitant demands, there was Peggy Roche ruefully confessing the shortcomings of NOBBY's director and there was, mercifully obscured, the final scene— Madeleine's body crumpled on a closet floor.

At the end of an hour's hard work, Charlie was convinced.

"It all fits," he finally acknowledged. "And it explains everything. But you do realize, John, that there's not a scintilla of proof?"

Exhausted by his logical exposition, Thatcher had slumped in his chair and was staring dreamily at the ceiling.

"Not yet," he said in a faraway voice. "That's the beauty of this, though. If I'm right, the police have their proof. If I'm wrong, they haven't made any waves. After all, we not only know where to look, but what to look for."

Charlie felt it was too early to rest on their laurels. Reaching out a hand, he pushed the desk phone closer to Thatcher.

"Then maybe, John," he said gently, "it's time to let Reardon in on this."

24. Chug-a-Lug

WITHIN TWENTY-FOUR hours the police had confirmed Thatcher's theory and it remained only to flush out the killer. Fortunately, the ideal occasion for misdirection was at hand.

The hoopla surrounding the joint announcement of the Rugby-NOBBY settlement would have turned Madeleine Underwood green with envy. Promised another appearance by Theresa Dominguez, a proven human-interest feature, the media was willing to turn out in force. And with this enticement Elmer Rugby had no difficulty securing the presence of a swarm of illustrious guests, all scenting an opportunity to make their views public. To extend the event as long as possible, a bar and refreshment table were waiting in the wings while the microphones had been arranged to accommodate three speakers—Elmer Rugby, Iona Perez and Theresa.

At first Iona had objected to this selection.

"You should be the one up there," she told Peggy Roche.

"Oh, no, you don't. As long as that girl is wearing a neck brace, we're going to show the world that NOBBY has taken its knocks, too."

So Elmer, flanked by two battle casualties, looked ruddier and healthier than ever. Making full use of his position as official host, he got his shots in first but he did so without straining anyone's patience. After briefly outlining the details of the college fund, he told the world that Rugby's was only too happy to waive its legal claims on behalf of its misused employee.

Iona Perez did not match his brevity. Reminding everybody of NOBBY's impeccable record prior to the riot, she produced the long-delayed *mea culpa* that should have been forthcoming that night.

". . . one grievous moment of misconduct on the part of our late director . . . deplored by us all . . . never to be repeated . . . willing to accept our responsibility to the unfortunate victims of this mishap."

Then, with a deep breath, she sounded the drums for the new NOBBY.

"Our first and foremost concern has always been the welfare of youth. Nothing could please us more than an agreement allowing us to make restitution in a form that promises long-term benefits to such a deserving young person."

Everybody was champing at the bit by the time she finished. Then, predictably, Theresa Dominguez and her mother stole the show. If they had been attractive at the hospital, they were irresistible in their moment of joy. Theresa stood revealed as the possessor of enormous shining dark eyes and Mrs. Dominguez, bowed by privation and toil, was incandescent with a glow that transcended all language barriers.

It was the stuff of which reporters dream, as Roger Vandermeer explained at length to Thatcher as soon as the official program was over.

"That's a smart move by Rugby, particularly when he's developing the Northeast market. The PR will be worth millions to him."

"And NOBBY isn't coming out of this badly either."

"Turning bad publicity into good publicity, that's a real trick," Vandermeer said sagely. "I didn't think they had it in them."

Unfortunately he felt impelled to repeat every syllable of his commendation when Peggy Roche appeared with Harry Hull in tow. Having her own reasons for keeping SDI sweet, she listened with every evidence of gratified interest.

"So you think we should keep in touch with her while she's in college in case there's a chance for additional publicity?"

"I'll bet Rugby will."

But Peggy, in spite of her apparent docility, was keeping an eye on the passing parade. As soon as Alec Moore and Claudia Fentiman came into view, she broke off her own remarks to hail them.

"We owe you a personal apology for Madeleine's conduct at the hearings. As for those private detectives, let me assure you that the board knew as little about that as we did about her plans for Rugby's."

"We could tell you had a real fruitcake on your hands," Alec responded cheerfully.

"You're right there. And what annoys me the most is that I called Madeleine at her home the night before the riot. If I'd known half of what she had in mind I could have stopped her in her tracks. But she didn't tell me a thing, she didn't even tell me she'd moved into a hotel. Instead she jabbered about the clothes that she was going to wear."

Claudia Fentiman handsomely remarked that knowing what was in Madeleine Underwood's mind had been beyond the capacity of any sane person. Alec Moore, however, choosing to ignore this exchange, explained that the basic conflict continued.

"We're selling Quax and you're trying to stop us," he said to Peggy, as if this had escaped her attention. "Sending the Dominguez girl to college doesn't make any difference. You may have scored a few points today, but so what?"

"Everybody knows that, Alec," Claudia said crisply. "But now is not the ideal moment to say so."

"I don't see why not. The facts are simple enough. Underwood never had any real ammunition because Quax is perfectly harmless. And now that NOBBY's backing off from violence, they're dead in the water."

And bestowing a sunny smile on the gathering, he drew Claudia off toward the refreshment area.

Moore, Thatcher reflected, was perfectly capable of alienating the press and, through them, the entire American consumer market. But his jab had found its mark.

"People don't forget, do they?" Peggy Roche lamented. "We'll be paying for Madeleine's last two days forever."

Automatically Vandermeer reverted to his role as her mentor.

"Look, there are always unexpected foul-ups. The name of the game is learning how to make a decent recovery."

217

"And that's what we expect to do," she replied, neatly modulating into her real theme. "I think you'll find that this wave of publicity is just what we need to make our national drive a success. With all the networks here, there will be coverage in . . ."

Over her shoulder Harry Hull exchanged a glance of fellow suffering with Thatcher and jerked his chin suggestively toward the door. Together the two men gently drifted away.

"I'll say one thing for that NOBBY bunch. They never give up," Hull grunted as soon as they were safely out of earshot. "She'll be handing Roger a hard sell for the next ten minutes."

"And she may well be successful."

For a moment Hull looked dubious, then: "I suppose you could be right. No matter what happens, Roger has to worry about selling soft drinks, so it may work with him. I doubt if it will with Leon, though. He's still gun-shy."

But to speak of Leon Rossi was to look for him. When Hull caught sight of the chairman surrounded by a mob of reporters, he hastily made his farewells and set off across the room.

Free at last of companions busily pursuing their own interests, Thatcher was able to make his way to the bar, where he found Elmer Rugby happily presiding over his guests.

"A very nice job, Elmer," Thatcher said warmly. "You not only got your big turnout, but the press is still here picking up quotes."

It seemed as if, in every corner of the room, someone was expressing public approval of the day's work. Unseen, but perfectly audible, Dean Kichsel was announcing his satisfaction in a deep, baying tone.

"Of course the Kichsel Brewery is pleased. We recognize that there is always room for the expression of differing sentiments. I have no quarrel with NOBBY's activities as long as they remain responsible and law-abiding. And no better purpose could be served by this settlement than by giving young Miss Dominguez a real chance at fulfilling her potential."

Closer to hand, Iona Perez was supplying a musical accompaniment.

"So happy that everything has worked out this way . . . membership really excited about the opportunity to perform such a valuable service . . . always glad to see one of our young people set-ting out on the right track."

But as she had been largely unavailable since the break-in, the press wanted more from her than views on the settlement. Soon she was describing her ordeal.

"It was too dark for anything except a general impression . . . yes, of course, I was terrified . . . think I'm lucky to have nothing worse than a broken wrist . . ."

Elmer, who insisted on parading around the room with a propri-etary air, was exultant when the largest group of reporters was dis-covered clustered around the Dominguez women.

"You don't think they could use a little support from you?" Thatcher asked.

"Just listen to her," was the reply. "That little girl doesn't need help from anybody."

And from the middle of the group came a breathless, excited voice.

"I don't know yet. There are so many colleges and I never thought I could go. So, you see, I never found out much about them."

Then, loud and clear, the voice expanded on a wave of enthusi-asm.

"But the guidance counselor at Rugby's has been advising me. She says my marks are good enough to apply anywhere. Even to Harvard and Stanford!"

Thatcher examined Elmer Rugby with new appreciation. "I didn't know you had guidance counselors."

Elmer was smug. "We hire a lot of inner-city kids who don't know which way is up. So we started the program in San Antonio, where there's a feeder college on public transport. Of course, usually the counselor concentrates on making them finish high school and maybe go on to a vocational course. Not many of them are like Theresa."

"It was still a good idea to tell her to push your program."

"Like hell," said a reproachful Rugby. "With some people you have to break your back explaining what you want. Theresa knows without your saying a word. And she understands in her bones the principle of giving good value."

"Her mother is no slouch either," remarked a new voice as Charlie Trinkam materialized from the throng. "I've just been listening to her explain, in broken English, that naturally they'll all miss Theresa. But Elena is such a good girl and she's going to take Theresa's place. That's the next daughter."

"I know," Elmer riposted. "She's starting work for us next month."

"Well, you're certainly playing this right," Charlie congratulated his client, "but you were damned lucky in your victim."

"Don't I know it. The busboy who was standing behind Theresa when the glass went is a real washout. We couldn't have done a thing with him. But this family is a find."

Elmer's fervor had made Charlie suspicious.

"Just how far ahead are you thinking?"

Elmer was as near smirking as was possible for him. "I haven't broken it to NOBBY, but Theresa intends to do pre-med."

While Charlie expostulated, Thatcher found himself wondering if even that was to be the end of it. Or was Elmer planning to work his way through the whole string of Mrs. Dominguez's offspring? This settlement, Thatcher decided, was unique. Theresa Dominguez might be the chief beneficiary on paper, but NOBBY and Elmer were almost as pleased with their lot. And how often does that happen?

But Elmer, even on a tide of well-being, had not forgotten other items on his list.

"Good, there's Cushing," he announced, indicating the NOBBY administrator making his way over to the congressional contingent. "I've been trying to get hold of him."

"Nine chances out of ten he's there to sell them on NOBBY," Charlie warned.

"I don't care what he does on the side, but first he's got business with me. The settlement is fine, but I want to see that money in the escrow account."

When one has invited the press, however, they have to take pride of place. Settling himself directly in front of Sean Cushing, Rugby was obliged to wait out Harry Hull's informal comments to the nation.

". . . heartening to see the real good that can be accomplished when confrontation gives way to negotiation. Miss Dominguez is not the only winner here today," he said, blithely ignoring the fact that, if such had been the case, there would have been no settlement. "Both parties to this agreement can be proud of what they have accomplished."

Every trade has its own standards.

"Good," said Leon Rossi as soon as the press had departed to find fodder elsewhere. "You managed to avoid mentioning NOBBY at all."

"Oh, come on," protested Cushing. "NOBBY's going to come out of this smelling like roses."

"It will as soon as we get all the details tied up," said Rugby, seizing his moment. "I still don't understand why we have to let two days pass before my accountants can get together with you."

A week ago Sean Cushing had been tensing at the sound of every accusatory voice but, like almost everybody else in the room, he was enjoying a new access of confidence. Feet spread, chest out, he had been examining the crowd benignly as Harry Hull delivered his set piece. Now he was almost indulgent.

"But I told you Madeleine's son has arranged the funeral for the day after tomorrow. It's way the hell out in New Jersey and we'll be tied up all day. There's no way I can duck, not with this big an affair. You might consider coming yourself."

Thatcher was amused to see Leon Rossi's eyebrows vigorously signaling to his younger colleague. Apparently this was going to be the one public funeral in the metropolitan area that would not be graced by the chairman's presence. He was probably busily inventing a prior commitment, but Elmer was more direct.

"Fat chance," he said stoutly. "All right, I'll give you Thursday, but what's wrong with tomorrow?"

"Bill Underwood doesn't have that much time and he wants to get Madeleine's house ready so they can auction off the contents. I said I'd go out there with him tomorrow and haul away the NOBBY stuff."

Rugby frowned in suspicion. "Mrs. Perez told me she was going to do that."

"I persuaded her not to," Sean said blandly. "Does she look in any condition to do heavy lifting? There'll probably be cartons of the stuff. But I can be with you bright and early on Friday."

Even Elmer could scarcely characterize two solid days with the bereaved as goldbricking. Grumbling, he yielded the point and was even capable of sardonic amusement when Sean immediately returned to the attack on Leon Rossi, assuring him that NOBBY's future obligations to Miss Dominguez would be met with maximum fanfare.

"You know it was that little Perez woman who saw the possibilities in this settlement right off the bat," Rugby told his companions as soon as they left the congressmen to their fate. "And she's done a fine job selling the rest of her bunch."

His good humor was further restored when he himself became the target of roving microphones with questions about Rugby's guidance counselors.

". . . in all metropolitan areas . . . minimum-wage jobs are no solution to the problem . . . teenagers present a special case, particularly if the job can be used to slot them into an ongoing education program . . ."

"God, Elmer will go on as long as anybody will listen to him," Charlie muttered in an undertone.

"And he doesn't need our help to do it," Thatcher replied, striding firmly off.

They were rewarded several moments later when they found Iona Perez exercising her persuasive talents on an unlikely subject.

"Eleven o'clock at the Presbyterian church," she was saying as Theo Benda scribbled in his appointment book. "The cemetery is some distance away, but we'll have plenty of extra cars on tap."

Charlie, incredulous, moved forward as soon as she sped off on her recruitment rounds.

"Are you really going to trek all the way out there for this shindig?"

"It might not be a bad idea," Benda said soberly. "We came here today to spread sweetness and light, but it isn't easy with Alec behaving like a horse's ass."

"I heard him briefly myself," Thatcher observed absently, registering Benda's first open criticism of Quax's division manager. Of course the change in approach was understandable. As long as Alec

Moore was a police target, Kichsel itself was threatened, and solidarity was the name of the game. Now that those clouds had dissipated, frankness was permissible.

Charlie had swiveled to examine the crowd. "Moore doesn't seem to be in action anymore."

"Claudia took him away. She's probably explaining to him somewhere that it isn't a good idea to rain on your customer's parade."

"Then she did the right thing," Charlie said.

"I told her to. Alec doesn't realize that we're all walking on tiptoe today. It was smart of Rugby to provide all this dilution," Benda continued, waving at the surrounding crowd, "but it doesn't alter the situation. Camouflage or not, he's brought together every single person concerned with Madeleine Underwood's murder."

Nodding silently, neither Thatcher nor Charlie felt obliged to point out the one significant absentee.

Inspector Timothy Reardon was a long way away.

25. With a Chaser

E VEN AS THE BAIT was being dangled during Elmer Rugby's conference, the police were arming the trap in New Jersey. Inspector Reardon had been surprised at the early hours prescribed by the local force.

"Rugby's promised to keep things going until six," he pointed out. "Nobody can possibly get here before seven-thirty."

"It's the neighbors I'm worried about," the chief replied. "If we pile into that house and remove our car, the whole block will know it's a police bust. They'll sit up all night with lights blazing to watch. Hell, they'll probably lay on a buffet and invite friends over."

Reardon, accustomed to the mass anonymity of Manhattan, welcomed any information he could get on suburban customs. "Whatever you say."

"Then we'll use some camouflage and be in place by five-thirty."

Accordingly Reardon arrived in a truck emblazoned with the logo of the cleaning firm employed by Madeleine Underwood.

"Everybody knows the house is going up for sale. They'll just think we're getting it in shape," explained the chief, virtually invisible behind the carpet shampooer he had hoisted to the shoulder of his coveralls.

To Reardon's critical eye the Underwood house seemed ideal for their purposes. It was a substantial Colonial in the older part of town. Set on half an acre, it was surrounded by well-established landscaping that included lofty trees and mature bushes. On the street side a semicircular drive, defined by massive plantings of flowering shrubbery, swept up to the front door. Toward the rear, shade trees could be seen towering above the garage. As soon as the sun began its descent, the whole area would be dappled in shade that deepened as dusk progressed.

Under the chief's direction the exit of the mock cleaning crew was accompanied by such confusion that the neighbors were unlikely to realize that, when the truck finally pulled away, two men remained inside.

"Is this the way most of your robberies are pulled off?" asked a professionally interested Reardon.

"It depends on the season. The really busy time for us is in the summer. That's when the families with school kids pull up stakes and it's when the others go away on vacation. So the favorite trick is to arrive in a giant moving van and gut the whole house. At other seasons they pretend to be appliance repair people, delivery crews, re-upholsterers."

There was something to be said for high-rises, Reardon reflected. In his own territory the common run of burglaries involved a smashed lock and the disappearance of money, jewelry, furs and other portables. It was rare indeed that anybody tried shifting furniture and rugs down fourteen or fifteen flights.

The chief broke into these musings, saying, "It's a shame my boys didn't find that tape when they looked through this place before."

"It was my fault, not theirs," Reardon said for at least the fifth time. "I didn't realize she'd been back here."

Forty-eight hours ago a phone call from John Thatcher had caused Captain Reardon to kick himself and he had continued the process ever since.

"It was sitting out there the whole time and I never saw it," he admitted. "There was a woman who checked into a hotel on the spur of the moment because she had a busy public schedule for days ahead. She sure as hell wasn't going to make do by buying a toothbrush."

"The hotel should have mentioned it," the chief said supportively, "but that's witnesses for you."

"They were never asked the right questions, thanks to me. Instead of wasting time on records of outgoing calls, I should have concentrated on the obvious. As soon as I did, I got what I wanted."

Indeed the reception clerk had been surprised he had to ask. The reason Madeleine Underwood had explained her sudden decision to the front desk was because she was checking in without luggage. Further police prodding had produced a bellboy who remembered carrying her suitcase in the elevator at ten-thirty that Monday evening.

"If I hadn't been so damn thick," Reardon continued his self-flagellation, "I would have had this place torn apart the minute I heard about the break-in at NOBBY. Instead I waited until yesterday."

"Well, you got the tape and that's the important thing. Right now we'd better make sure that window is unlocked," the chief said, leading the way down the hall.

They were heading for the room in back that had been the target of yesterday's belated efforts. Like every other square inch of the large home, it had received the ministrations of a fashionable decorator. Originally designed as a study for Madeleine's lawyer husband, it boasted all the usual paraphernalia. There were leather club chairs before the fireplace, dark barrister bookcases along two walls and Daumier prints above the mantel. But another personality had long since taken over, dispelling any aura of leisured masculinity. The seating area had been compacted to allow the introduction of all the modern office machinery so dear to Madeleine's heart, with each item on its own metal stand. The small end tables designed to support a chaste snifter of brandy or the latest issue of the *Harvard Law Review* housed tattered copies of *House Beautiful* while the bookcases, bereft of their ranks of law reports, now overflowed with heaps of fax material. Even the mahogany kneehole desk had virtually disappeared under a jumble of correspondence topped by a casually discarded tape recorder.

Yesterday, after discovering the recorder was empty, Reardon had stared at the masses of material in dismay. "My God, she didn't organize a thing. This is even worse than the NOBBY office. We may have to listen to every single one of those," he said, pointing to the stacks of cassettes gathering dust in odd nooks and crannies.

But the head of the search team did not agree. He had strolled over to the desk to double-check the tape recorder, then remained stock-still as he sniffed the air for the ghostly scent of the room's untidy owner.

"Maybe not," he said, turning his back on the whole sorry mess to drift into the hall.

The essence of being a gifted searcher is the ability to know instinctively what people do with things. This one stood in the archway of the living room surveying the decor before he marched straight to an ornate armoire and swung open its doors, revealing a complicated array of expensive electronic equipment.

"But that's her entertainment system," Reardon had protested.

Ignoring him, the expert trailed a finger past amplifiers and speakers, a VCR and a CD player, to pop open the cassette player.

"Aha!" he grunted in satisfaction. "Here's the one she played last. You did say she'd realized her tape was important, didn't you?"

"Important enough for a wow of a press conference," Reardon confirmed.

"Then she wanted the best audio definition she could get. That's why she brought it in here."

This might be logical, thought Reardon dubiously, but logic had never been Madeleine's forte. Furthermore he had approached closely enough to see cassettes featuring Vivaldi and *The Phantom of the Opera* in the adjacent tray. In spite of these doubts, however, he was waiting with bated breath by the time the expert had rewound the tape and punched the play button.

One minute was enough to tell him this was the right tape. It took almost fifteen minutes, however, of listening to two voices rising and fading away before—unmistakably clear—the motive for Madeleine Underwood's murder proclaimed itself.

"By God, I've got to hand it to Thatcher," the inspector had exclaimed in a burst of relief. "He was absolutely right."

And today the fruits of victory would be harvested, but only after long dreary hours had passed. Outside, the familiar orchestration of a suburb on a workday evening was proceeding. Dominating everything was the sound of cars. From the main highway far away there came a mighty background roar. Lesser tributaries contributed the unending din of idling motors backed up at intersections while closer at hand the thinning trickles invaded nearby residential streets. Car doors slammed and voices rose in greeting as local commuters arrived first, to be followed by those from more distant outposts. And even before the last stragglers from New York City were in their garages, the mighty surge of teenagers began, heralded by gunned engines, squealing brakes and blaring radios.

From five-thirty to seven-thirty Reardon and the chief discussed exhaustively every single aspect of the New York Yankees, Knicks and Rangers, covering past performance, future prospects and rumored trades. The monotony was broken only once with a phone call for Reardon.

"They've picked up the punk who broke into NOBBY," he announced. "The dumb slob never realized he was getting involved in a murder until he saw the headlines the next day. He's been holed up, scared to death, and now he's singing his heart out."

"Between the tape and the witnesses, you've got plenty to tie your man to the killing even if he doesn't show up here."

"Yeah, but we can put a hell of a lot more pressure on him if we arrest him on the spot. You can take him right down to the slammer and I can give him the good news that we've heard the tape. That's enough additional leverage to make this stakeout worthwhile."

"Oh, I see the benefits, but do you think he'll really come?"

Reardon shrugged. "This guy has already killed one woman and hired a thug who sent another to the hospital—all because of that tape. I think he's too rattled to sit still now, but you never can tell. The thing is, I've got no idea what time he'll choose."

It was a problem on which the chief was happy to expand. "Well, he's got to come by car. If it was me and I didn't know the area, I'd pull into town during rush hour and pick up a local map at a crowded store. Then I'd locate this house and case the immediate area. Since you can't park around here and walk away without attracting attention, I'd leave the car in that shopping strip on the main drag three blocks over. Then I'd wait until it was dark enough so I couldn't be easily recognized but still early enough so a man walking alone isn't conspicuous. After that it's a piece of cake. With all these trees and bushes I'd slip through the shadows and pray there's an unlocked window."

"Well, we've left one open for him so he won't have to break anything. But if you're that sure of what he'll do, we ought to have someone at that shopping strip."

The chief produced a thin smile. "We do."

"Then all we have to do is wait."

The chief, however, was still coining refinements for his perfect burglary. "You know, if this guy had enough time to prepare, it wouldn't be a bad idea to bring a beagle along. You can walk on these streets anywhere, at any time, if you're just on the end of a leash."

Kindly but firmly Reardon ended this fantasy. "I don't think he's had enough time to equip himself."

At eight o'clock the chief's authoritative certainty was more than justified with a phone call from the shopping strip. Their suspect had just pulled into the supermarket parking lot. Upon hearing this, Reardon congratulated himself on the caliber of his ally and, with an early-warning system now in place, went so far as to don headphones and tune his transistor to the game at Yankee Stadium.

But as the late-spring evening progressed, his attention wandered more and more to the changing patterns of light. The pools of shadow were gradually lengthening, at first striping the lawn with a brilliant motley of green and black under the clear azure sky. With the blue steadily darkening, however, the colors were soon leached from the scene, leaving only a spectrum of grays. The last squeals of nearby children playing in their yards died away, the street lamps suddenly came on and the final roseate glow in the western sky sank below the horizon. By nine-thirty the house was engulfed in a sea of unrelieved black.

At ten the police chief stirred impatiently. "What's he waiting for? Do you think he's got cold feet?"

"He didn't drive all this way to spend the night outside a supermarket," Reardon argued. "Maybe he's decided to try it in the small hours."

"Then he's crazy. If he waits until one or two he'll have the local crime watch flooding the station with calls."

Momentarily distracted by this insistence on constant suburban alertness, Reardon tried to imagine a New York City where every law-abiding citizen called the police upon observing a stranger in the area, an unfamiliar car parked on the street, a lone pedestrian after midnight. But even this daunting prospect could not hold him. With nerves increasingly on edge he tracked the almost imperceptible advance of the minute hand on his watch to ten-fifteen, to ten-thirty, to beyond.

Finally the phone chirped again.

"Yeah? . . . And high time! . . . What's that? . . . I'll be damned . . . Well, you stay in position until you hear from me."

Turning to Reardon, the chief reported, "Your guy's on his way. And whadda you know? He's figured out a substitute for that beagle."

"What's he come up with?"

"He's wearing a jogging suit and running shoes. That's pretty smart. We've got a lot of people in town who do a couple of miles every day."

Sensing some obscure criticism of city dwellers, Reardon said, "We have joggers, too. You should see Fifth Avenue at six in the morning."

"Out here some of them do it before bedtime."

Reardon did not feel called upon to explain that sensible New Yorkers avoided solitary workouts late at night. Instead he reached for one of the dusty cassettes. "I'll just slip this dummy into the recorder. If possible, I'd like to slap the cuffs on him while he's got it in his hands."

With this preparation complete, the two men took up stations in the hall outside the study and achieved practiced stillness. In the unnatural silence they became aware of an insect banging into a screen, of a late bus rumbling along a distant street. Filtering out these minor disturbances, they waited with straining ears for the sounds that finally came—running steps on the street outside approaching in steady rhythm, then slowing appreciably, finally faltering as the runner tired.

No one would think twice about those sounds. The mind's eye would create its own picture of an exhausted figure leaning against a support, then limping noiselessly home. Even with every sense on the alert, the invisible watchers barely heard the faint rustling in the shrubbery that told of a circuit to the rear of the house. After that the intruder's movements were preordained. The faint metallic *ping* of a door handle being tested was followed by a duller resonance from the kitchen window. There remained only one more window facing the backyard, the one in the study that had been carefully left un-latched.

More in imagination than in actuality Reardon traced the soft footfalls covering those last fifteen feet and waited breathlessly for the welcome *whoosh* as the lower half of the window was raised. The dim light reflected from a distant street lamp was barely sufficient to disclose the shapeless form clambering over the sill. Then, star-tling to eyes accustomed to the stygian interior, a hooded flashlight clicked on. Its narrowed beam traversed the floor, picking out the furniture, seizing on the kneehole desk. After a gentle slither of approaching movement the small ray of light played along the clutter, capturing a pile of memos, moving to the jumble of corre-spondence, catching a corner of the discarded tape recorder. Then it circled back to center on its target. A hand moved into view over the recorder just as Inspector Reardon threw the wall switch oper-ating the large lamp on the desk.

"Hold it!"

For a bare second the figure in a blue-and-silver running suit froze. Then the heavy flashlight sailed through the air directly toward Reardon's face while the other hand swept the tape recorder across the lamp, plunging the room once again into darkness.

Instinctively ducking, Reardon collided with an end table to stumble and fall full-length on the floor. From this foreshortened perspective he saw a gigantic black shroud briefly obscure the win-dow and then disappear. As he scrambled to his feet and hurled him-self toward the window to half-fall through it, he involuntarily yelped in pain. Furious at the triumph slipping through his fingers, he ignored his twisted ankle to crash around the side of the build-ing, so absorbed in his pursuit that he was barely conscious of an ap-proaching din.

Once he reached the front, however, he was brought up short by an astonishing spectacle. Pounding around a corner into the street directly ahead came a disorganized array of twenty-five or thirty men. The *pad, pad, pad* of their feet was the only sound as they bore down on the house, menacing in their single-minded intentness. For one confused moment Reardon wondered if this anti-crime community regularly unleashed bands of vigilantes.

Then the leaders passed into a patch of light and he saw they were wearing shorts and singlets, steadily pumping muscles already glistening with sweat. Even as he identified them as innocent joggers, a blue-and-silver figure slipped from the last shrub on the driveway to join the pack and disappear with it around a curve in the road.

Hampered by injury, encumbered by street clothes, Reardon was in no condition to give chase. He had not even managed to cry out in the few seconds required for the phantom apparition to sweep by. He was still cursing in mortification when the police chief emerged from the front door and advanced at an unhurried pace.

"Not to worry," he said affably. "He'll peel off that mob and circle around to his car. I sent some backup over there."

It was the wrong note to strike with Reardon at that particular moment.

"What the hell was going on out there?" he demanded with an enfeebled wave at the now empty street.

"Sorry about that," the chief replied offhandedly. "They're having a Ten K on Saturday for the hospital. One of the local clubs scheduled a practice run tonight. They had it posted all over town."

"You mean you knew about this all the time?" Reardon choked.

"I forgot," the chief said, his thoughts elsewhere. Then, complacency in every syllable, he exclaimed. "I'll bet that's why the guy waited as late as he did. He must have seen the announcements too. They even had a diagram of the route."

Gritting his teeth, Reardon tried, and failed, to remember the necessity for cordial relations with fellow police departments.

"We may have blown the whole operation," he snarled.

"What's the big deal? The guy can't walk all the way to New York. He's got to go back to the supermarket."

"All you can think about is cars."

"Cars are what matter around here."

"If you know so goddamned much about around here, why didn't you tell me about this practice run?"

They could have argued in circles forever. Nothing was capable of placating Inspector Reardon—nothing except the news that arrived fifteen endless minutes later.

Congressman Harry Hull had been arrested in the parking lot, still clutching Madeleine Underwood's tape recorder.

26. Capping It Off

ARLY-MORNING TELEVISION told the world the next day that Harry Hull had been charged with murder, enabling the other subjects of recent police attention to breathe sighs of relief. Thereafter, however, reactions varied. Dean Kichsel and Alec Moore, without a second thought, caught the first plane home to plunge into their neglected duties. Elmer Rugby was not far behind them, pausing only long enough to say, "That guy never had the balls to be a Texas politician. What gave him the idea he could get away with being a killer?"

But at NOBBY they were unable to put the past behind them so speedily. They had questions by the score, and because one good turn deserves another, they had the right to demand some answers.

"After all, we're the ones who set up the trap," Peggy Roche said as soon as Charlie Trinkam ushered the NOBBY delegation into Thatcher's office.

"And did it very well," Thatcher congratulated her warmly.

"But Elmer Rugby was the real star," Sean Cushing conceded. "I didn't expect him to make my taking Iona's place in New Jersey sound suspicious. He almost got me rattled."

Iona's systematic mind wanted to start at the beginning. Moreover, she was still offended at not having been included in the play-acting at the Rugby settlement.

"I think Mr. Thatcher should explain how he came to suspect the congressman. This is all a surprise to me," she said, gently underlining the last word. "In Washington I realized Harry Hull could simply walk away from the whole Quax issue whenever he wanted to. He seemed to have the least to lose."

"You made the same mistake we all did," Thatcher began. "Because the fundamental issue was a struggle for market share, we thought in those terms. Even the police were sucked into that overly rational approach. But Mrs. Underwood was the central figure and she didn't see her cause in that light at all. In front of Rugby's she made her views very clear. Quite simply, her enemies were money-grubbing exploiters while NOBBY was inspired by sheer altruism."

Suddenly Thatcher turned to Sean Cushing for a personal aside. "That of course was the reason she resisted knowing details of corporate contributions. The recognition that there were commercial interests on her side, too, would have destroyed the dream vision."

"Well, I always figured it was something like that," Cushing agreed. "Madeleine was full of that sort of baloney."

Both Peggy Roche and Iona Perez, feeling the need to justify Madeleine's role at NOBBY, burst forth with reminders of her valuable services.

"We have over ten thousand members," Peggy declared, "and almost every one of them joined after exposure to Madeleine."

"Whenever she spoke it was a shot in the arm to the volunteers," Iona chimed in. "I could always count on a rush to sign up after one of her speeches."

Thatcher nodded. "Oh, she knew how to be effective. Until shortly before her death she was careful to present her program so that it was attractive to the people she was recruiting. After the riot it may have been expedient for you to emphasize NOBBY's irreproachable history, but it was still the truth."

"And she never intended to start a riot at Rugby's," Iona continued the defense. "I was furious at her irresponsibility but I did realize that her idea, however insane, simply involved blocking the entrance."

"Which puts her right up there with the anti-abortion thugs," Peggy muttered unforgivingly.

"She was like all those armchair generals," Charlie expanded. "They're always coming up with some decisive stroke that would have changed everything, but they fail to allow for some equally creative counterstroke."

Iona wagged her head solemnly. "Madeleine never did consider other people's reactions."

"Nonetheless, the change in policy was unlikely to recommend itself to NOBBY's members," Thatcher continued his argument. "Why then did she do it?"

"She was doing a lot of things she'd never done before," Cushing protested. "Chasing the Kichsel people and having public brawls wasn't her style either."

"That's what Reardon finally fastened on—the complete reversal in tactics that made it impossible for anyone to deal with her. She may have been difficult before, but you managed to work with her for over a year."

A reminiscent gleam appeared in Cushing's eye. "You just had to know how to handle her."

"That's right," Iona supported him. "You couldn't criticize even the silliest suggestions. I always pretended to accept them and then modified them as I went along."

"Same thing with her writing," Sean said instantly. "Mostly it was garbage, but you just took it and changed it all around."

"As long as you called it polishing, you could get away with anything," Iona chanted rhythmically.

Sean then produced a chuckle. "It wasn't all that hard. Even Cheryl had figured out how to do it."

They were alternating with smooth efficiency. By now it had become a game with Iona and Cushing, to be played whenever one of NOBBY's governors was present. Listening to them, Thatcher decided that NOBBY's board was once again in danger of being manipulated by its hired help.

"So we had a silly, self-centered, but perfectly normal woman," Thatcher said, returning them to the subject, "who suddenly underwent an astonishing transformation between Monday at dinnertime and the next day."

"It had sure happened by the time she lit into me on Tuesday morning," Sean acknowledged ruefully. "I'd never heard her like that before, claiming I'd betrayed her, that I'd undermined her position."

Even as he listened, Thatcher marveled that Cushing should be so deaf to the implications of his own words. Leveling a reproachful finger, he said, "And didn't you ask yourself how she had suddenly become so knowledgeable? How did she find out?"

The first impatient reply died on Sean's lips.

"You know, I never thought about that," he finally admitted.

Thatcher's sternness did not abate. "Even more important, she was alive to the consequences of SDI financing. You told the police you were surprised she had grasped the vulnerability of her position."

"I just figured that was why she was going off like a rocket."

"But someone had gotten through to her," Thatcher insisted, drilling his point home. "Someone managed to puncture her self-importance."

"Then hats off to him," Sean riposted. "I certainly didn't make a dent."

"Neither did I," Iona offered. "In the ladies' room she was shrugging off everything I said."

"And I assume you were both too angry to be tactful," Thatcher suggested.

Sean's face lit up. "I called her an incompetent bitch."

"Then it's safe to say enlightenment came to her in some form that abandoned the usual proprieties of conversation."

"So what?" Sean demanded. "Until you knew who she was with Monday night, that doesn't tell you anything."

This obtuseness, Thatcher decided, underlined how much of a maverick Mrs. Underwood had been. "On the contrary, it tells us a good deal. At five o'clock on Monday, Madeleine was perfectly content. By the next morning she had been told the financial realities with such brutal candor that she was frightened enough to launch into totally uncharacteristic conduct."

"Now wait a minute," Sean objected. "What makes you think she was scared? She was acting like hell on wheels."

"The woman's whole identity centered on NOBBY. That was what was important to her, and that was being threatened. From then on her constant theme was betrayal. When you add the fact that every suspect was alibied for Monday night, you understand Inspector Reardon's dismay when he learned she had been in her own

237

home. If his suspects didn't have an opportunity to see her in the city, they certainly didn't have time to run out to New Jersey."

"Then Sean's right," Iona declared. "It's a bigger mystery than ever."

"It was until Charlie straightened us out. Mrs. Underwood was such a menace when she was on the warpath that we all focused on her aggressive behavior. But Charlie pointed out she was behaving abnormally before she came roaring into NOBBY on Tuesday morning. He said that earlier she had been up when she should have been down. He was the only one of us who kept his eyes firmly fixed on the kind of woman she was."

Peggy Roche, sharing a sofa with Trinkam, allowed her gaze to drift sideways for a long, measuring look.

"I'm not surprised," she announced.

Charlie, choosing to interpret this ambivalent remark as a compliment, beamed at her.

"Yes, yes," Thatcher said hastily. "And the place where this anomaly was most apparent was in Harry Hull's room. Roger Vandermeer had unceremoniously excluded Madeleine from a strategy session about the anti-Quax campaign. By all rights she should have been seething."

"But she was planning to come back and pump Harry Hull," Peggy explained. "She thought she'd outwitted Vandermeer by leaving her briefcase behind."

Inexorably Thatcher corrected her. "If that had been her plan, it failed. Vandermeer's contemptuous dismissal was followed by a brush-off from Hull. Yet instead of being resentful, she was, according to both Hull and a nearby chambermaid, as chipper as hell. What could possibly have made her so cheerful except the knowledge that she really had outwitted them?"

He then came to a full stop, regarding his visitors with kindly anticipation. As the seconds ticked by, Peggy Roche's bewilderment increased, but Iona and Sean began exchanging glances of dawning comprehension.

"Oh, Lord," Iona moaned, "you don't think she had the nerve to—"

"It would have been just like her," Sean interrupted on a rising tide of certainty. "And don't you see? It explains the break-in."

Peggy, viewing them both in exasperation, seemed almost afraid to ask what Madeleine had had the nerve to do. But at last the suspense was too much for her.

"What are you two talking about?"

Too triumphant to be coherent, Sean blurted, "Those damn pocket recorders she carried around."

Thatcher was more explicit. "Mrs. Underwood left her open briefcase in an inconspicuous corner with a tape recorder running. In her eyes two subordinates were having a conversation she was entitled to know about."

With every new insight into Madeleine Underwood's methods Peggy became more appalled. "I had no idea she was so . . . so high-handed. When she asked me to have the governors make tapes for her I explained that our discussions were private. I suppose I should be grateful she didn't bug us."

"Maybe she did," suggested Sean, grinning broadly.

"Oh my God, I wonder what we said."

Predictably Iona was the one who refused to be diverted. "That doesn't matter anymore. But I'm beginning to understand why Madeleine went ballistic. When I was in Washington, Roger Vandermeer didn't make any bones about his next moves but he was reasonably polite about it. Talking to Harry Hull, particularly after Madeleine's show at the hearings, he would have been a lot more unbuttoned."

"Indeed he was," Thatcher assured her. "The first fifteen minutes on the tape consist of some blunt remarks about Mrs. Underwood's incompetence, together with his plans for the future. Either NOBBY acquired a new director or he'd launch a rival consumer group. As far as he was concerned, Mrs. Underwood was history."

"Madeleine must have been devastated," Iona murmured soberly.

"No doubt. But if the beginning of the tape was a body blow, the last five minutes gave her a powerful weapon. In the event that a new organization was necessary, Vandermeer was offering to increase his under-the-table payments to Harry Hull. They even bargained about the amount Hull needed for his reelection campaign. That information was a godsend to Madeleine."

Frowning in thought, Iona said, "That explains the press conference. But why the riot?"

Thatcher, refusing to pretend that he understood every twist of Mrs. Underwood's overheated imagination, could only speculate. "I think that, like you, she knew the value of an army already in the field. This time she was not trying to recruit new members, she was proving that she had a viable organization ready to do her bidding. Of course the riot was intended as the first half of a one-two punch. The next day she would go public at the hearings."

Iona was reliving the last few moments at the committee. "She must have been wild when the adjournment was announced."

"I'll bet she blamed that on Harry Hull. That would be why she decided to wipe the smile off his face by telling him her intentions," Sean reasoned.

Charlie Trinkam nodded. "That would do it, all right."

"And so he killed her." Iona's slight frame was convulsed by a shudder. "He seemed like the last man in the world to suspect."

"Oh, I wouldn't say that," Thatcher disagreed. "First and foremost we had all those references to betrayal, which eliminated Kichsel and Elmer Rugby. It's not your enemies who betray you, it's your friends. In the absence of embezzlement and with Mrs. Underwood on the verge of dismissal, there wasn't any motive at NOBBY. That left Vandermeer and Hull. Of the two there was no doubt who was the more imperiled. Vandermeer wouldn't enjoy being part of a bribery scandal but he would survive. Hull wouldn't."

Peggy had an objection. "Until you found the tape, you couldn't be sure there was any bribery."

"No, but there were ominous indications. Every time Hull appeared with Madeleine he had to protect his own position, yet he went out of his way to give her exposure. He suggested her for the hearings even though she had already demonstrated her incapacity on a radio show for which he'd sponsored her."

"I wondered about that myself," Sean admitted. "That's why, when we were all upstate, I asked Hull how she did in Philadelphia. I couldn't understand him proposing her as a witness unless she'd done a bang-up job. He probably didn't like that question."

Once again Thatcher was startled at the selective nature of Cushing's memory. The young man had a gift for coming close to essential points, then stopping. "Maybe not. But it was another statement by you that almost gave him a heart attack. You told him that Madeleine's last tape had shown up at NOBBY and been confiscated by the police."

"Christ!" Sean exploded after a moment's blankness. "That was when he had a coughing fit."

"You'd just kicked him in the groin," Charlie explained succinctly. "It took him a second to realize you were talking about a tape she'd dictated. But you should have smelled something fishy in the fact that he was having lunch with you at all. At that stage both Vandermeer and Hull should have been staying as far away from NOBBY as they could get."

"That's certainly what they indicated in Washington," Iona confirmed. "I was surprised when they continued to take an interest, but I put it down to curiosity."

Thatcher's voice was grim. "A very specialized form of curiosity. They'd organized a break-in to steal the incriminating tape and failed. If it surfaced, they wanted early warning. That's why two busy men both made unscheduled stays in New York after their trip to Mohawk Crossing."

"Say what you will, this is still just guesswork," complained a discontented Peggy. "I'm surprised it was enough to make the police act."

"I was merely asking them to search the house in New Jersey. The trap wasn't arranged until after the tape had been found. Besides, Inspector Reardon had always favored Hull as the murderer, but he was stumped for a motive. Like any American citizen, the inspector could easily postulate chicanery in Washington. But he couldn't imagine how an ignorant outsider like Mrs. Underwood could obtain specific information, let alone hard evidence."

All references to the trap made Iona stiffly resistant. "Why in the world would he single out Congressman Hull?"

"Just think a moment. What was the reason for putting Madeleine's body in the closet?"

"That's self-evident," Peggy said promptly. "To gain time."

For once she received some support from NOBBY's staff.

"The last thing the killer wanted was a hue and cry while he was still in the elevator or the lobby," Sean reasoned.

Thatcher shook his head. "Being in the elevator or lobby might be bad but being caught manhandling the corpse would be far worse. Bear in mind the killer was supposed to know where to find Madeleine because her appointment with Hull was made in public. By the same token the killer should have expected Hull to appear at any moment. Furthermore, anybody unfamiliar with the committee's housekeeping arrangements couldn't know the staff was gone for good. It was two o'clock and they might have been out to lunch. For everybody else, safety meant fleeing instantly. Only Hull could have been certain enough of privacy to risk lingering. And, as he had to admit being at the scene, he had the most to gain from a stage set allowing him to claim he'd noticed nothing unusual. That's why the body was moved."

Thatcher had phrased his last sentence as delicately as possible. Nonetheless the unspoken vision of Madeleine Underwood stuffed into a closet like a discarded doll provoked a murmur of distress from Peggy Roche.

"Poor Madeleine! She probably needled Hull into a homicidal rage and never even noticed until he swung on her."

Sean Cushing was seeing the same image. "Maybe she didn't have time to notice anything," he said.

But Iona's thoughts were elsewhere. "And all this—about the bribe, I mean—will become public?"

"Almost immediately, I would expect," Thatcher agreed on a note of inquiry.

She was nodding to herself. "Then Roger Vandermeer will get fired. I'd better approach SDI directly about their funding."

Peggy gasped in outrage. "Look what happened the last time we had dealings with them."

Nobody could complain that Iona Perez was blind to other people's reactions. Her normally pale features were suffused with pink as she quite deliberately misread Peggy's objection. "They thought they could yank our chain because they were our only big institutional donor. This time I'll see to it that SDI is lost in a crowd. After all, we agreed to get back to them as soon as the audit and settlement were behind us. And nothing has changed," the quiet voice continued with absolute conviction, "except for the better. I think I should make an appointment as soon as possible to . . ."

CLAUDIA FENTIMAN AND Theo Benda did not share the instant detachment achieved by their colleagues at Kichsel. However, they took the precaution of scooping Paul Jackson into their net before descending on the Sloan.

"I've been talking to the boys in the prosecutor's office," Jackson explained as soon as he was seated, "so I've got all the inside info."

But Paul, too, believed in the principle of quid pro quo. This was his chance to recount his feats in the manner of *Ludlum versus Kichsel.* His captive audience listened restively to the superb skill with which he had timed one damning revelation after another. The Ludlums had wired money to their son on Cape Cod the night of his arrest for drunken driving. And, while the Ludlum household was indeed completely dry, it was because the father was in AA.

"Daddy was a drunk until his son was fifteen."

"All right, all right, Paul. The whole thing was brilliant," Charlie said perfunctorily. "And you got your verdict. Now on to what's really important."

Mentally Jackson reviewed his fund of information. "Let's see. Did you know that the cops picked up Vandermeer the minute he left the settlement party?"

"I can't see Vandermeer protecting anybody at the expense of his own skin," Thatcher ventured.

"Hell, no," Jackson agreed cordially. "And in a sense you can't blame him. He didn't know a thing until Mrs. Perez came to Washington and announced to Hull that she was about to prune Madeleine Underwood's files. Then Hull, in a panic, told Vandermeer and admitted killing Underwood because she had a tape of them talking about the bribe. So there Vandermeer was, mixed up in a murder whether he liked it or not. That's why he set up a meeting between Hull and the punk who broke into NOBBY."

"Vandermeer must have loved it when the break-in went sour," Charlie suggested. "They ended up without the tape and with all the cops in New York City looking for one."

"Yeah, he admits getting edgy. All he could do was cozy up to Cushing, asking to be kept abreast. And the minute the cops put the arm on him, Vandermeer gave them the name of the punk in DC."

"So even before Hull got to that house in New Jersey Inspector Reardon had Vandermeer's testimony," Theo Benda said appreciatively.

"More than that. He had the punk, too."

Claudia had been listening to this exchange with mounting impatience. "Wait a minute. You're leaving out the most interesting part," she objected. "They said on the news that Harry Hull was caught breaking into Underwood's house. Were the police waiting for him? Was it a trap?"

"Yes, and it was laid at Elmer's party," Thatcher told her. "In fact, the first part of the bait was planted right in front of you when Peggy Roche called you and Moore over to apologize. It gave her a chance to fabricate that tale about calling Mrs. Underwood so Hull would know Madeleine had gone home. Then, because Reardon didn't want to allow enough time to hire another professional, Elmer Rugby and Cushing announced that the house would be stripped of all NOBBY material the next day. If Hull wanted a crack at the tape, he had to act that night."

Paul Jackson was indicating sage approval. "The cops know the value of arresting somebody in the act of committing a felony and doing it late enough so lawyers and judges are hard to come by."

"Well, it worked," Charlie acknowledged. "They got him red-handed."

"Red-handed enough so he's trying to cop a plea," Jackson said brightly. "His lawyer is pulling the irresistible-urge defense. According to him, Hull never intended to murder anybody. He was happy as a clam when he arrived for his meeting with Underwood. Then she sprang her big surprise and things happened fast. He'd just taken in the fact that she was going to destroy him at an open press conference when she reached for the phone to tell NOBBY's board what she was planning. Everything went black and, without knowing what he was doing, he grabbed the bookend and swatted her. By the time the cloud cleared he had a body at his feet."

It sounded all too possible to Thatcher. "The use of the bookend and the cleaning of the phone are both confirmation of sorts," he remarked.

"Hull claims what really drove him insane was the way she didn't recognize what she was doing to him," Jackson continued. "He didn't go over the edge because she was prepared to sacrifice him but because she didn't acknowledge his position at all."

Theo Benda was moved to disapproval. "It sounds to me as if Mrs. Underwood and Roger Vandermeer were two of a kind. She started to run amok when he decided to eliminate her from the movement and treat her as a nonperson. Then she turns around and pulls the same stunt on Hull. The difference, of course, is that his idea of running amok was to kill her."

Emboldened by Benda's venture into theorizing, Claudia had an addition of her own. "Status was another difference. Hull had gotten himself onto the fast track, heading for the big time. Then this nonentity of a woman was ready to wipe him out as casually as if she was stepping on a bug. It was just too unnatural to tolerate."

"Lèse-majesté," Charlie supplied kindly.

Paul Jackson was almost twitching with annoyance at these amateurish divagations. With a tremendous clearing of the throat he returned them to essentials.

"The lawyer is skating over the whole business of the tape to avoid any suggestion of premeditation," he said when he had reduced everyone else to silence. "If Hull went into shock when Madeleine told him what she had on him, he really flaked afterward. With her explaining jubilantly that she always carried her recorder in her briefcase, he assumed that's where the tape was. When he discovered it wasn't, all he could do was sit tight. The first twenty-four hours he must have been expecting the cops on his doorstep every minute. From then on it was a roller-coaster. Every time he relaxed, another threat came along. First Mrs. Perez intends to comb through the NOBBY files, so he tries the break-in. After the dust has settled from that one, he's told the tape is sitting out in New Jersey. The guy's blood pressure must have been going through the roof."

"He did a good job of hiding it, at least compared to Alec. We had two men collapsing all over the place and I only noticed one." Claudia ended her self-criticism with an expectant gaze at Paul Jackson. "I still don't know what Alec was in such a sweat about."

Jackson liked nothing better than being the repository of confidential information. "And you aren't going to find out," he said smugly.

He had preened himself too soon.

"Oh, I don't know about that," Benda said gently.

Suspecting a bluff, Jackson decided to stand pat. "Moore said he didn't tell anyone."

Instead of replying directly to this challenge, Benda addressed himself to Thatcher and Charlie. "You wouldn't know this, but back home we have a rich lady called Eileen Tyler. When her husband took off she decided to sow her wild oats far and wide. She's been working her way through the country-club crowd for about two years."

"Eileen's a byword," Claudia agreed with a puzzled frown. "She even had Alec in tow last fall. Eileen makes sure the ladies' locker room is current with her tally of scalps. But what does that have to do with anything?"

"You've been spending too much time in San Antonio and New York," Benda told her. "It pays to keep up with the local gossip. About a month ago Eileen tested HIV positive and the word went out to everyone who might be affected."

Claudia was visibly counting months on her fingers. "Good God—Alec!" she cried.

"Exactly," said Benda. "When Alec pulled all that cloak-and-dagger stuff about what he was doing at the time of the murder, I figured he might have been getting himself tested in New York, so word wouldn't leak out to the company. Of course I wasn't sure until he started to unravel completely. And when he was suddenly on top of the world, the situation spoke for itself."

Charlie, listening with bated breath, nodded. "No wonder he didn't care if he was charged with murder. The poor slob wasn't sure he'd live long enough for a trial. That was it, wasn't it, Paul?"

Paul Jackson made no attempt to hide his chagrin. "Moore didn't mention that everybody in Illinois knows about this. In general, you've got it right," he said grudgingly to Benda, "but you're wrong on details. Actually, Moore had hopped over to New York for the tests earlier. The results were supposed to be ready on the day of the murder. Then he got socked with two terrific jolts. First, when Madeleine Underwood was chewing him out, it sounded as if she'd found out his little secret. Then—"

He was allowed to proceed no further. Claudia Fentiman had straightened with an explosive snort. "I knew she'd rocked him," she exclaimed. "Alec wasn't defending me when he ripped back at her. But where did he get the idea that she knew?"

Jackson was once again in the saddle.

"You probably don't remember, but Underwood used the word 'infected' when she was ranting about his moral corruption. That was enough, particularly when she'd sicced private detectives on him. Moore was afraid he'd been tailed on his first visit to the clinic. Anyway, he was still reeling from that blow when the doctors told him that there'd been a glitch at the clinic and his test results had gone missing. He was going to have to sweat it out until they were found."

Many things were becoming clear to Charlie. "No wonder he started to hit the bottle. I'll bet he'd disciplined himself to wait the standard two weeks, but the extra strain made him come apart at the seams."

"That was it," Jackson agreed. "As the days went by, he managed to convince himself that he had full-blown AIDS and everything was over."

Claudia was staring at Benda as if she had never seen him before. "And you kept quiet about this, Theo? That was very generous of you," she said, unable to banish incredulity from her voice.

"No, it wasn't," said Benda, amused. "Alec's been behaving like a horse's behind. While he's been scurrying a thousand miles for his tests, Eileen's blabbed her head off, trying to get sympathy from everybody in sight. The only reason Dean didn't find out was because Dottie Kichsel has been out of town. Now that she's back, I'll bet she got the whole story before she reached the tenth tee."

247

"And," said Thatcher, beginning to understand Benda's methods, "Dean Kichsel isn't going to appreciate the fact that Alec Moore was a prime murder suspect because of an AIDS test."

Claudia, apparently consumed with outrage, had lost all sympathy for her superior. "To hell with that," she said forthrightly. "Kichsel's looking for a new CEO. The board won't think much about the common sense of a man who doesn't take precautions with Eileen Tyler—precautions every teenager knows about."

Thatcher could not tell whether her indignation was genuine or whether Mrs. Fentiman felt impelled to acknowledge the rising sun.

Certainly Benda, his face wrapped in a beatific smile, found no fault with her prediction.

"You know, I kind of thought that myself," he murmured softly.

Charlie Trinkam, bending closer to Thatcher, said in an undertone, "This should take care of Lancer's worry about the succession."

"Yes, yes," Thatcher agreed absently.

He was thinking about Iona Perez. Her busy brain was at this very moment concocting schemes to defeat Alec Moore—schemes of a subtlety that would have been beyond Madeleine Underwood. But Iona, like Charlie's armchair generals, might have forgotten that Kichsel could shift strategy as well. In the past the conflict about Quax had resembled a toe-to-toe slugging match. Under these two new champions, the conflict promised to become a good deal more artful.

Thatcher looked forward to seeing who would make the first move.